James Shearer

Prinkle and His Friends

A novel. Part 3

James Shearer

Prinkle and His Friends
A novel. Part 3

ISBN/EAN: 9783337045630

Printed in Europe, USA, Canada, Australia, Japan

Cover: Foto ©Andreas Hilbeck / pixelio.de

More available books at **www.hansebooks.com**

PRINKLE AND HIS FRIENDS.

VOL. III.

PRINKLE
AND HIS FRIENDS.

A Novel.

BY JAMES SHEARAR.

'For every worm beneath the moon
Draws different threads, and late and soon
Spins, toiling out his own cocoon.'—TENNYSON.

IN THREE VOLUMES.
VOL. III.

LONDON:
TINSLEY BROTHERS, 8, CATHERINE ST., STRAND.
1877.

CONTENTS OF VOL. III.

CONTENTS.

PRINKLE AND HIS FRIENDS.

CHAPTER I.

BLUNT HONEST JOE.

AFTER lunch, when Trevor, Joe Alton, Mary, and Maud, came out to enjoy themselves among the fine old trees, the last-mentioned renewed her proposal that they should seek out the Prinkles; and, in spite of the ridicule which it had already elicited from Mary, she again pressed it upon her as a duty. But Miss Alton kept the position which she had taken up, and in which she was now supported by Bob, who characterized Maud's proposal as a piece of superfluous courtesy.

'Why,' he said, 'if you only knew Prinkle half so well as I do, you would not give another thought to this affair. The fellow was made to be laughed at! And, if we did as you wish us to do, it would only inflate him with conceit, and for the remainder of his sojourn here he would be insufferable to us all.'

'But,' she pleaded, 'for his wife's sake! You know very well what trials she has had already;

and if we cannot lighten her burden, surely there is no reason why we should add to it.'

'You go on, Miss Clayton,' interposed Joe, 'I'll back you.'

'Nonsense! Maud,' cried Mary. 'She has too much common sense to fret over such a small matter. Besides, say what you like, we must keep our dignity.'

'But, for our own dignity we should set it right,' argued Maud. 'If we had kept our dignity, the affair would never have taken place.'

'Dear, dear,' laughed Mary, 'what dignity would there be in stooping to Peter Prinkle?'

Joe, who was standing by, listening to both sides, snorted dryly at his cousin's remark, but remained silent.

'Of course,' Trevor persisted, taking up the idea. 'Dignity does not stoop! Where's your good sense, Maud?'

'I beg your pardon,' she replied, slightly stung by his overbearing manner. 'Insolence never does; but Dignity is all the more graceful when she stoops!'

'Bravo!' shouted Joe, throwing away the stump of a cigar. 'I'll back Miss Clayton against the field! I don't know much about what you call dignity, and polish, and what not, in this old world of yours; but I boast a smattering of knowledge of human nature, and I judge it'll be pretty much the same here as it is with us over the water. It was a deuced shame, Mary, the way you treated

Prinkle, especially when you know he meant no offence, and the least thing you can do is to go and square matters with his wife. Trevor, you brought common sense aboard. Well, I'll back Miss Clayton for that, against you both! And if Miss Clayton is good enough to accept my escort, you two can go where you like, and we shall go to the lodge to see the Prinkles. And I promise you a new bonnet, Mary; and you, Trevor, a new hat, if you are able to remark, when we return, a loss of dignity in either of us! Is that fair?'

This outburst was as genuine as it was unexpected, and they all eyed him curiously, for Joe's bashfulness was proverbial. Maud was somewhat staggered by his abruptness of manner, and, as no one spoke for astonishment, Joe became very red and flustered.

'Thank you, Mr Joe,' cried Maud, extending her hand, which he took. 'We are sworn allies! I have tried hard to get recruits, but I've got a stout one at last.'

'Rather a raw one!' laughed Mary.

'But a ready one!' said Joe. But after that, he relapsed into his normal state of silence.

Trevor and Mary were quite as well pleased that they should get the afternoon to themselves, and they were not slow to take the other two at their word.

'Now, Joe,' laughed Mary, by way of encouragement, 'be a man! And if you don't have

our presence, you have, both of you, our best
wishes.'

'*Au revoir!*' said Trevor, raising his hat.
'We shall leave you alone in your glory.' And
they turned down towards the river.

It must be confessed that Joe did not look very
much like glory, for as soon as they were left alone,
he was covered with embarrassment, and Maud was
perplexed. As it appeared to her, the whole thing
looked like a plot to throw them into each other's
company, and under this aspect she did not care
for it.

Maud was not so blind as to fail to note that
Mr Joe, with all his vagaries, had invariably shown
a special inclination towards herself, nor did she
dislike this, by any means, for her eyes were also
open to the fact that he held her in the utmost
respect. It is comparatively an easy matter to
gain a man's love, but to secure his admiration is
quite another thing; and when a woman can
reckon upon both of these, she is mistress of the
situation, and she may turn a man as she likes.
Perhaps that is saying too much; but any woman
who can put two thoughts together knows that,
in the management of a man, his love for her is an
element of weakness on his own side if he would
withstand her, and she also knows that she lives
in a tower of strength if she is able to command
his high respect. Maud knew this; and she was
confident that, if Joe attempted to embrace this
opportunity for the purpose of advancing his

affection, she would be quite able to turn him from
his intent without any loss of respect for herself
or disparagement to him.   It may be objected that
Maud was looking rather far before her, but it
must be remembered that it was no secret among
Joe's friends that he had come from the West for
the express purpose of selecting a wife; and as his
stay in England was certain to be limited, it needed
no very great stretch of imagination on the part
of Maud to believe that there was a method in the
by-play of attentions of which she had been made
the object.   If she had entertained a doubt on this
point, it would certainly have been dispelled had
she overheard a part of the conversation which
then took place between Bob and Mary.

Mary was highly amused at the predicament
in which they had left them.

'I'm sure,' she said, 'that Joe intends something.   I know he'll do something dreadful!'

'Do you think so?   Do you think he has his
eye on Maud?'

'I'm sure of it.   And more than that, I believe,
if he were to get rid of that bashfulness, and
speak out with less fear, he would have a very
good chance.'

'I'm not so sanguine as you are.   I'm afraid
it would require more tact than Joe possesses to
catch Maud.'

'Nonsense! Bob.   He has plenty of money;
he's an honest soul; he has a good appearance; a
good heart; and what more would a girl have!'

Although this was spoken without a moment's forethought, we wonder if any one, after any amount of consideration, could have stated the desires of a woman with greater truth, and in more perfect order, than Mary set them before Bob.

Meanwhile, Joe and Maud were wandering away towards the lodge, by way of a narrow path which was almost hid by the overhanging trees. His very proximity to Maud was a source of embarrassment to him, and he had not gone many steps before he devoutly wished that he had pocketed his chivalry. But he lit a fresh cigar, if so be that he might appear more at his ease.

'The fact is, Mr Joe,' she said, 'from the way we parted with Mr Prinkle on the forenoon, I'm afraid he may magnify our unintentional rudeness to his wife. She is one of those women for whom you cannot help entertaining a downright respect, and I should be sorry were she needlessly hurt by any thoughtlessness of ours.'

'Naturally, naturally,' he replied, contemplating the end of his cigar. 'It is very natural.'

'But you take it meekly, Mr Joe. Do *you* think I am making too much of a small matter?'

He lifted his eyes as far as her chin, but dropped them instantly.

'No, Miss Clayton. You are doing what is right, and you deserve credit.'

'Oh, no. It is my duty, and I deserve no credit.'

'By George!' he exclaimed. 'We're beset by so many things to distract us, that if a fellow does his duty, he deserves all the credit going! I—' but he stopped, and the intelligence that brightened his eye was withdrawn.

Maud noticed this, and she was interested.

'You were about to say something, Mr Joe?'

'Eh? No—how do you know I was?' he asked, with a confused look.

'Because I saw it in your eye. Were you not?'

'I was,' he replied. 'But who cares what I say or think?'

'I do. You speak so seldom, that I begin to believe you are one of the wise men who speak little.'

'No. I don't say much. Then, what I do say comes out in such a rough-and-tumble fashion! But I can't help it.'

'And why should you try? Good common sense never sounds so fresh and healthy as when it is spoken in that same rough-and-tumble way.'

'Do you think so, Miss Clayton?'

'I do,' she answered.

'Then, by George!—I beg your pardon;—but you are the first who has confessed so much to me.' And his gratitude brought away more words. 'I know that the majority of Mary's friends look upon me as a large, good-natured ninny—good enough for the West Indies, but rather an awkward specimen for a London ball-room! And I know that their maternal instincts are often quickened on my account, for they do nothing but twitter and talk nonsense to me, as if I were a three-year-old, lumpy boy!'

Joe was fast becoming wroth, and it was with difficulty Maud could cloak her amusement. But she appeared to listen with interest, and this drew him out the more.

'I know,' he said, 'that my cousin Mary has a good deal to do with this. But I don't blame her—she's a spoilt child! For she twits me like the rest; and, taking undue advantage of her position as my cousin and a lady, she pokes fun at me to such an extent that, if she were a man, I'd—by George!—I'd punch her head!'

'Come, come, Mr Joe,' she cried, laughing heartily, 'that is too much!'

'I beg your pardon,' he replied. 'A vast number of ladies employ a style of satirical language towards gentlemen, which is highly offensive, knowing well that their opponent, being a man of manners, would not use like weapons in reply; while, if he cared to lay aside his dignity for a moment, he could double up his assailant with two words!'

'Oh, Mr Joe, Mr Joe!' cried Maud, with a ringing laugh. 'Why didn't you come out in this style before? How I should have enjoyed your company! You are positively entertaining!'

'Miss Clayton, give me your hand! I believe it would have been much better for myself, had I been thrown more into company such as yours. The rough stone might have got some points of beauty, after all, from having been brought in contact with the diamond!'

Maud was amused, but responded frankly. 'My hand, Mr Joe; but the less we ordinary mortals indulge in figurative language, I think, the better.'

Joe grasped her extended hand, and we are afraid that nothing short of a figure of speech would adequately express the sensation that passed up his arm from the touch. But it was momentary, for who should turn the corner of the secluded walk but Mr Prinkle and his wife!

'Ho!' cried the former, taking in the whole scene at a glance, and bundling his wife about without ceremony. 'Go on,' he shouted encouragingly, with his back to them. 'Go on, we have no wish to intrude on such an interesting occasion!'

'Come here, Mr Prinkle. Come here,' cried Maud, blushing at the *contretemps*. 'Really, I assure you, you don't intrude! Call on them, Mr Joe. Please do!'

Joe made a frantic rush, and took Prinkle by the arm. 'Really, my good fellow, you are quite mistaken. Do come back. Upon my soul, there is no occasion! Miss Clayton wishes you both. See; she is coming.'

Nell took the hand which Maud offered her, but Peter was inclined to be waggish, and his

face was bright and happy as if never a cloud had
rested on it.

'Bless me, you know, Miss Clayton,' he said,
as she came up. 'It is very awkward, you know,
—But, really, is there no occasion ?'

'None, Mr Prinkle. And if you ask Mr Joe
he will tell you that we were just on the way to
visit you and your good wife. Really, Mr Prinkle,
you have no need to look so sceptical. It is the
truth, I assure you.'

And Peter suffered himself to be convinced,
under the reservation that he thought it very
queer. 'My wife and I,' he said, 'were taking a
quiet stroll, for the last time, through the policies
of Ashfield; and you must admit that, to come
suddenly on a likely couple, in a likely place,
holding on at each other's hands, is rather a sug-
gestive piece of business !'

'Indeed, Mr Prinkle,' exclaimed Maud, glad
to get an opportunity of turning the conversation.
'How, for the last time? Are you leaving us so
soon ?'

'We are,' he answered shortly.

'What a pity! You know, Mr Prinkle,
though I have seen comparatively little of you, I
have spent many pleasant hours with your wife.'

'I believe you, Miss. One only requires to
know my wife to be pleased with her.'

Nell's face wore an aspect of delight, but she
mildly deprecated such flattery before strangers.

'Not a bit !' he cried stoutly. 'I don't care

who knows it! Besides, Mr Joe isn't a stranger.
He and I have spent a deal of time among the
cocks and hens! Haven't we, Mr Joe?'

'We have, Mr Prinkle.'

'Of course, I haven't seen much of Miss Clayton,' he added, 'although I did meet her this
morning.'

'Yes, Mr Prinkle, and I'm afraid you must
have formed a very poor opinion of us. You must
know,' she said, turning to Nell, 'that we met
your husband this forenoon, and on account of a
remark he made about Mr Trevor's relation to
Miss Alton, and the humorous way he put it,
Mary and I could not maintain our gravity, and
we laughed outright. Now, Mr Prinkle, answer
me candidly. Is it on account of our rudeness
that you are leaving Ashfield so soon?'

Peter rested on one leg, and then on the other.
'I don't blame you, Miss Clayton,' he answered.
'It was the other one.'

'But, if you would look at it in the right light,
you would see that there is no one to blame.'

'Of course,' interposed Nell, with a laugh.
'And my husband knows that, too! But you
have no idea the trouble he gives me, pretending
he can't understand a thing, when all the time he
is laughing in his sleeve at the pains you are
taking to make him understand!'

Prinkle felt that this statement set him in
rather a favourable light, and he winked at Joe,
as much as to say, '*You* can understand me.'

'Look here, Mr Prinkle,' said Joe, taking him by both shoulders. 'Don't you say another word about going home. Stay on for a few days more, and I'll take you to places to which you have never been.'

'Can't,'Mr Joe! It's quite impossible. My mind's made up!'

'Can't you make it down again?'

'No, sir. It's like the Medes and Persians— unalterable!'

And, indeed, they found it so; for there was no inducement which they could throw out that in any way shook his determination; and when they appealed to Nell, she answered that it was her own desire to stay, only she would submit herself to her husband. After about an hour's pleasant chat, Maud and Joe parted with them, down by the river, and Prinkle assured them both that he had no ill-feeling. But as soon as he was alone with his wife, he asked her, somewhat mysteriously, 'Nell, I wonder what made these two press us so much to stay?'

'I suppose it was their kind nature, dear.'

'Not a bit of it,' he rejoined, somewhat sharply. 'They've a motive to serve; and I wouldn't wonder if it's a dodge to keep me away from the warehouse at the present time!'

'How can it be that, dear, when it was only then that they knew of your intention?'

'Nell,' he answered, 'say no more. There's wheels within wheels!' And he allowed her to digest this bit of mystery as best she might.

Maud and Joe were anything but pleased with their want of success, and the former gave expression to her dissatisfaction.

'I fear, Mr Joe,' she said, 'that the laugh won't be on our side when we meet Bob and Mary. They'll deride us, and say we have got our trouble for our pains!'

'Very likely,' he replied. 'But there is not much in a lover's laugh.'

She was amused. 'How do you mean, Mr Joe?'

'I mean that, when a person is in the condition of Bob or Mary, his opinion or laugh is not worth much.'

'But you talk in riddles. I cannot understand you.'

'I am afraid you are like Prinkle, taking a quiet laugh in your sleeve!'

'I protest, Mr Joe. I am not.'

'Well,' he rejoined, making an effort to be plain. 'These two are so engrossed with each other that it is impossible for them to bestow two consecutive thoughts on any subject outside their own little circle. Consequently, they receive anything which pleases them, with rapturous delight, while they dismiss, with a sneer or a laugh, better things which, for the time, they are too selfish to appreciate.'

'I am afraid, Mr Joe, that you are too severe.

Have you ever been in love?' she inquired, glancing up in his face with simplicity.

He was staggered by the question, but he righted himself instantly; and as he answered her frankly, she was greatly astonished at the gathering confidence with which he spoke.

'If you mean by love, a passion that makes a man too maudlin to appreciate aright the true excellencies of a woman, while it renders him blind to her most glaring demerits, I have not known what love is.'

Maud opened her eyes, and regarded him archly. 'I begin to think, Mr Joe, that you *are* a philosopher! But, really, have you ever been in love?'

'Well—once; only once. And that was for a very short time.'

'Indeed! Then you were inconstant?'

'No. Hardly that. But my love did not blind me.'

'Ah, I understand! You noted her defects, weighed them against her excellencies, and found her wanting! Mr Joe, you are too matter-of-fact ever to get a wife.'

'Indeed, Miss Clayton, I assure you the very opposite was the case. I observed her excellencies, and my admiration exceeded my love.'

'You are the most extraordinary man I have ever met!'

He removed his hat. 'Am I to receive that as a compliment, or otherwise?'

'Oh, Mr Joe, you are too much of a philosopher to care for compliments; but I did not mean it otherwise.'

'Thank you,' he replied. 'I am too human to regard lightly the opinion of one whom I respect.'

'Really, Mr Joe, I wish you would come down from the clouds and explain yourself. I cannot understand what you would be at!'

'On one condition, I shall.'

'Name it.'

'That we go back to the house by a more circuitous route than this—say by the waterfall. I shall tell you my story, but it won't bear interruption, especially such as we have encountered already in Mr Prinkle.'

Maud seemed to think that this condition required consideration, for she hesitated. Indeed, she was beginning to regard Joe in quite a different light from that in which she had held him hitherto. The striking way in which a closer acquaintance had dispelled his wonted awkwardness had raised him so high in her estimation that she began to doubt if a prolonged conversation would be advisable.

'Do you agree?' he inquired.

'Is it not rather late, Mr Joe?'

'I do not think so; but it is for you to say,' he replied.

Maud looked him full in the eyes, for a moment, as if to read him; but it was impossible, for Joe could look as unintelligent as a cow when it suited him to do so.

Women in general are not cowards, and
Maud in particular was far from being one;
so, without more words, she turned into the
narrow walk that led to the waterfall. This
walk was more secluded than the rest, and the
foliage of the trees on either side mingled overhead and darkened on the path with a dim syl-
van beauty, while the air was musical with that
indescribable chord of contentedness which is only
struck by a stream that is heard and hid. It was
such a scene as lovers might wish to linger in, but
it was not in unison with the thoughts of these two.
For Maud regarded Joe with undisguised curiosity
rather than with affection; while, on the other
hand, he regarded her with too much matter-of-
fact honesty to be charged with love.

In the parlance of Ashfield, 'Round by the
Waterfall' included the idea of a delightful lounge
on the mossy bank that stretched out from the foot
of a series of little precipices, over which the rivu-
let trickled and splashed like some fairy genius
throwing diamonds in the sun. Reaching this,
Joe at once assumed the mock-heroic. Stretch-
ing forth his arm, he began to address Maud
in a manner that astonished her more and
more.

'Lady, behold the beauty of the place. Not
often do the crags look down on one so fair; the
streams are joyful in thy presence; the mighty
trees droop down to make obeisance; and, out of
every crevice, even the ferns peep out to look at

thee! The Spirit of the place displays its hospitable shades, and supplicates—'

'For goodness' sake, Mr Joe,' Maud interrupted, with a stamp of her little foot, ' will you talk sense! ' And then she blushed, for she knew that by so expressing herself she had narrowly compromised her dignity as a lady.

By the rules of society, ladies are not allowed to swear, but even the best of them do employ a style of language which is couched in the spirit of a round masculine oath.

' I'll be sensible, Miss Clayton, if you rest with me here for a little. I'm about to give you some of my experience—and you know that experience is profitable in all things.'

Maud's curiosity ran high, and she arranged herself on an inviting couch of moss; and Joe accommodated himself near her on the same bank.

' You will pardon me,' he began, looking up to her, ' if I remark the increasing astonishment with which you have regarded me since we set out in search of Prinkle and his wife ; but I assure you, Miss Clayton, that it is a matter of wonderment to myself to be found sitting here and talking to you in the collected manner in which I now do. (You will pardon me if I am egotistical.) I have always considered myself a bashful man,—in the presence of two ladies I am nowhere, alone with one—the odds are against me. I know that, ever since the time I met you, I have appeared to disadvantage in your eyes—the cause of this I shall explain to you afterwards,—and, seeing that my time in this country is now so very limited, I have determined that I shall employ it so that, in parting with you, I may be able to believe that you respect me honestly as I admire you surely.'

'But, Mr Joe,' she interposed, 'indeed there is no necessity for this; you have my respect already.'

'I am glad of that,' he replied, fidgeting where he sat, for his face showed that he was very much in earnest. 'I am glad of that, but—really, you know, your respect for me is a very recent thing.'

Maud made no reply, but the hesitation in her face showed that there was at least a grain of truth in what he said.

'You need not confess it, for it is quite patent, and I have myself to blame; although, perhaps, there is some excuse for me, too. I was born in the West Indies, and all the education I have, I got there. My father was the owner of extensive plantations; and, when I came to be overseer, I was little over twenty years of age, as accustomed to the rough-and-tumble of Colonial life as I was unaccustomed to the manners of polite society when I first landed in England. On my father's death, the estate fell to me as heir. I was lonely, and began to think of marriage; and it is the plain truth I tell you, that three different times I have come to England to seek out a wife, and for the third time I am about to leave its shores a bachelor. You may look incredulous, but it is a fact.'

'You must be hard to please, Mr Joe.'

'Well, you see, it is rather a ticklish business the choice of a wife, and I own that I am the least bit particular.'

'But you may be too particular.'

'I think not. I'd sooner have my back broken with my chance for life than be yoked with a bad mate. One can't be too particular; for once a wife, always a wife!'

'But, Mr Joe, among the hundred girls you have met, has there never appeared *one* whom you could really like?'

Joe shirked the question.

'The fact is,' he said, 'my cousin Mary, who has been the means of introducing me to all the ladies I have known, has a very cousinly way of taking her fun off her big relation. No sooner am I introduced to a girl, than she whispers into that girl's ear that Cousin Joe is on the look-out for a wife; and knowing this, I am naturally out of joint, so to speak, with that girl ever afterwards. And it stands to reason that the same girl looks upon me from a certain point of view; the consequence is that, if she is a clever girl, she makes game of me, or if she is amiable, we are mutually awkward. Now, I am not referring to any isolated case, for it has been the same all round.'

'Well, certainly, it is too bad of Mary; not only for your own sake, Mr Joe, for there is no saying what girl might have been a happy wife ere this!'

'I don't know if it would have gone that length,' he answered, 'yet, there was the chance.'

'But, Mr Joe,' she said coaxingly; 'you promised to tell me of the girl you really loved. Since you spoke of her, I have been wondering all about her. Come, you must tell me your story.'

'Do you wish me to speak of her?'

'I think I do;—at least, I should like to know by what process your love was overcome.'

Joe looked at her steadily, for a moment.

'Is it out of honest interest you wish to know, or is it for banter?'

Maud hinted that the insinuation of the latter motive was, if anything, unkind.

'I beg you will pardon me. It is so unusual for me to meet with one who is interested in me that I had forgot. But it is a delicate matter, and you must bear with me if I handle it in my own rough way.' And he continued: 'I never cared for balls and evening parties, and towards the end of this last winter I was heartily disgusted with them, and I would have left off attending them entirely, but that, living with my uncle, I was under the necessity of trotting out Mary as a matter of course. They told me, too, that these were the places where I should be able to judge of ladies to the best advantage; indeed, I began to see that the ball-room holds the same position in Society that the market does among those who deal in cattle. A lady is for sale; her qualifications are whispered about in the drawing-rooms; and she is expected to show off her fine points there. But I have found that the sex sinks in my estimation when I see an amiable and, it may be, a good girl, in one night, whirled about in the arms of a dozen different men, half of whom she has never seen before; and I cannot admire a lady when I see her sipping wine till the flush heightens on her cheek. Of course, there are many exceptions to this; but nothing tries the dignity of a lady more severely than the heat and excitement of a ball-room. Yet it was at a dancing-party where I first saw, and, I may say candidly, loved this one of whom I spoke. But there were a grace and loftiness in her manner which defy description. Nowhere have I seen such a beautiful woman!'

'Were you introduced?'

'I was.'

'And, as soon as she spoke, I suppose she would tumble down in your estimation like a castle of cards?'

'The very opposite, I assure you. I came to know her, and, graceful as I thought her on that night, I have since seen her acting with more infinite grace.'

'How? When?' she inquired, somewhat eagerly, for she was interested.

'When I saw her,' he replied firmly, but with softness too, 'carrying a small basket of fresh eggs to the door of a poor widow in Ashfield!'

In a moment, Maud was on her feet; her face

crimson, but she did not speak. Joe rose as quickly, and stood beside her.

'Miss Clayton, you will not be so ungenerous as to charge me with flattery when I tell you that I have no motive in the wide world to serve. Ten days hence, I shall have left this country, and it is probable that I shall never see you again on this side of time!'

'I did not expect this, Mr Joe,' she answered tremulously.

'I know you did not, but I was determined if ever you thought of me when I was away that it would not be as the senseless clod I have seemed to be! I tell you frankly that I loved you with a passion that was strange to me, but when I began to know you in other scenes than those of the ball-room, I was not blind to the disparity existing between your lofty nature and mine; but while I must control my love I need not restrain my homage. Your sphere of usefulness is far removed above that of the wife of a West Indian planter. I know not what is before you; but, in my heart of hearts, I believe you will scatter smiles and blessings wherever you go!'

Joe's blood was fired, and the strong sincerity with which he spoke thrilled through every fibre of Maud's nature. Her thoughts went back to Frank Grierly and the noble tender of affection which he made, and she was struck with the similitude between this and that! Here was a man, a few weeks past, and she would likely never see his face again; yet, on the very threshold of his departure, and without a selfish motive, he offers her his highest regard! The flood of thoughts which came in upon her with these two scenes before her eyes, might well overpower her; but she bowed her head in her hands and tried to hide her agitation.

Joe, meanwhile, brought from his pocket a bit of blue ribbon with a diamond cross attached. He placed one hand on her shoulder and held out the other before her.

'Here is a little thing, Miss Clayton, that I got for you. I wish you to wear it, when I am away, as a token of the respect with which I shall never cease to regard you.'

'I cannot take it,' she cried. 'I cannot.' And her handkerchief was raised to her eyes, for her feelings found vent with her words.

He still kept it before her.

'It is the only favour I shall ever ask of you,' he said, without any urging; and when he saw that she was silent, he tied the ribbon on her neck. His hand was as unsteady as his voice when he did so.

Maud made no answer, but she did not oppose him; for the thought came to her heart, 'Love is so sweet, generosity so strong, life too short to slight them.'

For days she was uneasy in the secret possession of the cross, but when the giver was beyond the sea, she brought it from its hiding.

Years afterwards, when harsh experience told her that love may be repaid with hate, and goodness with distrust, she would sit and muse over the token; and her heart would receive sweet solace, from a recollection of the scene by the waterfall, with blunt, honest Joe!

CHAPTER II.

THE DISSOLUTION.

NEXT morning, Mr Prinkle bade farewell to Ashfield. Old Willie, the gardener, accompanied them to the station, and while he presented Nell with a bouquet that might have graced the hand of a duchess, he testified how much he had enjoyed their good company at the lodge.

'Well, Mister Scott,' said Prinkle, shaking him warmly by the hand, 'I must tell you that I've been very agreeably disappointed in you. I could not have believed that a Scotchman could be such a jolly old chap as you are, and I like you very much. Any time when you are in London, be sure and look us up, and I can assure you of a hearty welcome.'

'Thankye, Mr Prinkle. But you'll no catch me in London in a hurry. I canna put up wi' the reek and roar o' the City. Be sure and come back. Good-bye, Mrs Prinkle; and my best wish

is that you may baith bend before the blast and
ne'er break.'

Peter seemed to have a very indistinct idea of
the meaning of this, for he signified to Willie
that he yet hoped to be spared to punch the
blast's head !

'Good-bye. Good-bye, Mister Scott ! God
bless you ! '

And the train was just starting, when who
should rush into the station but Mr Joe, red and
flustered from a sharp trot. He had only time to
bundle a small hamper in by the carriage-win-
dow, crying out,

'That's for your wife, Mr Prinkle. They'll
be good—roast or boiled ! Good-bye, both ! '

Peter was greatly gratified by Mr Joe's kindness, and it put him into such good-humour that
he kept his fellow-passengers in amusement all
the way, by the manner in which he tried to make
himself intelligible to a brace of fat fowls in the
basket.

When they arrived in London, he went home
with his wife; and, after having helped her to
put a few things in order, he started for the
warehouse.

Here he found masters and servants over head
and ears in work. Goods were being turned out
of shelves and piled on the floor ; clerks from the
office were hurrying about with slips of paper in
their hands; others were jotting down to the dic-
tation of warehousemen ; and everything and

everybody helped to add to the confusion of stock-taking. Up-stairs and down-stairs, every one was busy; and, beyond a few congratulations he received from his more intimate friends, Mr Prinkle's return was unnoticed.

This was no ordinary stock-taking; for it was well known to be the last under the existing firm of Alton and Hendry, but no one knew better than Peter Prinkle how much depended on the way it should be done. He had not forgotten the incident with Mary in the garden, for the impression had gone deeper than even his wife imagined, and he was naturally anxious to ascertain how things had been going on in his absence. But, in the mean time, he was too busy to prosecute the investigation, which he intended to do with the utmost care. The vision of the villa by the Thames was still present with him, and he remembered, too, that he had priced gold watches and work-boxes for Nell.

One thing that struck him very particularly on the day of his return was the absence of Gregory. This was so unusual, especially at such a busy time, that he remarked it to a fellow-warehouseman.

'Oh,' was the answer, 'I can't tell what's come over Gregory at all; but for the last three weeks—shortly after you left for Sandhaven—he's been oftener out than in. Between you and me, Mr Prinkle, I've an idea that they're going to open another place.'

'How, Robson? what makes you think that?'

'Well, you see,' answered Robson, taking him behind some goods and whispering, 'you've no idea how anxious they were to re-engage all the hands here. Two days after you left, there was not a man among us but put our names to a three-years' engagement, to serve the firm either here, in Manchester, or in Glasgow. And, mind you, they've come down handsome! I suppose it was to balk Hendry, and to retain all the chaps that know the business! By Jingo! Hendry 'll be riled!'

'Yes—yes,' said Prinkle, anxiously. 'But what about opening a new place?'

'Ah, that's only a conjecture. But immediately on our engagements being signed, they commenced sending out—'

'Yes, yes—well?'

'—large quantities of new goods,—as if—'

'Well—well? Go on,' he cried eagerly.

'What a face you've got, to be sure, Mr Prinkle. You're as pale as a ghost!'

'Go on,' he whispered. 'Go on. You were saying that large quantities of new goods were being sent out as if—as if what?'

'As if for customers' orders; but they weren't! They were sent to stores, and I believe they'll send them on to Manchester or Glasgow, after a bit.'

'Robson,' whispered Prinkle, nervously taking hold of the collar of his coat. 'For God's sake, never mention this! It's a plot; and it may bring

the whole place about our ears! Speak of the devil
—there's Gregory himself! I'll tell you more
about it again, Robson; but, for Heaven's sake,
keep it quiet. *I know where Gregory's been!*'

'Well, Prinkle,' said Gregory, somewhat
boisterously, 'you've got back again, and are
idling as usual. There's a great deal to be done,
and you must make up for lost time. We'll have
no laziness here.'

'Very likely, sir. At least not in me,' he
answered sharply.

'Now, look here, my fine fellow. No speaking back. We won't tolerate that. You go along
to your work.'

Prinkle was about to answer him again, but
recollecting that he had an end to serve, he turned
silently away.

Some time later in the afternoon, Mr Alton
came up to him, as it was only then he had leisure
to welcome him.

'I'm glad to see you back,' he said, giving him
his hand. 'You are looking well. I did not expect you would leave Ashfield so suddenly, but
you were quite right to return to your work as
soon as you felt able.'

Prinkle was intensely gratified that he should
shake his hand in the presence of so many of the
warehousemen, and he was about to thank him in
his choicest words for his kindness at Ashfield,
when Mr Alton cut him short by calling him into
the private room. This room inevitably associated

itself with a certain conversation in Prinkle's mind, and he became very red, as he followed his master with that alacrity which is characteristic of a consciously guilty dog. In fact, ever since he had set himself to watch the actions of his master in business, he had felt an irresistible demoralization creeping over him.

In the matter of concealment, man differs widely from the magpie. The latter waxes sprightly over a secret, but the former thinks of it with guilt, then fear, then abhorrence, till the hidden thing becomes gaunt and hateful to contemplate, and the years establish it as the skeleton in his closet.

Prinkle, therefore, was visibly relieved when Mr Alton stated why he wanted him.

'I'm glad you're back, Prinkle,' he said, dropping the customary civility. 'You're looking strong; and it is well, for you have enough of work before you for the next ten days.' He then drew a paper from his desk. 'I suppose you know that the co-partnery existing between myself and Mr Hendry terminates with the present month?'

'Yes, sir. Yes.'

'Well, I intend to assume Mr Gregory as partner, and I wish to know if you care to renew your engagement and continue in my employ. I see you have been in the receipt of £90 a year; but you have been very correct and assiduous in your work, and I propose a three-years' engage-

ment—£110 for the first, with a rise of £20 on
each year. What do you say to it?'

Prinkle's little eyes at once began to sparkle
with gratitude and surprise, for the proposal was
liberal as it was unexpected.

'But, sir,' he blurted out, 'are you sure it isn't
too much ?'

His master smiled at this unheard-of objection,
which, coming from a less single-minded man,
would have been the veriest irony.

'Well, Prinkle,' he replied, 'I'm rather astonished that you should put such a question ; but I
may tell you that I like honesty in my servants,
and that can only be insured by a master paying
honest wages. The figure I have named is an
honest valuation of your services. I am pushed
for time,' he said, looking at his watch, 'and I
should have liked a plain yes or no ; but if you
wish to consult with your wife, I shall leave the
offer open till to-morrow.'

'Bless my soul, Mr Alton !' he cried, the
muscles of his face twitching with agitation. 'Do
you think I am an idiot or a fool to refuse your
kindness ! No, sir ; and I accept your offer.
There is no master whom I would wish to serve
but you ; and I must take this opportunity of
thanking you for the tremenjus kindnesses with
which you've covered me, sir ! Both at Sandhaven
and Ashfield, sir, we've been living on your bounty;
and it has been a source of great happiness to my
wife and me, for there is nothing half so full of joy

in this world as to feel that you are overhead in debts of gratitude! And please, sir, would you thank Mr Joe for the fowls, sir? One of the hens was a cock, sir, and I'm going to keep it alive for laying eggs!'

'What, Mr Prinkle?'

'Mr Hodge, sir, in the flannel department, is a farmer's son, and he tells me that cocks' eggs is always the best, sir.'

He smiled incredulously. 'I am afraid there is a mistake,' he said.

'Well, sir, it's Hodge's opinion.'

'It may be so, Mr Prinkle,' he answered calmly, striving to hide his amusement. 'Opinions may do a great deal; but not all the opinions in all the world could make a cock lay a single egg!'

The comical twitch at the corner of Mr Alton's mouth caused Prinkle to reflect for a moment, and when it dawned upon him that he had rendered himself ridiculous, he silently determined that Hodge should pay for it, the first opportunity!

'You must watch these fellows, Mr Prinkle. They are greedy of fun, and they don't care much how they get it.'

'I know that, sir, and it's very aggravating. But I'll laugh at them all yet! There's a spirit slumbering within me, and it's—'

'Yes, yes, Mr Prinkle, I know that. But I want to give you a bit of advice. I can see, from the complaints you have been bringing me all along, that you have your own to do to keep the

peace with these fellows. I spoke to them all on
the subject, when they were signing their engagements, and they have each promised to desist for
the future. But you know that human nature is
stronger than any promise, and it is quite likely
they may not keep their word; so, if they should
commence again, just make an effort to take no
notice of it, and as soon as they see that they cannot provoke you, they are certain to desist.'

'Well, sir, I'll promise to try. But human
nature is as strong on my side as theirs, and it's
just likely that I'll break *my* promise!' And
Prinkle laughed at his own little joke.

'All right, Mr Prinkle. Whatever comes of
it, you won't break your heart.'

'Certainly not, sir. My heart's easily melted,
but it's not easily broken.' And he laughed
briskly again.

'Well, will you kindly sign this sheet? I'll
read it over if you wish.'

'Oh, no; not at all, Mr Alton. It'll be quite
correct, and I know you would not ask me to do
anything that is not for my own good.'

'Thank you, Mr Prinkle.' And when he had
signed, 'There, that is done. Let us shake
hands. Our interests are identical.'

And while Prinkle gratefully wrung his
master's hand, there was not a Judas-like thought
in all his nature.

When Nell heard of the terms of her husband's
re-engagement, she was filled with delight; not so

much on account of the addition it would make to
their little store, but that it had the effect of
making Prinkle think and speak in the most
kindly way of his master. In view of any difficulty arising with regard to the knowledge ac-
quired so guiltily by her husband, she had greater
confidence that he would act in a manner consistent with his respect and love for Mr Alton, and
that he would not adopt the course he had, at one
time, threatened.

But Mr Prinkle, with all his regard for his
master, and in spite of the double tax on his
working powers, was not inobservant of the fact
that there were suspicious proceedings taking
place under his very nose. Large quantities of
goods were disappearing, being sent out for unknown destinations, and he commenced taking
notes. Bit by bit his curiosity became excited, so
that he was not satisfied with the information he
was able to gain by his own observation, and with
the aid of the lad in the office who had done like
things for him before, he got a very good idea of
what stuff had been sent out during his absence;
and when he compared these order numbers with
his key, he found that some of them were fictitious,
though not all.

It was a rule in the warehouse that a stock-
sheet should be made out each Monday, and sent
to Manchester for Mr Hendry's guidance; and
Prinkle observed that immense quantities of these
new goods had never appeared in the sheets at all.

It happened in this way; and we give an instance.
On Monday night the stock-list was sent to Manchester in the usual way, and on Tuesday forenoon
three hundred and fifteen pieces of the fine new
winter patterns were received.   Immediately on
their being delivered, Gregory and a couple of
warehousemen set to and checked the lengths,
re-numbered the pieces as if by a customer's instructions, entered them against No. 74 in the
day-book,—which No. 74, according to Prinkle's
key, represented a firm in Montreal,—packed them
in trusses, and sent them out the following day to
a calender in the City to wait instructions; so
that, when Monday came round again, these goods,
not being in stock, were not represented to Mr
Hendry in the list sent to him ; and, consequently,
he was not aware that they had ever been received.
In those instances where fictitious numbers were
used, Prinkle had no doubt that they were spurious
consignments, unless, indeed, some new names had
been added to the books which were not yet in his
private key.   In view of this, he had no other
course than to wait till after the dissolution, when,
if Mr Alton had agreed to Gregory's nefarious
scheme as he suspected, these goods would be returned piece-meal from the calenders, stores, and
other places, to which they had been consigned.

As the balancing day—that fixed for the dissolution of partnership—drew near, Mr Alton became
shorter in his temper, his face wore an expression
of unwonted anxiety, and altogether he was a

changed man. The prospect of that day seemed to hang over him with as much gloom as if it were to be a veritable day of judgment for him. Nor did he only retain this anxious bearing when at business, for he carried it home with him to Ashfield, and it soon began to arouse the solicitude of his wife and daughter. We have already stated that the whole course of Mr and Mrs Alton's married life had been one of uninterrupted happiness, and indeed it could hardly have been otherwise, seeing that the former was invariably of a frank, open, and kindly disposition, while the latter, by her whole demeanour, showed that she appreciated to the full her husband's efforts for the welfare of his home. But now it was evident that a change was setting in. Night after night did Mr Alton bring Gregory with him to Ashfield; and night after night did they retire together, after dinner, to the library, where they would talk over private matters as if they wished to eschew other company than their own. Naturally Mrs Alton's heart was troubled by this, for she could not help contrasting it with the time when her husband would eagerly untwist himself from the coils of business, and seek a pleasant repose in the conversation of his wife and daughter. As naturally did she conceive an aversion to Mr George Gregory, who, she deemed, was in some manner the cause of her husband's disquietude. Mary, for the same reason, treated this man with open dislike; and she resented, unmistakably, every approach he

made to friendship. Indeed, Mr Alton had to in-
terpose at times, and request that his daughter
should act more becomingly to a chosen friend of
his own. Mary, on one occasion, replied with perhaps more insight than paternal regard,

'I cannot pay proper respect to Mr Gregory,
papa, when I believe there is no good thing in him.'

'What right have you to make such an insinuation as this on a mere whim of dislike, Mary?'
he inquired, somewhat sharply. 'I insist that you
be more dutiful to your father's friends. I *insist*,
I say; and see that you obey!'

It was many a long year since Mr Alton had
spoken to his daughter in this manner, and she felt
it keenly.

'Now, Mary,' he added, still more harshly, when
he saw her put her handkerchief to her eyes. 'Remember that I insist on this; and I hope that these
tears are for your own folly.'

Mary tried to suppress a sob as she turned
away, but her father heard her. It was late at
night, and she betook herself to her mother's room,
where Mrs Alton was undressed and in bed. The
mother saw that there was grief in her daughter's
face; and, when she inquired the cause, Mary fell
upon the bed beside her, clasping her round the
neck, and burst into sobs.

'I wish, I wish, mamma,' she cried, 'that this
cruel time were over.'

A while after, when returning to her own room,
she glanced into that in which she had parted from

her father. The lights were out, but she saw that he was still there at the window looking out into the night. She slipped in, and caught him by the hand.

'Do you forgive me, papa? I am very sorry.'

Mr Alton turned to her, and his face was as white as the shining moon. He put his arm around her shoulder affectionately.

'Mary, my child!' he said in a tremulous voice. 'You are my only child. Good night.'

There was a strange, sad love in these simple words; and they went to Mary's heart. If she had waited a minute after he kissed her, she might have seen his pale cheeks quiver in the light, as he muttered deeply, 'But it has gone too far—too far.'

The day preceding, and the two days following the dissolution of partnership, there were brisk times of it in the private room. Mr Alton, Mr Gregory, and Mr Hendry were there, and there was also a grand reckoning. Musty-fusty books which had not seen the light for years, were lying open for consultation on the tables. These were the records of the new religion! Balancing papers were strewed about the desks in regardless confusion; every now and then high words were spoken, neither very graceful nor complimentary; and to crown all, up-stairs, in his desk enclosure, Mr Peter Prinkle, flushed and excited with his old tricks again, was perched like a recording angel at the pipe!

Mr Hendry, it may be supposed, was not so blind as to overlook the fact that immense quantities of new goods had been disposed of, at prices which would leave no profit, and he was roused accordingly; but he bottled his wrath till the balance was struck, showing a fearful deficit.

'I can understand this,' he said, turning sharply on Mr Alton. 'I expected as much. I observe all along, and especially towards the end, that you have been sending out large deliveries of these new goods. I did not expect you would be able, or even try, to sell winter stock so early in the season, but I see that your prices would have tempted anybody. Do you mean to tell me,' he inquired, 'that you have sold these goods at no profit at all?'

'I do,' said Gregory.

'I beg your pardon, Mr Gregory,' he replied curtly. 'My business is not with you. It is with Mr Alton.'

Mr Alton thus appealed to, signified that such was the case, but he was not master of the effrontery which his manager displayed.

Hendry was excited beyond measure, and he hastily turned over the stock-sheets; but there was nothing in these to allay his fears.

'I see that all the new winter's goods have been received, and yet there are only eleven hundred and thirty pieces left in stock ! What is the meaning of this?'

'They are sold,' answered Mr Alton, striving hard to maintain his composure.

'Sold! And what am I to do for new stock?'

'That is your own business, not 'ours. Mr Gregory and I have made our arrangements in view of the coming season.'

'We'll sell you a lot if you like,' said Gregory, with an insulting laugh; but Mr Hendry turned from him disdainfully.

'Why was I not informed of this? You have misrepresented the lists.'

'Mr Hendry,' said Alton, biting his lip, 'you must adopt another tone, or I shall bring to your recollection the fact that this place is mine, not yours. If you ask explanations with regard to anything in these papers, I am at your service.'

'Tell me why these goods do not appear in the stock-list?' he demanded.

'Simply for the reason that goods received and sold within the week, cannot be entered there.'

'But I should have been informed of this. You knew how much depended upon it.'

'Certainly!' laughed Gregory. 'That is why we were silent.'

'Mr Alton, I ask of you,—Do you think this was honest?'

Mr Alton fired up when he replied. 'You must put your question in another form. If you speak of honesty or dishonesty, I demand that these books be closed at once, so far as we are personally concerned, and that they be put into agents' hands for examination!'

Mr Hendry modified his tone on hearing this, and Gregory nodded approval to his partner.

'Do you mean, Mr Alton, to tell me you think this was right?'

'I mean to tell you,' he replied, 'that, in the circumstances, it was both legally and morally right; but I acknowledge that, had we been alone in this matter, we should have been morally wrong. But we were not alone, Mr Hendry; and it is my turn to inquire of you why the balance in Manchester, for the last nine months, comes out on the wrong side? You have kept no stock whatever; you have had your goods transferred, as you required them, from London; but you have been selling at prices quite inadequate, as you well know; and, consequently, the balance in Manchester shows a considerable loss to me.'

'I admit that the balance is on the wrong side; but—'

'And you know the reason of it! You have been selling at the lowest prices, to curry favour with customers against the day of dissolution. You are fond of referring to Scripture, sir; and I may tell you that it is the unjust steward all over! We were watching for ·this, and revenged ourselves upon you with your own weapons. The only difference is that you were selling *old* goods, while we were selling *new*. That is the whole story; and if you begin again to speak of honesty or dishonesty, I shall certainly demand that these books be closed till the law of the land opens them, and

I am confident to leave the verdict in the hands of Justice!'

It was quite evident that, in view of the matter having gone too far, Mr Alton had thoroughly prepared himself against this charge of Hendry's, for he spoke out what he had to say with such a straightforward expression of injured innocence that even George Gregory was silent with admiration. Mr Hendry stood like one deeply chagrined, as indeed he was, for he had not suspected for a moment that Mr Alton would have condescended to so sharp a trick; and in the emergency he was quite powerless, for the weapons he had to contend with were his own turned against him.

When in Manchester, Mr Hendry had noticed that none of the goods were appearing on the weekly stock-list, but he accounted for this by thinking that none of these goods had been delivered; and he had therefore hoped that he would have exactly half of the new stock that had been ordered up, with which to commence business on his own account and that of his son. The fact was, he had been giving Alton credit for being a much more honest man than he himself was; for, while he was disposing of old goods in Manchester at the most inadequate prices—thus currying favour with customers, as Mr Alton had said, with an eye to the future,—he had not thought that Mr Alton might be doing exactly the same thing in London, with new goods, and for the same reason. And now that the fact had been discovered, he knew that he had

no hold whatever on his partner, for the simple
reason that goods bought in the name of Alton
and Hendry were justly saleable by either member
of that firm. But, at this time, Mr Hendry again
gave Mr Alton more credit as an honest man than
he really deserved, for he quite overlooked the
possibility that these sales might not be *bonâ-fide*
after all. At this juncture, time was money to him ;
and he lost not a moment in seeking out his son,
Mr David Hendry, who was then in London
superintending the fitting up of their new premises,
and with him he set about to order a new stock in
lieu of that sold by Mr Alton. But in walking
the markets, these gentlemen ascertained a fact
which would prove detrimental to their realizing
any good profit from their first season in business ;
and this was that all classes of these goods had
risen from twelve and a half to fifteen *per cent.*
in value ! Chagrined, however, as they undoubt-
edly were, they bought in largely, being determined
to show a strong opposition to Alton and Gregory,
even although it should be at a great loss to
themselves.

Mr Hendry was impatient that this opposition
should begin at once ; and the balancing was
hurried through, with much ill-feeling manifested
on both sides ; and in other four days, stock was
declared, and the balance struck.

All sorts of vehicles were employed for the
carrying away of Mr Hendry's share of the stuff ;
and, as load after load disappeared round the

corner of the street, Mr Alton breathed more freely, for with them he believed that his trial was passing away.

His last interview with Hendry was cold in the extreme ; and as they shook hands and expressed a wish for each other's welfare, you might have seen the twinkle of irony in Mr Alton's eye, which met with bitter hatred in that of the other.

When Mr Hendry left the warehouse, George Gregory, who was standing by the door, offered him his hand, but the former disregarded it, and made no other sign than that of a stiff bow in passing out.

George Gregory ejaculated a contemptuous 'Hah ! ' as a parting kick ; and thus the partnership of Alton and Hendry was dissolved at last.

Prinkle, who was a witness of Gregory's discomfiture, could not restrain a smirk of satisfaction as he peeped past the corner of a pile of goods. For this his master ordered him off to his work, and characterized him as an idle sneak !

'Sneak, or no sneak,' muttered Prinkle to himself, 'time'll show which of us is the better man ! '

Immediately after this, changes began to take place. Circulars were sent to their numerous correspondents, acquainting them that Mr Alton had assumed his well-tried and faithful manager, Mr George Gregory, as partner, and that the future designation of the firm should be ALTON AND GREGORY. Brass plates were taken down and

set up again with the new name upon them; in-
voice, and other forms, were lithographed for the
same purpose; and all these changes the well-
tried and faithful Gregory regarded with compla-
cent satisfaction.

The designation of DAVID HENDRY AND SON
burst out in all the glow of burnished brass, on
their new warehouse in Cannon Street, over which
Master David, Junior, was left to preside. The
elder Mr Hendry returned to Manchester, and by
the hard way he wrought for the welfare of his
new firm, we have reason to believe that the
Society for the Evangelization of the benighted
Heathen in remote lands, had no cause to congratulate themselves on this last shuffle of the commercial cards.

It is not here that we desire to write in full
with regard to the younger Hendry. Suffice to
say that he left his paternal home in Manchester
with a spotless character, so far as we know; and
if half what the clergyman said of him that Sunday morning, in his Bible class, when he bade him
farewell as a disciple, were true, then James, and
John, and Peter, and the apostle Paul, were
miserable sinners compared with him.

Yet we believe, on our life, that the old
clergyman's heart went along with his words
when he said, presenting him with a pocket Bible,
and hardly able to articulate for the tremor in
his voice, 'In London you will face the Giant of
all unrighteousness in his most hideous form, and

I do trust that this Book may be as a sling and a stone in your hand, and that, in the name of God, you shall conquer and subdue. Finally, David, be strong in the Lord and in the power of His might.'

Whether David acted up to this last injunction we know not; but this we know, he took up his new quarters in the City, mightily strong in his own esteem.

Before Mr Joe Alton sailed for his western home, he was glad to see that all his uncle's good spirits were returning; and the anxiety which had kept him in England a fortnight longer than he had intended,—anxiety that all was not well with Mr Alton's business, was completely dispelled.

Whatever misgivings Mr Alton had entertained with regard to these transactions of his with Gregory, were soon dissipated; and he satisfied himself with the make-believe that it was only a series of clever tricks, and nothing more. His step regained its elasticity, his face its smile, and he congratulated himself that he had been able to steer the barque of his integrity, thus far, through the troubled waters of commercial life. His evenings with his wife and daughter were now of the happiest description, and they, good souls, enjoyed them all the more for the temporary disquietude which had passed away.

But what, may be asked, was Prinkle doing all this time?

Not much. His movements were none the

less furtive; his hearing was as acute as ever; and
he was rapidly becoming proficient in short-hand.
He stood Gregory's insults with commendable patience, but he was quietly writing up a score
against that gentleman, determined to make him
pay it off at the first opportunity.

CHAPTER III.

' SIRS, BE MERCIFUL ! '

Not many weeks passed by, before Prinkle's
investigation began to yield its fruit.   Knowledge
came, and with it the consciousness of power.
There was not a bale of goods brought into the
place, but what he examined carefully; and, by a
large portion of them, his worst suspicions were
confirmed.   True, the packing, marks, and numbers
were changed; but, from the notes he had taken
previously, he found no difficulty in identifying
the goods as those which had been sent out, pre-
sumably for customers' orders, during the reign of
the old firm.   Every day saw a delivery of these
suspected goods, nor was he the only observer, for
they called forth disrespectful remarks from others
among the warehousemen.

'It's very queer,' said one of them to Prinkle—
the same who had hinted strange things when he
returned from Ashfield—as they were looking over

the contents of a bale newly arrived, 'but I'll take my oath that these identical goods were in the warehouse two months ago! It's very queer, I say : and it don't look like the correct thing.'

'You must be mistaken,' replied Prinkle; but he negatived the effect of this by putting his finger to the tip of his nose. 'Surely you don't think Mr Alton would commit a fraud!'

The warehouseman looked at the goods more closely, shook his head, but made no reply.

By-and-by, the prosecution of these researches encroached so much on his master's time, that he began to neglect his proper work. Mistakes were made that came under the notice of Gregory, who reproached him in the most severe terms; but Prinkle could afford to brook even Gregory's wrath and the inflammatory names he used. This man Gregory neglected no opportunity of harassing him, gave him more work to do than he could possibly accomplish; and to crown all, taunted him with his intentions regarding Nell.

'Come now, Prinkle,' he would say, 'get on with your work. You know your wife will never be a lady if you don't stir about more nimbly! You were late this morning : it won't do. Ah, let me see; there's an explanation; a woman's hair sticking on the collar of your coat!' and he would pretend to pick it off, and puff it in the air with his breath.

Of course, the warehousemen, in deference to Gregory, would laugh at such an exhibition; and

poor Prinkle had no resource but to submit.
Once, however, he replied pretty sharply to his
tormentor,

'If, sir, in a moment of weakness, before I
knew what you were, I treated you with confidence,
it says very little for you to go back on these conversations as you do.'

'Now, Prinkle, cease talking and commence
your work.'   .

'If you would leave me to my work, sir, I
would work. But you torment me as if I had as
little of a heart as you have yourself, sir.'

'No impertinence, Prinkle! I'll not stand it.
You must treat me with respect. I'm your master.'

'Perhaps you are, sir, but there never was a
master yet who could force respect by a passionate
demand. You heard these fellows laugh,' he said,
pointing to some of the warehousemen who were
near. 'Ask them if there was any respect for you
in that laugh!'

Gregory was about to answer him angrily, when
Mr Alton passed into the department in which they
were, and the quarrel ended for the time. Gregory,
however, waited his opportunity in which to let
Prinkle feel the lash of his tongue. In the mean
time, however, he resorted to rather an undignified
method of tormenting him.

Some of the lads in the counting-house were
working late in the evening, after the majority of
the warehousemen had gone, and Mr Gregory
waited a short time writing letters in his room.

His own work finished, he came out and chatted with the boys, and was much amused by their recounting some of the scenes they had when tormenting Prinkle.

'I remember,' he said, 'when I was a boy like you, there was a trick we frequently played. We would take the coat of one of the warehouse fellows and put it in the copying-press and leave it over the night, and in the morning we would have great amusement when he put it on. I don't advise you to try it, mind; but it was great fun!'

This hint was sufficient for the boys, and one, who was more ingenious than the rest, bought some sugar and dissolved it in water. He then took Prinkle's warehouse coat that was hanging on a peg, saturated it with the solution, folded it, and put it in the press and screwed it firmly down. Early next morning he took it out stiff and dry, and hung it up on its peg to wait the arrival of its owner. An unusually large number of the warehousemen were in Prinkle's department when he came, and when he put on his coat, their glee was great.

'Dash it,' he exclaimed; 'it's been frost last night. My coat is quite stiff, I declare! What are you laughing at?' and then, when he recollected that it was a fine August morning, he suspected there was something wrong.

'God bless me! There's two of my buttons broken!' he ejaculated; and he pulled his papers

from his pocket to find that they were all sticky
and stiff, and that his lead pencil was split.

'You're a set of rascals,' he cried; and I'll
sift this matter to the bottom. Can't you let a
fellow alone? If there's a man among you, let
him stand out, and I'll fight him!'

This challenge was received by all with a shout
of derision, and poor Prinkle had to hold his head,
for it was aching badly.

A day or two after, one of the counting-house
lads hinted to Prinkle that Gregory was the insti-
gator of the trick; he believed this, and determined to have his revenge at the earliest opportunity.

Gregory, meanwhile, lost none of his hatred for
his subordinate, so, when they next met, it was the
meeting of fire and water.

The packing-room was deserted by its usual
occupants, and Prinkle was alone with a bale of
suspected goods, busy as a crow over a carcass,
when who should slip quietly in but Mr George
Gregory! He watched him a moment bending
over the goods and taking notes, and then a
suspicion flashed across him.

'What are you doing there?' he cried,
rushing forward in a passion. 'Get out of
this. You are a lazy, meddling hound. Be
off!'

Prinkle rose to his full height, put his notes
carefully in his breast-pocket, suddenly becoming
pale, and eyed Gregory who was quivering with

wrath. But Peter felt that his hour was come,
and he met it calmly for the moment.

' What did you say, sir ? '

' Are you deaf? I called you a hound ! You
are a dog and a vagabond ! '

' Well, sir; I've stood many a thing since I
came to this warehouse, but I will not stand being
called a hound and a vagabond by one who is worse,
perhaps ! '

' What do you mean?' cried Gregory, grasping
furiously at the collar of his coat. ' What do you
mean, you dog ? '

' I mean,' shrieked Prinkle, striking out his fist
like a man, ' I mean that I'll be a dog no longer ;
or, if a dog, I'll change my master ! Gregory—
George Gregory, let go ! ' and with a wild wrench
he was free ; but the lappet of his coat was left in
his master's hand. On seeing this, his rage was
fearful to behold. His small eyes darted fire, and
there were white spots on his cheek.

' My God ! My coat ! Gregory, you fraudulent
rascal, you'll pay for this ! Let me pass, let me
pass ! '

But Gregory stood in his way, and the noise
attracted the warehousemen, who ran in, in time
to see Prinkle dancing madly before his master.

' Do you hear him, men ? He calls me a hound
and a vagabond ! Damn you, sir, let me pass or
I'll be death to you ! ' and with this shriek he
rushed on Gregory furiously ; but that gentleman
dealt him a blow on the breast that made him

stagger back. Suddenly Mr Alton appeared on
the scene, white but calm, and demanded,

'What is this?'

Prinkle was standing, panting from the stroke,
and could not speak for the moment. Gregory
knew that he had raised the devil, and he was
speechless.

'What is this? I ask,' he again demanded.

Prinkle tried to speak.

'Oh—oh—oh, Mr Alton, I wish to God you
alone were my master! Did you hear him, sir?
did you hear him? Sir, sir!' he cried, 'is thy
servant a dog?'

'What is the meaning of this? I ask,' he demanded, looking from the one to the other; but still
there was no explanation.

'What do you mean, Prinkle? Is this a way
to conduct yourself? Are you mad again?'

This was a climax; and Prinkle rushed past
him with a scream. They followed, and saw him
take his coat from the peg.

'What are you doing, Prinkle? and where are
you going?' demanded Mr Alton again.

'Sir,' replied Peter, striving to calm himself.
'If I'm mad you are well quit of me, if I am a
vagabond I suppose I can wander, and if I am a
dog I can bite! More than that, Gregory and you
shall know in time!'

'Prinkle, you are forgetting your engagement.
You are breaking it.'

'Breaking it!' And he laughed shrill like a

maniac, as he made for the door. 'Breaking my engagement! I'll break your business and your hearts!' And with a howl he shook his fist and parted from them.

The cool air did not calm Mr Prinkle in the least degree, for he rushed like a madman through St Paul's Churchyard, turned into Cannon Street, and made for the Hendrys' new warehouse, but his excitement carried him away beyond it into Tower Street, and he did not halt till he was near the Tower. Here he became aware that he had left his hat behind, and he began to understand what made people turn to look at him as they had done. Even the attention of the police had been called to the excited man who ran barcheaded with a poor coat on his back and a good one on his arm; and if these guardians of property had allowed their sense of duty to overcome their indolence, Prinkle should certainly have been apprehended on suspicion of theft.

Utterly exhausted, and scarcely knowing what he did, he sat himself on the curb-stone, and began to wipe the perspiration from his face, when he received a friendly tap on the shoulder, and an awkward-looking man bent over him.

'Hallo, Guv'r'nor! Here's a go! What's up now?'

'Dear me,' cried Prinkle with a crackling laugh. 'Victor Cole! Bless my soul!' And immediately he noticed that his words rhymed, and he exclaimed further, 'God bless me! I'm a poet!'

' Wich you are, Mr P., and a reg'lar mad 'un.'
The brow clouded.

' Don't say I'm mad, Victor. I've had enough
of that. But you don't mean it;—give us your
hand. I'm Bunyan out of the "Pilgrim's Progress,"
and I'm fleeing from the wrath to come ! '

' So you seem,' was the reply; ' but you're fleeing with a wery dirty face. You've been swab-
bing yer brows with a duster ! '

' Bless me, so I have.' And he stuffed the
duster into a pocket, and rose and grasped Victor's
hand. Victor could not understand his appearance,
but he could feel for it.

' Look 'ere, sir ; my mother's house is near by.
Come and see the old woman ; she'll be glad of a
wisit ; and you can get yer face washed, and cool
down at yer conwenience.'

Prinkle accepted this offer at once, for he
wished to make a favourable impression on young
Mr Hendry, and he judged rightly that such a
dirty face would not enhance his comeliness.

' Thank you, Victor. Thank you ; I'll go.'
So Victor took his arm and led him off.

As they walked along, the poor fellow blurted
out his sorrows and his hopes, and he found that
there was sympathy in Victor's breast.

' Well, Mr Prinkle, I allus war sorry for the
way as I tormented you when we was in the old
place together, and I ax yer pardon. I allus
know'd as you was good at the heart.'

' Thank you, Victor ; thank you. I have a

warm heart; and warm hearts like to be told such things as that. How's your mother, Victor?'

'Wery well, I thank you. Same as ever. Allus moaning and groaning arter the old Cole, as if the young Cole warn't better than the old 'un! Strikes me, if a man wants his widder to 'old him in 'fectionate remembrance w'en he's dead, he's only got to drink hard and wallop her well when he's in life!'

Victor had grown very big and clumsy, but he was evidently as laconic as ever.

His mother lived in a quiet way, her house was little better than a cellar, but everything in the place, from the corners of the floor to the white napkin over her shoulders, was clean and tidy. Her personal appearance was anything but imposing, for she was squat-built, but there was a pleasantness about her face, especially when she contemplated her only son, that would draw out the good-will, even of a stranger. Prinkle was made very welcome, and a sign from Victor made her set a basin of hot water with soap on a chair. Our friend performed his ablutions with pleasure to himself, and sat down by the fire, clean and beaming like a Christian.

'Yes, Mrs Cole, you ought to be proud of your son. *I* know what he is, and there's not many like him.'

'Please God, sir, I'm wery proud;' and she put her arm round Victor's shoulder. 'He's a good

son, sir, and allus minds me of the old Cole—so
broad and so tall he is, sir!'

Victor knit his brows.

'Why d'yer moan about the old Cole? Come,
mother, please don't be so 'fectionate; mind there's
a stranger a looking on. Why d'yer moan about
the old Cole, mother? Ain't the young 'un good
enough that you must be 'lastingly raking up the
old 'un's name. It's all along of my being out
of a sitiwation, *I* know; but I tries all I can,
mother; and a fellow can't make his destiny move
on as he would vish—it aint like an 'and-cart that
you can shove along—you must wait on it!'

The old lady seemed to adore these laconic
sayings of her son, for she clasped her hands and
exclaimed that 'the old Cole might 'ave been a
honest man, and a broad and a tall man, but he
waren't a philosophy like the young 'un!'

'Now, mother, you go along, and don't be
drawring inwidious comparisons. If yer would
look up the grammar you'd find that inwidious
comparisons and superlatives is odious.'

This occasioned another outburst of adoration
on the part of the old lady for the learning of
her son, who was pleased but not proud. Victor
was not ignorant, neither was he a fool, and he
understood perfectly well that this last sentence of
his was pure nonsense; but he had a great love
for amusement as well as admiration, and if he
could gratify these two at the same time he looked
upon it as a good economy of his resources.

Prinkle had not heard, till now, that his friend was out of employment, and he referred to it. Victor told him frankly that he had not been comfortable with Mr Trevor for some time past, that his salary had not advanced in proportion to the prosperity of the business, that he had complained of this, that high words had ensued, and, lastly, that he had thrown up his place in great dudgeon.

'I ain't an adwenturer,' explained Victor, 'but I ain't a fine piece of sculpture to stick up in a niche till an earthquake comes, so I jest stept down from my pedestal, and 'ere I am.'

'By my soul,' cried Prinkle, and he gleamed with pomposity. 'I think I could give you a situation. I'm not, just yet, in need of a clerk, but I've no doubt Mr Hendry, who is now forming a new house, will be able to make room for you one way or another when I represent your case to him. I know he will do anything for me.'

Thus showing that, if he was sanguine, he was also generous.

'It is wery good of you,' said Mrs Cole, wiping her eyes, 'and I'm sure I wish my boy to be settled, for it ain't good for a young 'un to be idle, 'cos it breeds mischief. My boy is wery honest, and he's wery broad and tall; and what more would a master 'ave?'

'You go along, mother. It ain't no credit to me that I'm broad and tall, but it's wery hard to be honest, *I* know.'

'Ah!' exclaimed the old lady, rapturously

kissing her son's brow, 'if my Victor waren't honest, I should die, *I* know!'

Surely, surely, when the life of one has passed before us, scenes long forgotten rise with wonderful significance in the light of accomplished facts; and, by a half-remembered sentence, we might mete the standard of the man!

It was still forenoon, although much had been done and the crises of some lives had been reached that day; and Mr Prinkle, rested and refreshed, again bethought himself of the work he had to do. The return walk to the Hendrys' warehouse was not a long one, and in a few minutes he was at the door. It so happened that the elder, as well as the younger Hendry, was in town, and Mr Prinkle had an audience of the two. Our pen would fail to describe the astonishment with which they listened to his story, which he related calmly and clearly; and as fact after fact was corroborated by the multitude of notes he had taken and now produced, these gentlemen quickly got rid of the suspicion they at first entertained that the whole thing was the wild vagary of a mad brain.

'Gentlemen,' said Prinkle, only becoming agitated now that the murder was out. 'Gentlemen, these are the facts of the case. The investigation has cost me many a night's sleep, and the excitement has driven me to the verge of insanity; my telling the truth to you has deprived me of the means of life, and it only remains for you to do your duty by me as I have done my duty towards you. If you doubt my word, there are the written facts. Go to the stores where these goods were stowed away, and make every inquiry; go to the houses whose names were used—there they are—and ask if they ever bought the goods or even heard of them;—it is a simple thing,—and, if you find '—here his voice rose to shrillness, 'if you find that I have said one thing that is untrue, come back and turn me on the street and I'll then be the vagabond they called me;—tell me that I'm a liar, and—and—my wife and I shall go down with sorrow to the grave!'

Poor Prinkle at last gave way, and he bowed himself on the desk, leaving the two to look and wonder.

Father and son consulted hurriedly together in undertones for a few minutes,—they might have spoken out for all the attention Prinkle paid them; and then the former gathered his notes together and hastened out.

Meanwhile the revulsion of feeling manifested by poor Peter was very terrible. In vain the son held out hopes of advancement for duty performed; in vain he pictured a long life of pleasure for our witless friend; and, taking his idea from the frantic cries, he expatiated on the comforts that would flow to his wife, Nell; but all in vain! Prinkle's fervid imagination had commenced to work. It was not the brutal master, or the facile dupe, that disturbed him now, but the thought of a broken-hearted wife and a distracted child!

What would he not have given to obliterate
the work of these last two hours! what, not have
dared!

'Ah! my God,' he cried with vehemence; 'if
I had only known! I would have begged my
bread from door to door to be saved from this!'

Young Mr Hendry's position was anything but
a pleasant one, and he was greatly relieved when
his father returned, bringing with him his man of
business, who was very professional and very stiff.

Mr Hendry had driven in a cab to several of the
places mentioned by Prinkle, and found a corrobo-
ration of his story in every particular. He thereupon dropped in upon Mr Alton, but we shall not
now describe the interview; and then he called
upon and took possession of his confidential adviser.

All this time, Prinkle had been sobbing on the
desk like a broken man, but when Mr Hendry returned, the scene again was terrible. He looked
up at them with wild red eyes; his hair was streaked
and wet; his sallow face twitched and quivered from
his temples to his chin; and altogether he looked
like an old man, old in disappointment, old in
misery, weary in his mind.

'Oh, sirs,' he piteously implored. 'An hour
ago, mine was the secret, mine the power! If my
last breath could buy it back, the ransom would be
paid! Sirs, be merciful! Think of the fearful
consequences of this! Think of a wife's shattered
heart, and of the sunny-haired child who has never
known a grief! Sirs, be merciful! Think of our

own eternal fate if mercy were withheld! Think
of me—it is I who have done it all! It is not for
Alton or Gregory, but, Great God, I have bathed
my hands in the innocent blood!'

_____

CHAPTER IV.

LIARS.

THE warehouse of Alton and Gregory had
witnessed many scenes in which Prinkle was a
conspicuous actor, but never one in which the in-
tensity of his nature was so manifest, and his demeanour so tragic, as in this last. The warehousemen were awe-struck, Mr Alton was confounded,
Mr Gregory was cowed, all by the whirlwind of
passion, the ominous threats, and the ecstasy of
rage which they had seen and heard. As the men
gathered together in knots, their whispering was
like the calm after the thunder-storm, and they
seemed afraid lest the action of their voice might
disturb the atmosphere and bring on the storm
afresh with all its fire and fury. Judging from
their faces, there was not one among them all who
would have dared to trifle with Prinkle now!

Gregory followed Alton to the private room,
and the door was shut. The latter took his seat at
his desk, but he bent forward and covered his face
with his hands, as if stricken with the fear of some

impending calamity. Gregory remained silent
for a time, then made a motion towards the door,
but immediately returned in guilty hesitancy, for
he feared to face the inquiring glances of his men.
But his partner's silence made him still more un-
comfortable, and he determined to brave it out in
the warehouse, rather than endure this irksome
silence longer.

'Stop, Gregory. Stop!' And Mr Alton
looked up with a painfully distraught countenance,
motioning him to remain.

'A moment, Gregory.' And he stopped for
breath. 'Does that madman—' and he clenched
his fist, and the words stuck in his throat, while
his eyes lighted up fearfully and his nostrils dilated. 'Does that madman know anything of
our crime?'

Gregory started. 'Crime, sir! what crime?'

Mr Alton brought down his fist on the desk
and repeated the word, but his voice was husky
and slow.

'Crime—George Gregory. Crime!'

His partner smarted for a moment, but immediately regained his effrontery.

'I have yet to learn, Mr Alton, that any action
of mine may be designated by that name.'

'Then, sir,' he cried, loudly and shrill, 'you
shall learn it now!' and he rose to his feet. 'You
shall learn it now, and I'll be your teacher!'

'For the love of Heaven, sir, beware! The
men must hear you, the walls are thin!'

Alton's voice broke into a sharp laugh, own
brother to Prinkle's mad one. 'Oh, they are
thin! But if we had our deserts, George Gregory,
they should be thick—thick and barred!'

'Do, Mr Alton—do be calm,' he pleaded,
pressing him back to his seat. 'Be rational.
The men may overhear you, and mischief may
come of it. That is right, sir; let us talk
rationally.'

Alton was quieted for the moment, and he
sank back in his chair. But his excitement was
still great, and he kept wiping the cold drops
from his brow; the colour had fled from his cheek,
and he licked his lips, for they were hot and dry.

'Gregory,' he said, in a hoarse whisper,
'there must be an end to this. I'm sick of it.
The time was when I could command the respect
of my servants, every one, but it is different now.
By lending myself to that trick, I have been de-
graded. I am stricken and harassed! I feel as if
every one suspected me! I can stand it no longer;
you may do what you like, but I'll have an account
drawn up, and Hendry shall be paid to the utter-
most farthing!'

Gregory was not astonished at this, nor could
he hide the contempt with which he regarded the
weakling.

'Mr Alton,' he said, drawing himself up like a
man who knew his position. 'You must recollect
that in exposing yourself to the scorn and ridicule
of the world it is not only you who would suffer,

but I along with you! And I would have you consider well, lest in a moment of weakness you should
whistle a life's reputation down the wind! One
thing is certain; if you willingly publish your
disgrace to the world, you shall have no sympa-
thizers, and you shall become an outcast and a by-
word wherever you are known! But I put it to
your calmer judgment, and I ask you, What have
we done that Hendry has not done? You may
call it honest or dishonest; but you, and I, and
Hendry, must stand or fall by the same term. If
there be guilt, then we are all three guilty; for
the simple reason, as I have told you often and
again, that goods bought by a firm are justly saleable by either or any member of that firm. That
is the whole affair. Hendry's mind, not being of
a very high order, he had no compunction in com-
mitting the theft,—for, morally speaking, it *was* a
theft,—of selling goods under cost. Had you
known this in time you might have refused to
part with the goods, but they were out of the
place, and delivered in Manchester, before you had
an opportunity of knowing. You had then no
hold on Hendry, and legally you had no redress;
and you had either to submit quietly to the loss,
or have recourse to the alternative of indemnifying
yourself, trick for trick. Your strong sense of
right made you accept the alternative, for then
your head was clear; but now, in a moment of
passionate blindness, you are guided by your
warmer instincts to deplore that which you have

done. I cannot blame you for this, for it is your innate high-mindedness and your lofty integrity which make you so unspeakably sorry that it was necessary for you to take the course you did. But it *was* necessary,' he exclaimed, gathering strength when he saw his partner becoming pliant to his voice. 'It *was* necessary, and although the course was unpleasant, the cause was just, and the nature of the circumstances such that the most noble mind would at once acquit you of having lent yourself to anything which was false or dishonourable!'

The human mind is eminently sophistical; and, in spite of all that genial Broad Church Deans and No-church moralists may say to the contrary, the heart is deceitful above all things and desperately wicked. The question which is represented as having been first put to man, was answered by a direct lie; the patriarchs were a 'loopy lot;' in his haste, the Psalmist king averred that all men were liars, but, as an old Scots divine laconically remarked, if he had lived in our day, he might have done so at his leisure! Lord Bacon was honest when he wrote '*Does any man doubt, that if there were taken out of men's minds vain opinions, flattering hopes, false valuations, imaginations as one would, and the like, but it would leave the minds of a number of men poor shrunken things.*' The exalted being who, with his hand on his heart, affirmed that he had never been guilty of an untruth, emitted, at that time, we believe, the

biggest lie on record. The fact is, gloss it as we
may, all men are liars; falsehood is an attribute
of humanity. And, as with all the attributes of
humanity, it seems to change, while it only
appears in different forms. There are those who
would scorn to perpetrate deception on their fellows, while they never cease to deceive themselves;
but by far the most common type of the liar is
the man who has a conscience, who finds it necessary for his own peace of mind to deceive himself
before he can be brought to practise deceit on his
neighbours; and to this class Mr Alton belonged.
Although in calmer moments he had argued from
all the circumstances of the case, and had settled
in his own mind that the part he was acting towards Mr Hendry was a dishonest one, the reiterated sophistry of Gregory was sufficient to calm
his scruples, and the blunt English honesty which
so lately made him designate their action as a
crime, was lulled to sleep by the soft rocking of
his partner's plausibleness! And yet Mr Alton
was not a bad specimen of humanity. Humanity!
Give to the psychologist the backbone of Self
and the heart of Fear, and if he knows aught of
his science he will be able to rig out on these the
ordinary trappings of Man! But why should we
say *these*, when Self and Fear are one!

Mr Alton was greatly ashamed of the vehemence with which he had spoken, and more so, for
the weakness which had prompted his words.

'But, Mr Gregory,' he said, 'supposing for the

moment that we *are* right, are you not afraid that Prinkle knows something of our proceedings? When he went out, these were strange threats he made.'

'Yes, they were strange. And you may yet be sorry for not acting on my advice and dismissing him. He is a fool, but a prying one!'

'What do you mean?'

'I mean that he knows a great deal too much.'

'How do you know this?' he cried, with something of his past excitement.

'Simply,' he replied, 'because all this noise is the result of my having caught him in the packing-room, busily inspecting a bale of returned goods and taking notes of its contents.'

'Hah! But, Gregory, that may be your fear!'

'Perhaps so. But what am I to think when, after I had questioned him, he turns viciously and calls me a fraudulent rascal?'

'What!' he exclaimed, starting to his feet, while all his passion returned. 'You knew this, and did not inform me at once! I tell you there is a curse on this house, Gregory! Why did you allow him to go?'

'I had my reasons,' he answered coolly. 'If I had betrayed anxiety, the warehousemen might have wondered—suspected,—and as for Prinkle, he—'

'Hang your reasons!' shouted the other, losing all sense of dignity and decency. 'You are a fool, Gregory! You are a—' and he stammered in his

wrath; but his partner stepped forward and struck
the table, interrupting him angrily.

'I am not a fool : I may be a knave : but you
are both ! No more, sir. Not another insulting
word! You and I are done with each other! I'll
go to Prinkle's now, and secure him before this
goes further, but recollect that I do so for my own
sake, not yours; and after I have quieted him, I
shall return and make my terms with you!'

With this threat Gregory passed out of the room
into the street. Alton stood, for a moment, as if
transfixed. The light of the summer's sun shim-
mered on his pale, wet face, and the roaring of the
busy street was, in his ears, but the ghost of a sound
a thousand miles away! Visions were flitting
through the light. Of Peace, fair and pleasant,
passing from his view. Of Truth, with sad eyes,
ashamed. Of Home— This dashed him merci-
lessly to his seat, and he moaned, with weary faltering, 'Fool—fool—fool !'

Gregory was not a fool ; he could calculate ; he
was a knave. When he got to the street, he inwardly acknowledged his indiscretion in having
answered Alton as he did. Not that he, in any
way, regretted having caused him pain, but that
it was possible he had fomented a quarrel which
might prove fatal to both in the present crisis.
He tried to curb his temper, knowing well that a
cool head was necessary at such a time. Prinkle
must be got, and sounded; and the rest, he thought,
was only a question of money, and the devising of

a plan how to involve him, so that his silence should be effectually secured.

But on reaching Prinkle's house, he was disappointed. He was not there. Nell was made anxious by the visit, but he calmed her with a lie or two.

'No,' she said, ' he has not come home, nor do I expect him till the evening.'

Although she suspected, she was not certain that this was Gregory, and she asked if he would leave his name.

'It is of no consequence,' he replied. 'I am an old friend of your husband's. I shall call again in the evening, for I should like to renew his acquaintance.'

And before she could put another question, Gregory wished her ' Good-day,' and turned from the door.

On his return to the warehouse, he found that Mr Alton had been out for some time, and he waited for him in the private room. In a little while he came in, and although he had been walking up and down the streets, trying to rid himself of the fantastic fears which had clouded all his mind, there were marked traces of agitation on him still. Gregory rose when he entered, and they eyed each other silently, as if not knowing what to do; but Mr Alton stepped forward and offered his hand.

'I hope you will pardon me, Gregory; I am sorry that I allowed myself to be carried away by excitement. The language I used was thoughtless, and extravagant in the extreme ! '

Gregory took his hand and begged to apologize in his turn.

'I have been to Prinkle's house,' he said, 'but he was not there. He had not been home.'

And they were on the point of entering on the discussion of their position, when a knock came to the door, and Mr Hendry, Senior, was announced.

Both were startled. Mr Alton seemed to waver, but Gregory set his teeth.

'Show him in,' he said ; and they had only time to pass on each other an ominous look, when Mr Hendry entered.

He bowed calmly, but stiffly, to the two men, who returned the bow with equal rigour. As neither offered him a seat, he remained standing in the middle of the floor with his hat in his hand.

'I have come,' he began, rigidly enough, with his eyes on the carpet, 'Gentleman, on an unpleasant errand.'

'State it,' said Gregory, sharply ; so sharply indeed that their visitor was startled from his callousness, and his eyes met those of the junior partner.

'With your permission, Mr Gregory, I shall, and in few words. You may perhaps remember, at the time of our balancing accounts, that I had reason to express myself in strong language when I became aware of the terms on which you had parted with the greater portion of our new goods.'

'Whether you had reason or not,' said Gregory, 'you did it.'

'I did. And facts have since come to my knowledge which show that my strictures on you and Mr Alton were not unmerited. Indeed, had I known then what I know now, in all likelihood I should have denounced your conduct as that of—'

'Of what?' exclaimed Gregory.

'Of swindlers!' he replied calmly, bowing to both gentlemen.

Alton clenched his fists at his side and shook as if he were being electrified, but Gregory uttered an oath, and stepped rudely up to their visitor.

'Look here, Hendry. We are not accustomed to that language here, and we won't stand it, even from one of such pious pretensions as yourself! Take care what you are about, or I shall be under the necessity of applying an argument to you of which you little dream.'

Mr Hendry stared at Gregory for a minute, as if he could hardly realize such assurance, but immediately turned from him with contempt, nor did he deign to look at him again.

'Mr Alton,' he said, still calmly, and with dignity, 'I am afraid that you wrong yourself in not speaking. You have known me too long to think that I would use words like these at random, or charge you unadvisedly; and I have known you too long to believe that a man of your rectitude would lend himself to a transaction

such as that to which you know I refer, unless
he were at the time the victim of some wild
hallucination; and it is out of consideration for
yourself, and for no other, that I now offer to let
the matter drop, if you agree to go into the case
with me, and promise that you will make every
reparation to myself and son for the loss we have
sustained.'

Alton was staggered, but surely he was infatuated.

'I—I do not know,' he said, 'to what you
refer;' and for the first time since he entered
business, Mr Alton stood self-convicted of a
direct lie. The downward course was easy now,
and he gathered momentum as he went along.

'You don't?' inquired Hendry, somewhat
firmly.

'I do not,' he replied, 'and it is better that
this interview should end at once. I believe you
have been fooled into coming here, by the idiot
statements of a servant whom we have just dis-
charged, but you have yet to learn that you may
not use with impunity the term which you have
applied to us. You know my man of business—Mr
Beeds; any further communication you may wish
to make, must be made through him; and it is un-
necessary for me to add that I shall immediately
give him instructions with regard to terms you
have thought fit to use in this office. I wish you
Good-morning.'

On hearing this, Mr Hendry bowed, and

paced slowly to the door, but turned for a moment.

'I am sorry, Mr Alton, that you have taken up your present position; but as it is your own desire that the matter be placed in the hands of professional gentlemen, I have no other recourse than to submit. It might have been settled more peacefully among ourselves; but as you have determined differently, you will please to recollect that I shall deal with you no longer directly, but through my solicitor, and my instructions to him shall be to deal justly and rigorously, and to abate not one jot or tittle of my lawful rights, for the comfort of you or yours!'

And so he went.

The interview was very short, but decisive; and Mr Alton stood still as if he had just risen from a dream. Not so, Gregory; for he understood well the import of Hendry's last words, and time was precious. He rushed out into the warehouse, but his excitement got the better of him; and in directing the attention of the warehousemen to the fatal goods, he gave such unheard-of orders with regard to them, that they were bewildered. They were to be re-packed, at once, and sent out of the place.

'Where shall we send them?' inquired one.

'Here, and there, and everywhere, you blockhead! Get them out of this!'

And then his calmness returned for the moment, and he tried to imagine what earthly advantage the sending out of the goods would serve. His mind was wandering; he was losing his head. Suddenly again he rushed into the room, to find Mr Alton seated at his desk with his face buried in his hands.

'What the deuce, sir! Why don't you get up and work? What's the good of moping here?' he cried, brutally denouncing his partner.

'What can we do?' cried Alton, wildly.

'What can we do?' he re-echoed, with a sharp rattle of a laugh. 'Why the devil don't you go to your Mr Beeds, and impeach Hendry for calling us swindlers? It would be better than sitting here. Get up and work!'

'What *can* I do?' he cried again.

'Do! Do!' he exclaimed. 'Do anything; get the goods out of the place!'

'What of that?'

'Throw them into the Thames! We'll cover it! Ay, we'll cover it, though we burn the place!'

'Gregory, stop! I'm in your power, but not so much as to do that!'

'You fool! If the swindle was only a clever trick, arson may be only a strong measure!' and he laughed harshly at his own wit.

'What about Prinkle?' inquired Alton, suddenly. 'Can you not try again to see him? Money will buy him! He may not have told them everything!'

This was the last chance for a drowning man, and Gregory clutched at the straw.

It was a relief to get into the street; any place

was better than that room and warehouse; and as
he knew that Prinkle would not likely be home
for some time yet, he rode about in a hansom
for an hour or two, trying to calm himself before
setting out in quest of him.

Meanwhile, Alton lay on the sofa prostrated
in mind and body. His fingers worked in his wet
hair; he bit his lips till the blood trickled on his
chin; his eyes were so bright that they seemed to
protrude; and his sunken cheeks told how terribly
he was taken in his sin!

Miserable man! What of thine own happiness,
what of thy wife's, what of thy child's? Is not
the gleaning of the grapes of Honesty better than
the whole vintage of Fraud?

What will the world say? Yes, this is another
case that shall tend to shake the confidence of
England in its own commercial morality. Commercial morality! Why, the term is obsolete,
except when used as a reproach! How many firms
there are, large and influential, composed of men
whose integrity has never been impeached, men
who stand high in the respect of the circles in
which they are known, whose opinions sway those
of a community, whose workings, if they were examined, would show that they had been raised
from a series of swindles! It is very fine to talk
of ' keen transactions,' ' clever strokes of business,'
and so forth, but were these investigated by an
unbiased and a conscientious mind, they would
be shown up to the world as unmitigated frauds.

Yes, that is the word! It is a good thing to call a spade a spade, and till this be done in the business world, irrespective of class or name, we must look in vain for a clean bill of commercial morality.

Many, we doubt not, who read this story, will aver that we have judged Alton and Gregory too severely in designating this little job of theirs a swindle; but we lay it before the uncommercial reader, who has had nothing of the sort to bias him, and ask confidently if we have judged them either harshly or wrongly!

'Oh!' exclaims the man of the world. 'It is no swindle. Why, such things are done every day!'

Though it may be on a smaller scale, such things *are* done every day, and with shame may it be confessed.

Had this affair not been discovered, it would still have been considered by this London firm as a clever trick, but now that it is brought to the light of open day, men will judge of it differently, and even the sophisticated minds of Alton and Gregory shall be made to look upon it in another light and be compelled to confess it under a harsher name!

CHAPTER V.

NOBLE NELL.

It seemed as if Nell were destined never to enjoy a day's peace on earth. The flying visit of Gregory had filled her mind with painful apprehensions, and she waited long and wearily before her husband came. At last he returned home, weak and jaded, and when the stranger who accompanied him was introduced as Mr David Hendry, Junior, she knew that the worst had happened. Prinkle told the story in a rambling way; Hendry praised his conduct in the most grandiloquent terms: it pleased her husband, but Nell was silent and sad. All pleasure in life had gone out of her; and, as she stood with her back to them looking away down through the fire, picturing the terrible consequences of the day's work, her feelings towards her husband were not unmingled with reproach. But she did not allow this to be expressed, either by word or manner, for, although she felt that a slight had been put upon her by Peter in rushing to this fatal extreme as he had done without consulting her, she knew better than any one else the abnormal nature of his mind, that the slightest reproach would be resented by him, that an open quarrel would result, and that by this, it was just possible the pity she had hitherto entertained for the man to whom she was

linked for weal or woe, might be changed to
querulousness and contempt !

Her first duty was to bear with him ; and by
far the hardest trial a woman can endure is to hold
the balance with a true heart and steady hand,
when in the one scale are laid a sense of superiority,
the desire to reproach, and the faintest feeling of
contempt, while, in the other, there is nothing left
but a rigid sense of duty, and the lingering remains
of an old love.

It was painful to hearken to the strained
flattery of Prinkle as spoken by Mr David Hendry,
and once or twice Nell could have ordered him to
desist, but for the wish to avert anything like un-
pleasantness between herself and husband.

'Ah! believe me,' exclaimed Mr David, ' there
are few men who would have acted as your husband has done. He has sacrificed himself at the
shrine of truth : not that he shall lose by it—oh,
dear, no ! But, madam, it is a proud thing to
reflect on the character of such a man ! '

Nell saw through Hendry to the wall : she
did not deign to notice his hint at Peter's prospects, but answered calmly,

' I know my husband well, and the praise of
a stranger is not necessary.'

This was enough, and Mr David harped on the
same string no more. He soon began to notice
that his company was not desired by Nell, and
towards the fall of the evening he rose to go.
She was not at all sorry for this, it may be

imagined, but when he told her it was necessary that her husband should accompany him, she was startled, and she demurred.

'Surely, sir, this is not necessary. You can understand the state of feeling into which I am plunged by these circumstances, and it is only natural I should wish for the society of my husband.'

'Yes, my good lady. Very true,' he replied, doing his utmost to be affable; 'but I am afraid it is requisite we should keep him beside us, for we are too well aware of the unscrupulous character of others connected with this affair.'

Nell looked him steadily in the face.

'I do not understand you,' she said. 'I do not understand why this should keep my husband from me. Let the character of others be what it may, how can that affect him or me?'

Mr David appeared to be taken at a disadvantage, for he hesitated before venturing a reply.

Men who are everlastingly suspecting are not desirable friends. If they have too much simplicity to try to hide their suspicions, they are, like Prinkle, ridiculous; or if their cunning allows them only to express their suspicions by way of insinuation, like Hendry, they ought to be kept at arm's length by every honest mortal.

His idea at this time was that Prinkle and his wife might not prove impervious to a bribe, if offered either by Alton or Gregory, but when he saw that she took him up so sharply, he tried to modify the effect of what he had said.

'By no means, my good lady. I—'

'Would you please to address me, sir, as Mrs Prinkle?'

'Oh! a—I beg your pardon! But I did not mean to suggest that the conduct of the other parties could affect you or your husband in any way. Only I think it would be better were Mr Prinkle placed beyond their reach, for a day or two, till our course of action shall have assumed a more definite form.'

'Well, Mr Hendry, you must acknowledge that I should have a word in this matter; and as you seem, by your fears, not to entertain the same idea of his truth and honesty which your flattering terms at first implied, I must tell you that my husband is safer here than with ten men!'

'Oh—really now, it is too bad of you, Mrs Prinkle, to take me up in that way. I only meant that it would be better for your husband's peace were he removed, as it would no doubt be very trying to his feelings were Mr Alton to come here and reproach him.' Hendry smiled most amiably in saying this, as if it were a very benevolent thing to propose.

Prinkle shook his head, and stated that he was afraid to look Alton in the face.

'You hear that!' cried Hendry, triumphantly appealing to Nell. 'You hear that! It is just what I say. It must be very trying.'

'No doubt,' she replied, 'but it would be much more trying to me to be parted from my husband, for days, at such a time as this.'

There was a tone in these words that went to Prinkle's heart.

'It's quite true, Mr Hendry,' he cried, 'what my wife says; and it'll be much better for me to go with you now, and explain to your father why I should remain at home; and then I can return here at night. It's quite true, sir; my first duty is to my wife.'

This was a very simple thing for Prinkle to say, but Nell heard it with gratefulness, and her feelings towards him were more kindly than they had been.

Hendry saw that it were worse than useless to press him against his will, so he accepted Prinkle's proposal to compromise the difficulty; and in a few minutes they were riding in a cab to the Bedford House, in Covent Garden, where the elder Hendry was residing.

On their departure, Nell began to bustle about her household affairs, but her heart was not in her work, and she sat down by the fireside to think.

These were dreary thoughts of hers. When her mind reverted to the happy times at Ashfield where she had lived on the kindness and grace of those who were now destined to be brought so low; when she revolved the sunny memories of these days, not so long ago either, when she was cheered in her distress by the untiring goodness of Mrs

Alton and her daughter Mary, who can tell how much her heart was wrung! What would she not have done to save them now! But her hand was powerless : she could only weep for them; and even that was painful, for her eyes were hot, and her tears dropped like blood.

A visitor had knocked twice at the door, but she was too deep in her sorrow to notice this ; and she was suddenly brought to herself when she knew that some one was there. She turned, and Gregory was before her.

With anxious bearing, he inquired if her husband had been here.

'He has just gone,' she replied, rising slowly, 'but where—I cannot tell.'

'Was anybody with him?' he asked, with quick breath.

'Mr David Hendry—the son.'

'Have you any idea where they have gone?'

'None,' she replied; and her eyes were not raised from the floor.

'Had they any conversation when here?' he inquired eagerly.

'They had,—and Mr Hendry knows all.'

'All?'

'All! George Gregory ; and you have yourself to blame.' And she stepped forward and looked him full in the face, while she laid her hand on the back of the chair. She was becoming excited. 'Oh! you need not be surprised; *I* knew it all long ago. You were the author of the crime; you concocted the scheme; you carried it out; and you, sir,' she cried vehemently, ' were the cause of its being exposed ! '

' I ! ' he exclaimed, retreating a step.

' Yes, *you !* ' she cried, opening her eyes wider as she brushed the tear from her cheek. ' I say you need not be surprised. You knew my husband's weakness and played upon it ; you tortured him with gibes and heaped insult upon him at every turn, before his face and behind his back ! In league with a lot of boys you vexed him with your miserable tricks ! You have been the bane and the torment of his life ! Think you,' she cried, ' that those arrows which you shot, perhaps in thoughtlessness, did not rankle in his bosom at home, till he cursed you in his dreams ? Yet,' she added, softly reproachfully, ' wherein had he wronged you ? what evil had he done ? Oh ! sir, you need not be surprised, having done all this, that the man should turn against you in the end ! You called him a dog, and did you not think that he might yet turn and bite the hand that tormented him ? '

Gregory stood astounded, and winced under her sarcasms.

' You judge me wrongly,' he said in a conciliatory tone. ' If I did anything of this, it was done in no spiteful or wicked spirit.'

Irritated at this, she replied, ' I can pity and forgive boys for their thoughtlessness in tormenting him, although what was fun to them was

bitter pain to him, and the cause of a world of
anguish to me! I can forgive *them*, I say; but,
when children of your age, George Gregory, stoop
to participate in the thoughtless pleasures of more
tender years, I cannot forgive! You have done
this; you have acted with the silly thoughtlessness
of a child, and I despise you for it!'

As she hurled this sarcasm at him the spirit
of revenge chased the tears from her eyes, and she
looked at him fearlessly, but her cheek was pale,
and her lip quivered with emotion.

'Use no more insolent language to me, woman!
or by—'

'No threats here!' she cried hurriedly. 'You
are cowardly as you are criminal, and I dare you!
I have longed to let you know the feelings of a
wife the simple nature of whose husband you have
outraged, and as I can defend him I can protect
myself! I heard you, sir! You are a coward and
a wicked man! Begone! My tears are not for your
exposure or my misfortune, but, that you have
brought desolation upon a happier hearth than
mine!'

During this, Gregory had retreated a pace; but
when she finished, he rushed upon her with his
cane uplifted, as if to strike. But Nell was ready
for him. Quick as thought she seized his arm,
and gave it a twist that extorted a cry of pain.

'Not so, Gregory! You have done enough
without using your stick.' And she let his arm
drop as she retreated to the door, still keeping her

flashing eyes fixed on his. She opened it, and pointed out. 'There is an open door. Begone of your own will, or mine shall force you!'

He saw that she was in earnest, and slunk out.

'Woman!' he hissed, as he passed her. 'You are mad.'

'I may be mad,' she cried after him, 'but, at any rate, I am honest!' and with this she slammed the door upon him as soon as he had his foot on the step.

Noble Nell! In speaking to Gregory, she had exerted herself far beyond her strength; excitement had chased away every feeling of pity and of pain, and had lent to her an almost superhuman power. As her thoughts were formed within her they were at once resolved into words, and with the same power she had hurled them, with a sarcastic sting that burned into the very heart of Gregory. But now that further need was over, her strength deserted her, and she was left helpless as a child. She sank on the bed-side, burying her face in the clothes; she gasped for breath, and panted heavily; but the fountains of her tears were dried up, and she was denied that which to womankind first brings relief.

When Gregory left Nell, he was crest-fallen and sore at heart. He was a man who could stand the threats, or worse, the sneers and taunts, of fifty of his class, but he quailed before the voice of this one honest woman!

He returned to Alton to find him in a worse plight than before.

The majority of the warehousemen had gone for the night, and he was lying alone in the private room tossing on the sofa. Gregory told him the result of his visit; but all he could get out of Alton was the cry,

'I am weary, weary of life!'

Gregory was too much subdued to be angry, but he urged on Mr Alton the necessity that he himself should try to get an interview with Prinkle.

'You may have more power with them than I,' he said.

'But how shall I find him, Gregory?'

This was rather a difficult question to answer, for both believed that the Hendrys would keep him near to them at such a time. It was arranged, however, that Gregory and the cashier, who, it may be remembered, was intimate with the plot from its commencement, should visit some of the hotels which they knew Mr Hendry frequented, and try if they could get any information regarding their movements.

It was not long before their search was crowned with a certain measure of success. Bedford House had been Mr Hendry's favourite Hotel for long, and to Covent Garden the spies accordingly went.

That individual who rejoices in the title of 'Boots' is not generally believed to be inexorable to a bribe, and he of this good old house was no exception to the rule. The touch of gold was to his hand what the key is to the lock; and in a moment he had begun to open up the mysteries of Mr Hendry's toilet, bed-room, and baths, when Mr Gregory motioned an adjournment to a more convenient place than that by the shadowy pillars of the Garden.

Boots would take the smallest possible nip of pale Brandy—''ot!' Gregory and the cashier ordered for themselves and him, but for the present they did not taste.

Gregory had just begun to make inquiry about Prinkle, and to describe him, when Boots interrupted him, gently laying his forefinger on his arm.

'Didn't I know it, gentle-men! Didn't I know it? First I sees 'em all come in, three abreast; they goes and has a eager talk: then the young 'un and the Jack-in-the-box man goes out for a while, and they comes back again; and they're all three up-stairs at the present moment. I know'd, gentlemen, as soon as ever I clapt eyes on him with the round 'ead and the peeping eyes, that he were a likely subjeck for a hinquiry, hand I was watching for you a coming round the corner to hask me. I know'd as how they was up to somethin'. Now, what d'ye want me for?'

Gregory smiled at this, and complimented the man, then stated they wished to know if it was at all likely that Prinkle would stay in the house over the night.

Boots at once decamped, and returned in three minutes.

'Beds ordered for two; supper for three, at ten o'clock,' was the laconic reply.

'Then,' said Gregory to the cashier, 'you go off to A. and tell him to hold himself in readiness at that time. I shall wait here for further news. You,' addressing boots, 'go back to your post; and, as soon as they show signs of breaking up, you'll bring me word sharply.'

''Alf now, and 'alf again?' inquired boots.

'Certainly,' said Gregory; and he tipped his cap and departed.

The cashier returned from his mission, sometime after; and the two passed the time together, smoking and drinking beer, while they waited for Boots.

Precisely at a quarter to eleven o'clock, Boots returned; and as he stood in the doorway with flushed face and dishevelled hair, Gregory associated his perquisite with his appearance.

'Gentle-men, supper's cleared; bullet-head's getting on his coat; young 'un's going with him —hic!'

In a moment Gregory was ready, and they passed over and stood under one of the arches opposite the hotel.

In a few minutes the younger Hendry and Prinkle appeared, and they stepped into a cab and drove off.

'Quick!' ejaculated Gregory, as he and the

cashier jumped into a hansom. 'Follow that cab;
but don't appear to do so!'

Cabby hinted that the latter injunction would
double his fare.

'All right,' cried Gregory. 'Drive on!'

But there was another objector, who stood
leaning forward with his hand on the splashboard.

''Alf again, you know,' said Boots. 'Honour
bright!'

'Ah!' cried Gregory, 'I forgot;' and he satisfied him. Boots leaped back on the pavement,
twirled a half-sovereign in the light of the lamp
and caught it in his mouth.

The cab whirled away along, up streets and
down streets, till it stopped at Prinkle's door.
Hendry Junior saw his charge safely into the
house, and returned with the vehicle. Gregory
and the cashier observed every movement, but
they drove right past the house till they made a
sudden turn, and their poor horse was goaded
like mad in the direction of the Hotel to which Alton had gone. This gentleman, on receiving the
news, took a fresh horse and directed himself to
Prinkle's. It was midnight before he arrived.
He knocked at the door, and Nell answered with
the question,—

'Who is there?'

'It is I—Mr Alton. I wish to see your husband for a little while.'

'Are you alone?'

'I am.'

On hearing this, Nell opened the door.

'I am sorry, sir, you cannot see my husband to-night; he is in bed.'

As she said this, Prinkle, who, on hearing his master's voice, had hurriedly risen and put on some clothes, came behind her and cried,

'Let him in, Nell; if Gregory isn't there.'

With this permission Nell opened the door; Mr Alton passed in, and master and servant met. It was evident that they were all deeply affected, for the three stood in the little room in silence, as if waiting to see which should break it.

'It is a sad business this,' said Mr Alton; and he swept his brow with his hand.

'Oh! sir, do not reproach him,' cried Nell, as she placed a chair; 'I am sure he is sorry for it now!'

Mr Alton saw that both were kindly disposed towards him, and he inquired how it was that the affair had become known.

Prinkle, in his simplest way, told him faithfully of the manner in which he had become acquainted with their proceedings, and how he had been goaded on to inform against him, by the gibes and insults of Gregory.

'Oh! sir,' he said, with tears in his eyes; 'it wasn't because I didn't like you, but because I hated Gregory. I heard him propose the whole thing to you, and know how he reasoned you into it. It's Gregory that's to blame, sir. He did it all; and if it hadn't been for the way he tormented

me, Mr Hendry would never have known nothing
of the matter ! '

The simple, sorrowful way in which Prinkle
said this, with his thin, piping voice, quite affected
Mr Alton.

' Oh ! sir,' he added, ' and I wouldn't have told,
neither, if I had thought at the time, as Nell says,
of your wife and family ! '

Mr Alton heaved a long sigh, and dropping his
brow on the palm of his hand, he shook his head
mournfully. Nell saw that he was moved, and
motioned her husband not to pursue the subject;
but he continued in the kindliest manner,

' Oh! sir, I am sorry for what I have done,
that I should have been the cause of what Nell
says will bring desolation on your family, but—'

His wife again knit her brows, and impatiently
motioned him to cease.

' Tut, dash it ! ' he cried to her angrily. ' I'll
say what I like. D'ye think I'm going to hold
my tongue because you—' but he checked himself
here, for he saw the bright tears gather in her eyes;
he stepped forward, and, as if no one had been in
the place but themselves, placed his hand affectionately on her shoulder and kissed her. It was a
simple thing to do, but it showed Prinkle's nature.

' Have you told Mr Hendry all ? ' inquired
Alton, not looking up.

' Yes, sir, I'm afraid I have.'

' But if you retract, the matter may blow past
in a quieter way,' he pleaded.

'Ah! sir, it's all true that I've told them, and I can't tell a lie now. Even if I did, it would do you no good.'

'But the whole state of the case cannot be imprinted on their minds, and, if you were out of the way for a time, it would put them in a difficulty, and they might never know how far matters have gone.'

'I can't, sir! I can't. It's too late to draw back. Even if I did run away, they would be sure to catch me. It would make them worse against you, and it would ruin me!'

'But think of what is in store for me,' cried Alton, piteously, 'if this goes farther! My reputation gone! My wife broken-hearted; and Mary—my only child—disgraced! Think, before you decide, of the terrible ruin entailed on me and mine if you do not help me! If you leave the country to-morrow, all this may be averted, but if you do not—' here his voice fairly broke. 'I can see no other results than desolation, and, perhaps, death!' He paused for a moment as he wiped the tears from his eyes with the back of his hand, and Prinkle and Nell wept on each other's neck.

'When you told Mr Hendry all this, did you never think of any little kindnesses I have shown you?'

'Oh! yes, sir, I did,' cried Prinkle. 'I know that you have been good—very good to me! I know that it was to you I was indebted all the time I was away in the country, but what was that when I thought of making Nell a lady!'

'What!' she exclaimed, starting back. 'What had I to do with it!'

'Oh! you expected to get a reward from Hendry, did you?' said Alton to him, affecting a smile. 'You'll get none. I know the man better than you do. As for money, I can supply you with what you wish,' he said, taking a handful of gold from his pocket; but Nell stepped quickly between them and struck the table violently.

'Put back your money, Mr Alton,' she cried excitedly. 'Whichever way this matter goes, I will not allow my husband to accept one farthing from you; and if Mr Hendry offers a reward, it shall be refused, though perhaps not in so mild terms as I would use to you! No, no. So long as I live in this house and entertain a rag of regard for truth and justice, the price of sin shall not enter it! I am sorry—very sorry that Mr Hendry should have known anything of this before you were warned, but since the matter has gone so far, my husband cannot retract, for in doing so his own honesty would be compromised, and that is all we have got to live by! Since you have mentioned your wife and daughter, I may tell you that no one grieves for them more than I do! Heaven knows the tears I have shed over this,' she cried, as they again started to her eyes. 'And I pray God sincerely that this trial may be lightened to them, and that you may yet live to repent

and be forgiven for the evil you have wrought! Put
back your money, sir; and learn from a poor
woman that Truth is better than wealth—that
Honesty is all in all!'

There is a fine ring in an honest voice, and it
is a grand thing to see a daughter of Eve repel
temptation as an insult to her dignity, and make
a bold stand, like Nell, for Justice and for Truth.

Not till now, did Alton feel so utterly de-
graded and hopeless! Even although this were to
blow past, as he said, how could he ever hold up
his head again? He was shorn of his integrity!
How could he ever mingle with those who had
known him when his name was without reproach?

He would see Gregory, he resolved, no more!
He felt himself to be an outcast from all society,
too disreputable for the good, too hateful of the
bad!

Through dark, dull streets—damp and clammy
and deserted—he wandered on, unheeding all! It
was as if the Angel of Fate were spreading her
dark wings behind him, and hurrying him to de-
struction; and that was a bitter ringing in his
ears—'Truth is better than wealth—Honesty is
all in all.'

CHAPTER VI.

It was evident that the desperate state of Mr Alton's affairs was not yet known at Ashfield.

On the day Prinkle left the warehouse, Mrs Alton had received a telegram from her husband stating that it would be impossible for him to come to Ashfield, owing to an unusual pressure of business, and a letter bearing the same date stating that even next day he might find it necessary to remain in London; but that she was not to be anxious, as he would certainly come on the day following, 'For,' as he said, 'I have not forgotten that it is the anniversary of our dear Mary's birthday, and the last she is likely to spend with us as our child.' This had reference to her approaching marriage with Trevor, for, although the day had not yet been definitely fixed, they all looked forward to it in the immediate future.

It had been customary, for some years past, at the Hall, to honour Mary's birthday with a dinner-party, but this year it was to be dispensed with, on account of the delicate state of Mrs Alton's health; and the only guests invited for the morrow were Robert Trevor and the rector. Very little preparation was made for them, for Mrs Alton wished to be homely on that day, and she only asked the rector as he was a homely

man, and because she thought it would be pleasant
to have with them one who was to take an im-
portant part in the approaching ceremony.

The day came, but with it no word of Mr
Alton. Dinner was to be served at 6 o'clock,
and in the afternoon Trevor arrived alone. Mrs
Alton fully expected that her husband would have
come with him, and she was grievously disappointed at his absence. Still she looked for him
confidently by the 5 o'clock train, as that was the
last arriving from London till a late hour.

Trevor waited for him at the station, but he
did not come; and Mrs Alton and Mary were in a
state of consternation when they saw Bob return
alone. What was to be done? What explanation were they to make to their guest? But it
was plain that in Mrs Alton's heart there was a
deeper solicitude than this; there was an apprehension lurking in her bosom that all was not
right; and, all she could do, her face would not
hide it.

'I wonder,' she said to Trevor, taking him
aside, 'why papa has stayed away from home
these three days. Do you know if there is anything wrong with the business?'

Bob, thus suddenly appealed to, was taken
aback, and Mrs Alton noticed this.

'Really,' he replied lightly, 'I can quite
understand how he may be detained. An unusual
stress of business would do it; and I see no reason
why you should be apprehensive.'

'But, have you heard of anything wrong?'

'Wrong! Certainly not! Why?'

'I do not know what it is, but I have a strange feeling,' she said pensively, and she raised her eyebrows inquiringly. 'Is it usual, Robert, for men who have been partners in the same business for years, after a dissolution, to hate each other so heartily as my husband does Mr Hendry?'

'Well,' he replied, 'it is not necessary, but it is very common. I have known men who have been the warmest friends for years, after a dissolution, refuse to kneel at the same communion.'

Mrs Alton was shocked.

'And were they honest, upright men?'

'To all appearance they were.'

'I do not think that men can carry their animosity so far, and remain honest. Either they are false to themselves, or to their religion.'

'Very likely,' laughed Bob; 'but you would be astonished had you an insight to the minds of some commercial men. I know one who is faultlessly upright, who bears the character of a religious man; I have sat beside him in church, and heard him loud and ready in his responses, but on the fly-leaf of his prayer-book I have seen him making calculations of cost and profit during sermon! The fact is, you may think Mr Alton's absence unaccountable, especially on such a day as this, but I can quite understand it. We, commercial men, are so worried, at times, that we have no thought either for ourselves or for others; business engrosses all our attention; we leave undone things which we ought to do, and, (hem! he coughed) 'it may be, do some things which we ought not.'

Perhaps Trevor thought he admitted too much, for he coughed again and became red.

'Surely,' said Mrs Alton, 'this is not right. But if a seemingly religious man can forget himself so far as to make calculations in church, as you tell me, it is quite possible that business affairs may so engross papa that he has forgotten what day this is, even although he mentioned it in his note the day before yesterday.'

'Of course,' replied Trevor, gratified at the easier tone. 'But he is sure to be home to-night with the last train.'

'I should expect so,' she said more hopefully. 'Yet I cannot help thinking it is very wrong in men to allow the cares of the world to obtain such a hold over them. In olden times, Religion was in the van, but it is now in the rear.'

'Yes,' said Trevor with a laugh. 'Our times are out of joint; or, as Prinkle used to say when he got into any trouble, somehow or other the world has bumped up against something, and got into the wrong groove.'

At this moment the hoofs of the rector's horse were heard on the gravel, and Mrs Alton went to receive her guest, and make what explanation she could for her husband's absence.

. A jolly, plump, lively little man was Dr

Thorley, the rector. Nobody was ever known to hate him, and that is enough to establish the character of a man fifty-seven years of age. His hair was perfectly white—had been so for seven or eight years, but his face was rosy red, and his mild blue eyes were pleasant to contemplate. True, he had always a kindly inclination for a good dinner, as he had for everything else that savoured well, and he regarded the practice of dining out as one of the most agreeable of his pastoral duties. His politics were conservative if anything, but he never allowed them to become the subject of contention. Politically speaking, he was all things to all men, for at one moment he would aver that Radicalism was driving the country to the dogs, and the next he would turn to a Nonconformist friend and declare that he didn't mind if the Church were disestablished to-morrow—so long as they didn't disendow it. 'It is fast becoming a question of political expediency, and it will be a ridiculous thing if ever an institution of God has to depend on the stubbornness of Tory Lords!'

The dinner passed over in a quiet way, but a really hearty enjoyment of it was wanting on account of the absence of Mr Alton. Nevertheless, the rector was cheery, and so was Trevor, but Mrs Alton, at times, was deeply dejected, as if labouring under anxiety. Mary chatted freely and pleasantly enough, but from the frequent glances she bestowed on her mother, it was evident that she, too, was ill at ease.

'Ah!' cried the rector, jokingly over his wine, to Trevor, 'you fellows in business are a sad lot. You stick to your work in spite of waiting wives at home; and one doesn't know what you would be after. I've often thought of preaching a sermon on commercial men, taking for my text "My soul, come not thou into their secret; unto their assembly, mine honour, be not thou united."'

'Very good, sir. And I know you would do them justice in spite of your text, for you would tell us how that men engaged in business deny themselves the comforts of home society in trying all they can to better the position of waiting wives!'

'I believe you, Mr Trevor, honestly, and joking aside. Somebody must bear the burden, and I think from what I know of them, that they do it less grudgingly than any other class. Of course there is a pleasure in it too, for I can conceive nothing more pleasant than to contemplate the working of the commercial machine, if the wheels go smoothly.'

'It is very true what you say, Doctor,' said Mrs Alton, 'but we women are selfish, and we become impatient when we are denied the company of those we love, even though we know that it is in our own behalf they are engaged.'

'Exactly,' he laughed. 'You think sometimes that they work at the machine for the mere pleasure of seeing it going, and you expect that a good machine should always go, even though they

be away from it; but you must remember there
are innumerable hitches ever occurring, making
the presence of a master-mind necessary. I've
no doubt Mr Alton will be home to-night to tell
you that his is in full roar. I like a man,' he
added, 'who, while he trusts Providence, keeps a
sharp eye on the books!'

Thus the evening passed in pleasant chat, and
at ten o'clock the rector's horse was ready. Mrs
Alton requested him to wait to see if her husband
came, but Dr Thorley shook his head good-na-
turedly, and reminded her that he had work before
him in view of the approaching Sunday, which
would see him astir very early in the morning. Of
course she did not press him, and after a little
while he cantered away.

Mrs Alton was anything but strong, and the
tension of their conversation had kept her up
hitherto; but, as soon as they were alone, she
showed unmistakable signs of nervousness; her
conversation became disjointed and wandering; till
at last she burst into tears, and had to seek the
retirement of her own room. Mary followed her,
and Trevor was alone.

It was a painful position for him to occupy;
for, in spite of himself, the apprehensiveness of
Mrs Alton begun to grow on him, forebodings
crowded in upon his mind, he tried to battle with
them and reason them away, but at the best he
was anxious and ill at ease. Faintly he recollected
something of an old story of Prinkle's about a plot

to defraud Mr Hendry, but he had paid no attention to it at the time, and merely reproved Peter
for entertaining another hallucination. For a time
he sat trying hard to recollect the particulars, but
could not; so he dismissed the affair from his mind,
and tried to laugh at himself for having given it
a single serious thought. But still, the short conversation he had with Mrs Alton, coupled with
her demeanour throughout the evening, set him
a-thinking strange things.

He rose, stepped into the window-space, drew
the curtains close behind him, raised the blind,
and looked out into the night, striving hard to rid
himself of unpleasant thoughts. And, surely, if
natural beauty could have brought him peace, he
would have had it to his heart's content. The
moon was at her best, shedding her pale glory on
the lawn; showing the tree-tops pencilled on the
sky; deepening their shadows into darkest night;
and shining on the river as it lay silent and still,
like a thread of silver tangled throughout the
scene. But his thoughts were not with these,
not with the glorious beauties of the autumnal
moon.

Mary came into the room, and, seeing no one,
she stepped up towards the window and peeped
through the curtain. She saw him, and drew it
aside, and entering, placed her arm affectionately
in his. Bob saw by the light of the moon that
tears were in her eyes, and he drew his arm around
her and inquired the cause.

Mary could give no explanation, except that she was sorry to see her mamma so sad.

'It is not only now,' she said, 'but for a long time past she has been liable to these moods—ever, I think, since papa took Gregory into partnership. Do you know what it is, Bob? When I ask her, it just brings a flood of tears into her eyes.'

'Mary, my darling, you should not trouble yourself with this. Likely enough your mamma may have thoughts which she would try to hide from you; but why should you be sad? A little while and all shall be well again.'

'I don't know that, Bob. I think it is something wrong with the business. I know, if anything goes wrong with papa, mamma will break her heart. Do *you* know what it is, dear?'

'No, Mary; indeed I do not. But why should we speak of these things? Cheer up! Let us admire the scenery. Does not the Ash look beautiful, wending along in the light of the silent moon?' he said, in a laughing, mock-poetical strain; but she heeded him not.

'What will become of us if anything goes wrong?'

Trevor smiled at the simplicity of the question, but answered her ironically, trying to rouse her into better spirits.

'If anything *does* go wrong, your father can still break stones on the roadside. As for you, you can sew,—I suppose the mil—'

'Ah, Bob,' she cried piteously. 'How can you

speak to me in that way when you know mamma is so anxious? If anything serious happens to her, it will be no laughing matter to me whatever it may be to you!'

Trevor saw that he had pained her, and was sorry. He drew her closer to himself and pressed her form to his.

'Mary, I am a fool! Forgive me. I did not mean to pain you—You know I did not. But really, why should we converse in this way? Your apprehensions are groundless, and if I did ridicule them, believe me, I did not mean to freshen your grief!'

Stroking back the loose hair from her brow, he looked with enthusiasm into her large, loving eyes. 'Mary, it is wrong to foster thoughts like these; but, should misfortune come upon your father's house, I have money—more than we should need for ourselves—to fall back upon; and whatever comes, nothing in the wide world shall ever separate me and thee!'

Mary's heart was full. She looked up to him silently, for a few seconds, as if every particle of her life were concentrated in her love-lit eyes. Unable to restrain them longer, her tears welled up afresh and trickled on her cheek, conveying her sense of gratitude more beautifully than words could do. She tried to speak, but could only lay her face on his arm and weep for joy.

But they were not long allowed the pleasure of this situation, for they were startled by seeing

in the distance a carriage with lamps lit, driving
rapidly along the avenue towards the house.
Mary clapped her hands like a child. 'It is
papa, after all!' she cried. 'I was sure he would
come! One moment, Bob, and I shall let mamma
know.' But Trevor restrained her.

'Better not go till you are sure. If it should
not be he, it will only disappoint her the more.'

So they waited two or three minutes till the
carriage passed the window, and they saw that
Mr Alton was not there. Trevor got one short
look at the face— It was George Gregory's!

'Wait here a moment, Mary, while I see what
is wanted,' and he hurriedly left the room. Gregory alighted as he appeared at the door.

'Is Mr Alton here?' inquired that gentleman
in an excited whisper.

'He is not. Is there anything wrong?'

'All is wrong! But, hush, here comes Miss
Alton. Good-evening, Miss Alton; I have come
on a flying visit, to say that your father cannot
come to-night as he expected, and you are not to
be the least alarmed if he should not appear to-
morrow. Business of the utmost importance will
in all likelihood detain him in the City.'

Mary was smitten with fear.

'Will you come in and rest, Mr Gregory?'
she said, in faltering tones. 'You must be tired.
Mamma is in bed, but I think she would like to
speak with you.'

'Indeed, Miss Alton, I should have been very

glad, for I require rest, having been so busy; but I cannot. I must go back with the late train, and even now I have run myself short of time!' He looked at his watch impatiently, going to the light of the lamp, though there was no need, for the moon was shining brightly. But Gregory knew that his face was ghastly by reason of protracted anxiety, excitement, and drink, and he wished to hide it.

Trevor saw this, and therefore did not press him.

'It is a pity,' he said, 'that you must go so hurriedly.'

'Really, I must,' he replied, placing his foot on the carriage step. 'I must go. Look here, Mr Trevor,' he whispered. 'If Mrs Alton is asleep, better not waken her to-night. We'll see what to-morrow does.'

Mary did not hear this remark, for she stood a little bit off in the door-way. It was well.

'But, won't you come in, Mr Gregory? I am sure mamma will be anxious when she knows you have been here, not having seen you!'

'Really, I cannot. I must return; and this is the last train.'

'But,' cried Mary, striving to restrain her tears in the presence of a man she disliked. 'We *are* anxious. We *are* alarmed. What is it all?'

But he leapt into the carriage, and vouchsafed her no reply. Trevor rushed into the hall for his hat.

'I'll be back in less than half-an-hour, Mary. Don't be alarmed more than you can help. Keep mamma as quiet as possible, and don't say a word to her of this visit!'

It cost him a pang to leave that beautiful ghost of a girl, pale from anxiety, alone with the terror of an impending grief; but what could he do, knowing so little of what he knew must be so much? He kissed her bloodless lip once—twice, joined Gregory, and in a moment the carriage bore them away.

Mary withdrew from the cold air—the cold air that never left her—gently closed the door, and retired to wait the return of him around whom she clung with all the fondness of a whole heart.

On the way to the station Gregory gave Trevor a rambling account of the state of the firm's affairs; saying that he had hunted up and down London for a whole day, but had seen nothing of Mr Alton since he left him on the previous night for the purpose of visiting Prinkle; and that the message he had delivered to Miss Alton was a pure fabrication to allay any apprehension which might have arisen on account of his hurried visit.

'The fact is,' he said, ' there is no saying what has happened.'

'Good God! You don't mean to insinuate that he has—'

'No, no! He wouldn't do that. But I believe he has left the country, and it will be a long while before we see him back again.'

'But what is to be done?'

'Bless me!' cried Gregory, as he leapt out on the station at that moment. 'There's my train going off! Good night. Meet me at twelve to-morrow on London Bridge. Good night!' and he had just time to take his seat when the train moved away.

No words of ours could describe the state of Trevor's feelings now he saw that the worst apprehensions of Mrs Alton were realized, that ruin stared them in the face. He contemplated the bitter prospects, the apparently inevitable desolation that overhung the inmates of Ashfield Hall. But, when he thought of Mary—Mary, the tender, true, and loving girl—when he thought of her guileless name being outraged by the misdemeanour of a father, it was too much—too much! Every recollection he had of Ashfield was fraught with pleasure and with peace, but now there was no beauty in the scene that he should desire it; no grandeur, as he walked back on that dreary night, in the rush, *hush*, of the breeze among the pines; no music for his ears in the gentle ripple of the stream; no joy in the sparkle of the waters as they danced and glanced along: but there was a weirdness of dread in his heart, a chill on his soul, as a man feels when his friend is dead!

The lodge was lighted as he passed. Willie was not asleep, for there arose an *eerie* voice, swelling into the wild melody of the Northern hills,—

'A thousand suns will stream on thee,
A thousand moons will quiver;
But not by thee my steps shall be,
For ever and for ever.'

The music died away, and Trevor remembered Mary when she said, 'It is not enough for Willie that he should read songs: he makes music of his own and sings them.'

Mrs Alton did not hear Trevor going, nor did she hear him return. Mary opened the door as gently as she had shut it. She had sat by a window watching all the while, and she opened for him before his foot was on the step. Bob could not look her in the face, nor could he speak; but he passed her silently, and entered the room in which they had been. It was still lighted; Mary followed him and caught his hand. He turned to look at her, and she was pale like a spectre.

'What is it all?' she asked; but his head hung upon his breast, and he made no reply.

'Speak to me, Bob!' she cried, as she ran to close the door. 'Tell me what it all means. This suspense is fearful. Tell me the worst—I can bear it!'

But still he was silent. Mary knelt before him and wrung his hand.

'I implore you, Bob. Why don't you speak? Can anything be worse than this? Speak—Is my father in prison?'

He started at this: the thought had not occurred to him; but he remained speechless.

'Tell me what you know! Ah!' she cried
beseechingly, as the scorching tears streamed upon
her cheeks, 'you would tell me if you love me
as you say you do!'.

He raised her to his arms and she clung to his
neck.

'Yes, Mary, I love you now, more fondly than
I ever loved you before. There is nothing that
flesh and blood can do, I would not do to give you
happiness, and avert from you pain and grief! I
have loved you so long and so well, that your life
is dearer to me than my own! You know I love
you, Mary; and, God knows! it is this love which
keeps me from saying aught that may bring you
sorrow!'

The trembling voice, the deep pathos in which
these words were spoken, thrilled through Mary's
soul. She knew his words were true, but they
carried with them a strange mixture of sweetness
and of bitterness.

'Mary,' he continued, turning his face to hers
while he kept his arm around her. 'You would
not urge me to say more. You know well that I
would not keep from your knowledge anything it
would be good for you to know.'

He stopped for a moment, for his voice was
broken; but again it rang out as clearly as a bell.
'Yet you may hear me in this! If happiness
should still shine upon you as it has done, that happiness shall be mine; but if misfortune should at
any time arise to cast a cloud upon your life, that

misfortune shall be mine, and I will share its gloom! Come prosperity or adversity, joy or grief, you shall never be ashamed that you have given to me the greatest gift a woman can bestow!'

Though the words were dear to her, they crushed out the little hope that lingered in her heart.

'My father! What of my father?' she cried; and he then began to tell her how some things were not right, how all was wrong. But what could he say? His thoughts were wild and distracted, his words were jolted and confused. But they were enough for Mary, who sobbed convulsively as she flung her hands on his shoulders and hung upon his breast.

Trevor was overcome; he did not try to speak any more; but he pressed his confiding lover to himself, with all the passion of a love that is strengthened by sorrow.

Neither of them spoke for a time, and the silence was broken only by the short, convulsive sobs of Mary, and the strokes of Midnight from the great clock on the stair.

CHAPTER VII.

A WEEK passed. Mrs Alton received a letter from her husband informing her of the whole affair, but before it came to hand, he was out on the Atlantic bound for America.

The grand crash came. Metropolitan and provincial papers had the whole story, and leading articles were written deprecating the state of commercial morality. But since then, swindles have been perpetrated and exposed, leading articles have been written again and again, yet there is no remedy. There was no attempt made to bring Mr Alton back, and although Gregory still remained in London, the law laid no hands upon him; but he was allowed to go forth into society unpunished, ready to poison, by sophistry, the minds of men to whom he was previously unknown; and, it might be, to bring desolation and ruin on the lives of those to whom happiness was only known before. Almost every day we read in newspapers of swindles that are exposed in the Bankruptcy Courts, yet how rarely do we hear of the bankrupt swindler being punished for his crime? A letter-book may be abstracted to hide an illegal transaction, and leading articles are written in fierce denunciation of the man, yet the law stands idly by, as if its majesty were not offended. The excitement caused by such cases soon dies down, but their evil effect rankles in the bosoms of those who have been defrauded, for many years, and is only brought to an end by the close of their ruined lives. It is without fear we affirm that one man of Gregory's stamp let loose upon the world, does more harm, ruins more lives, and causes more grief than all the pickpockets in the land!

It was a sad time at Ashfield Hall. Mrs Alton's health had never been robust, but when the evil news came, it told upon her with terrible effect; and high fever one day, succeeded by complete prostration the next, helped to shatter her constitution.

Medical men were powerless to cure, and all they tried was for the purpose of keeping up her strength: they could give no name to the disorder, but in a week they signified to Trevor that the worst might happen at any moment. By reason of constant watching, Mary's strength was greatly undermined, and she flitted about the house, slender and white, like the ghost of the bright girl she had been. Servants slipped along noiselessly and spoke in whispers, shunning to meet with any of the family friends, lest it might be thought they were prying into their distress. It seemed as if a death had taken place. Old Willie, the gardener, tended his flowers as usual, but no one knew how much he felt for the inmates of the Hall. Poor old man! his heart bled for Mary whom he had loved from childhood; and, God knows, he would

have given every drop of blood in his veins to pur-
chase for her a life of joy. Often would he rest on
his spade and sigh deeply as he looked at the old
grey walls, and the tear was quietly wiped from his
eye when he thought that the furniture might yet
be sold to the rabble in the midst of an auction-
mob. His flowers, too, he must part with them,
and he tended them all the more with a loving,
sorrowful care.

Trevor, when he stayed at Ashfield, used to
come along on the fine mornings and have a chat
with Willie, but since the crash came he had dis-
continued the practice; not that he had given up
visiting Ashfield, for he came the oftener now, but
because he felt loth to talk of Mr Alton out of doors.
This trial had a humanizing influence on Trevor,
and he seemed to be purged of that vanity which
he so frequently manifested, and which is, more or
less, a part of every man's nature; his generous
feelings were brought more freely into play, and
his devotion for Mary was more distinct, although
it was not avowed in words. His manner towards
her was tender and delicate as the waves of light
upon the sea, and his love was not the less strong
that it was unexpressed.

One morning, however, he strolled along to
where Willie was working, and stood beside him.
The gardener touched his cap, and wished him
good morning, in that subdued tone in which we
would address one whom we knew to be newly and
sorely bereaved.

'Good morning to you, Willie; I see you are the same as ever, taking a pleasure in your flowers.'

'Pleesur', sir, did ye ca't? Hech, ay, but it's a painfu' ane noo. But come what will, I'll aye tak' an interest in my flowers. They're awfu' like men,' he added, drawing to his favourite theme.

'I have often heard you say so, Willie; but the oftener I hear you, the truer, I think, does your saying appear.'

'Ay, ay. If there was mair studying o' flowers, it would be a better world this; men wad ha'e a fuller knowledge o' Nature and Nature's God; and if they had that, they wad act mair kindly to ane anither than they dae.'

This had particular reference to Mr Hendry's treatment of Mrs Alton and Mary. Since Mr Alton had left the country, that gentleman's solicitor had not ceased to worry the inmates of the Hall, for they were completely in his power. Inventory had been made of every article in the house, and so little regard had been paid to Mrs Alton that even the sick-room was not kept sacred for the time. Trevor had gone to Mr Hendry for the purpose of appealing to his better nature, if he had any, which was questionable; he represented to him the disastrous effect which the presence of a valuator might have on Mrs Alton in her illness, but he was obdurate, and said that it was at Mr Alton's own request that the affairs had been placed in the hands of a man of business, and he therefore declined to interfere. Mr Beeds, acting

for the family, had tried what he could, but Mr
Hendry's treatment of that gentleman was rude in
the extreme. Likely enough he recollected a
former episode in Esther Square when the lawyer
acted like a Samaritan and he as a Levite, and
perhaps the priestly nature was still strong upon
him, for it is said that priests, of all men, are the
least apt to forget. When the servants at Ashfield
heard that even the bed on which their mistress
was laid, was noted in the inventory by a man who
demanded entrance to her room, they were indignant, and gave expression to their feelings in a way
that made the fellow glad to beat a hasty retreat.
Even old Willie was roused to passion, and cried,
'Shame on him!' as he passed. Trevor had heard
of this, and could understand the reference which
the gardener made.

'Yes, Willie, it is very true. I think it was
your own poet who said that "Man's inhumanity
to man makes countless thousands mourn."'

'We've had many poets,' said the old man
respectfully, 'but oor ain Robby Burns ken't
weel the truth o' what he was sayin' when he
said that. He was a rough-gaun chiel Robby, but
he reads us a' a lesson when he tells how sorry he
was to crush a wee bit daisy afore his pleugh ! Oh,
ay ; there's mair in a flower than what pleases the
senses o' seein' and smellin'. When I let my
mind wander awa' amang them, strange thochts
and fancies and mysteries come into my heid.'
Willie stopped for a moment, and there was a re-

markable twitching in the wrinkles of his brow.
Trevor saw that he was thinking, and did not disturb the old man, whose restless eyes seemed to
flit about from one flower to another. 'If thae
flowers werena looked after they wad a' gang
wild; and it's just the same wi' man, for if a
higher hand didna guide him, often like the
flowers when he doesna ken o't, he wad gang a'
wrang thegither. D'ye see yon black stalk?' he
said, pointing to a dahlia that had been nipt by
the morning's frost. 'Weel, a short time gane,
it had a bonny stem, and there hung on it as fine
a flower as in a' the garden; but a frost came, it
was withered in a nicht, and noo it's deid. The
blackened stalk is like the body, for I'll cut it
doon and bury't in the earth; but I'll tak' the
root into the house wi' me for a season, and then
I'll plant it oot, maybe in anither garden, and it'll
put forth as fair a stem, that'll hang wi' flowers as
bonny, if no' bonnier, than ever sprang frae't
afore! Od, sir,' he said with enthusiasm, 'when I
think o' that, somehow or ither, I feel that it'll
come a' richt in the end wi' man when he's planted
in anither world! If a flower be blawn doon wi'
the wind, it maun be brocht back wi' a tender
hand and wi' the saftest tie; if you work wi' 't
roughly you'll break it, and so it is wi' man. If he
be blawn wrang by some bitter blast—for there's
many an angry sough blaws doon this weary vale
—he maun be brocht back to his auld place wi'
tenderness, and held there by the maist tender

ties : on the ither hand, if you treat him harshly
and cast his fau't in his face, he'll gang far'er
wrang than he was before ! Oh, ay ; if you saw and
thocht as much o' flowers as I dae, you wad believe
wi' me that men are just flowers o' anither sort,
the world's a garden, and God is the greatest and
best gardener of all ! '

Trevor was amazed, and could not help contrasting the rough exterior of the man with the
purity and simplicity of his mind. Willie's com-
parison of the blasted flower with man called up
the case of Mr Alton vividly before him, and he
was truly grateful for the tenderness with which
the old man spoke. There was silence between
them for a little while as the gardener wrought
away with his spade, till something compelled
Trevor to inquire why he had not asked about
Mrs Alton's health. Willie stopped work instantly, and caught him warmly by the hand,
while a tear glistened in his eye and ran down
the furrows of his cheek.

' Thank you for that ! Oh, sir, I didna care to
speer at you, although I wished ever sae much to
ken, frae you yersel, how the Mistress and Miss
Mary are keeping.'

Trevor informed him, and the old man brushed
away the tear with the back of his hand.

' It's a sad, sad business, sir, for he was a good
man i' the main, and Gude kens what I wad dae
for his wife and the bonny lass ! Heaven send

them a blessin' wi' their affliction, and may God's
hand bear them up ! '

Trevor was visibly affected, and he thanked
old Willie heartily.

' Sir,' he said, after a pause, ' we maun a' tak'
a lesson frae't. Dinna think that I wad hurt
yer feelin's, when I tell you that you canna tak'
ower much care o' yersel in business. I'm an auld
man noo, and I hae seen a gude wheen ups and
doons in life amang business men, and there's
naething for't but to hae a strict knowledge o'
what's richt and what's wrang, and stick weel
tae't. Gang wrang for a wee while and you'll
aye gang wrang ! Keep a tree richt when it *is*
richt, and you'll ne'er need to say that it's ta'en
the bend. But, sir, although he's gane wrang,
dinna be hard on Mr Alton, for the best o' us 'll
mak' a slip: if he comes back, entreat him
kindly, and remember that the best man is the
ane that rises straicht frae a fause step.'

' Thank you, Willie ; thank you,' said Trevor,
holding out his hand and taking the gardener's.
' During these sad times I have much need of
consolation, and I have found it where I least
expected it.'

' I'm glad, sir, if you have received what
you say frae me, but I have been bred in the
school of affliction, and they are profitable the
lessons that reverses teach us. Keep up your heart,
and, oh ! try an' do the same for Miss Mary :

she'll need a' yer kindness !   Pardon me, sir, for
giving way like this, but I've ken't her since she
was a wee bit thing; I've watched her as I wad
have watched a plant in its growth, and I've seen
each new beauty in her as it was unfolded to the
sun; but till this time cam, I didna ken that she
had crept sae close to my auld heart ! '

Trevor wrung the man's hand as he parted
from him, and in that bright morning he walked
back to the Hall with a lighter step; a new joy
had been given to him, inasmuch as he had found
a companion in his grief.

When a man loves he is extremely susceptible
to disinterested praise bestowed upon the object
of his affections.   Although Trevor had been
going very much about the house, he had not
spoken to Mary a single word, since the crash
came, with regard to their future prospects.   Their
relationship had been distant, and even restrained;
they had not been alone with each other for any
length of time, and at these periods they had
conversed on any subject but that which both
had so very much at heart.   To a third party,
Mary's unremitting attendance upon her mother
might account for this, but she herself viewed it
in a different light.   Love is proverbially blind,
and it did not lose this characteristic on Mary's
side.   Although Trevor's affection for her had
increased and deepened with her misfortune, she
never thought that this restraint proceeded otherwise than from the altered circumstances by which

they were surrounded, while, in fact, it proceeded entirely from a conceit which is not abnormal to a woman's love. At first she had thought it possible that this disgrace which had come upon her house might have the effect of estranging his love, and she had dwelt so much on this idea that, in spite of many and distinct manifestations to the contrary, she had come to regard it as a reality. Trevor, on the other hand, yearned towards her with too much love to entertain a doubt of her constancy; and with a delicacy that commends itself, he had hitherto refrained from touching on a topic which was sure to rouse her feelings, when he knew so well that, at this juncture, strong nerve, and not passionate feeling, was eminently necessary to carry her through. But this conversation with Willie had increased his yearning to such an extent, that he determined, on the first opportunity, to break down the wall between himself and Mary.

In the evening he sat by the bed-side of Mrs Alton, and although she was too weak to converse, she manifested an unmistakable pleasure in his presence, and her eye was never more bright, and her face never more calm, than when he was sitting there.

Bob had always been an especial favourite with Mrs Alton, and at periods when her mind was distracted with the present and filled with forebodings of the future, it was a great consolation for her to think that, if the worst did happen and she were taken away, she would leave her daughter in the hands of one for whom she entertained the highest regard.

Mary was continually flitting about, in close attendance on her mother, but little or no conversation passed between her and Bob. Later in the evening he retired to the parlour in which they were when Gregory drove up in that eventful night, and he was taking a last look at the newspaper before returning to rest. Mary happened to come in for something or other, and he spoke to her. She answered him coldly, and left the room. A few minutes after, she returned as if on an errand, and Trevor asked her,

'Won't you sit with me for a little while, Mary?'

She turned as if it had been the voice of a stranger that addressed her.

'Indeed, sir, I am busy; but I may return shortly.'

Trevor was astounded at the manner in which she spoke, and for the moment a feeling of resentment rose within him; but he waited patiently, and his heart beat fiercely till she came again. Timorously she asked, 'Did you wish to speak with me, sir?'

'Yes, Mary,' he replied softly. 'Won't you let me have a few words? Come and sit with me here.'

He was sitting on a couch, and Mary seemed to hesitate between that and a chair on the back of which she rested her hand. Eventually she seated herself beside him; and there was silence for a few minutes. Trevor's heart misgave him, but he drew nearer and allowed his hand to fall gently on her waist.

'No, no!' she cried, starting from the seat. 'That cannot be now!' and she stood panting before him.

Bob rose in astonishment at this; he was utterly confounded, so different was it from his fond anticipation.

'Mary, what does this mean?' he inquired anxiously, trying to articulate clearly, for his heart rose to his mouth. His words were uttered in a deep, broken pathos in which were mingled the feelings of anxiety, tenderness, and reproach.

'No, Mr Trevor, it cannot be. Circumstances have so altered since you declared your love for me that I cannot but release you from our engagement! All my life was pleasure, my father in a good position, and my prospects the brightest, when first I drew from you that happiness which love alone can yield! Now, all is changed. These prospects are shattered, all my pleasure in life is gone, and my father has had to flee from his country a ruined man. I know that your love is noble and disinterested, but I cannot believe that a ruined family, and a name disgraced, will not stand as a barrier in the course of the most noble love! No, it cannot be. My respect—my love for you is too great for me to allow your fair fame to be sullied by being linked with a name that has become a by-word, such as mine is; but I shall always cherish a fond regard for you, and remember, with a sore heart, the happiness which might have been ! '

Mary spoke these words as if her soul flowed in them, and as she finished she burst into tears. But what was it all ? It was nothing else than a fine frenzy raised upon a false idea. If, in these moments of exalted passion, the human mind could analyze the feelings from which they are born, what miserable and puny creatures would we seem, to ourselves, to be ! But we cannot wed the calm with the storm, and the analysis comes too late.

Bob repeatedly changed colour while she spoke, and conflicting passions tore him ; but when she finished his rage was high, and for a moment his love was chilled. At length he spoke in measured words that cut with severe keenness into Mary's heart.

'Mary Alton, I have never spoken a harsh word to you before, and if I do so now, it is because I am powerless to restrain myself. Your speech belies your thought; for when you say that my love was noble, you hold the possibility of its being chilled by adversity. You impute to it motives that are contemptible as they are mean, when you tell me that it was for your position in society, and not for your personal worth, that I sought you for a wife ! '

'No, no, not that!' she cried.

'I will not say more,' he continued, 'for I do not believe that you are past all feeling; but I cannot leave you without letting you know that I consider what you said about a ruined family, disgrace, and so forth, was nothing else than a flimsy pretence to be quit of your engagement. It may have been a weakness on my part, but I confess that I expected something very different from one on whom I had staked so much!'

Saying this he passed from the room, leaving her sobbing as if her heart would break. But he was no sooner in the lobby than all his love revived, and he cursed himself for having spoken to her as he did. He lingered at the door, and his heart called loudly for him to return. The parlour-door opened; it was Mary; and in an instant they were locked in a warm and passionate embrace.

Some of our fair readers will, doubtless, disapprove of Mary's motion towards reconciliation; and we can almost think we hear the stamping of some tiny foot, accompanied by the ebullition of some sweet distemper, 'If any man had spoken to me as Trevor did, he should have been the first to apologize!'

But, reader, you are wrong and Mary was right. She saw that she had spoken to him unworthily, and in spite of the heartless manner in which he had reproached her, the best thing she could do was to make the speediest reparation possible. It must be confessed that many friendships are broken, and many loves are chilled, by some petty thoughtlessness which the stubbornness of human nature forbids to acknowledge.

CHAPTER VIII.

GOING, GOING, GONE!

SINCE the failure of Alton and Gregory, Trevor had busied himself, in the interest of Mrs Alton, trying to get a settlement of affairs. This was no easy matter, for what with the pecuniary losses Mr Alton had already made, the mortgages which he had given over his estate, and the enormous bill of damages which his late partner brought against him, it was evident that a general liquidation of all his property must be resorted to. Mr Hendry persisted in following out the course which he had threatened, and he abated not one jot or tittle of his lawful rights, so that, in spite of Trevor's earnest endeavours to avert it, a sale by auction of all the furniture was announced, by placard and advertisement, to take place at Ashfield Hall, within a week. This was all the more unfortunate on account of Mrs Alton, for the doctors would not listen to any proposal for having her removed. As the day approached she gradually became worse, and the medical attendants now entertained not the slightest hope

of her recovery. At times she would lie quiet
for hours, and even smile resignedly amid the
ruin that surrounded her ; but in other moments,
goaded by the remembrance of better days, she
would give way to such wild paroxysms of grief,
that her friends saw too plainly that reason was
losing its hold.

The night before the sale, Trevor and Mary
were watching by her bed-side while she lay
calmly asleep. Mary's face wore an expression of
intense fatigue, and a new cough that troubled
her now caused the flush to come upon her cheek
at times. Trevor was pale from sleepless nights
and incessant watching, and he sat sorrowfully
contemplating the saddened beauty of Mary, and
noticing the varied expressions that flitted across
the face of her mother. Any words that passed
between the watchers—and these were few—were
spoken in a whisper that harmonized sadly with
the quietness of the room. As the great clock
in the hall began striking twelve, a smile lit up
the placid features of Mrs Alton, and she awoke.
She held out her hand to Mary, who rose and
leant over her.

'You have had a pleasant sleep, mamma,' she
said softly, holding the fevered hand in hers.

'I had a dream,' she answered slowly but distinctly, with a slight pause between her words.
'I dreamt that I had gone and was happy—once
more. Oh ! ' and she closed her eyes as if striving
to recall the rapture of her vision. She opened

them again, making a weak effort to look around.
'Is he here, Mary?'

'Who, mamma?'

Immediately Trevor was standing near her.
As soon as her eyes fell upon him, a gratified expression settled on her face. Holding out her
other hand, she asked, 'Why don't you come
nearer, Bob? I'll call you Bob, now, for it won't
be long.'

Trevor bent down and held her hand, while
Mary at his side was leaning affectionately over
her.

'I have often wished to speak with you, Bob,
on a subject which is near to my heart, and near
to your happiness and Mary's; and as my day
draws to its close the desire becomes stronger.'
She stopped for a minute, while Bob remained
silent, and then she continued, pausing at short
intervals for breath. 'I have watched your love
for Mary and have rejoiced in it. I know that
you will be kind to her, and it is a sweet solace for
me to think of this in these hours. You are honest, Bob; but oh, take care of yourself when you
are at work in London—I know you won't be
angry with me for saying this, for you know how
much I have been tried. Be sure that there is
something wrong when you cannot confide in your
wife a knowledge of your actions. It is a good
criterion this.' She paused here and breathed
heavily, as a bright hectic spot burned on her
cheek. 'I believe—I know that there would not

be half the amount of sin in the world if a more complete confidence were established between husband and wife! I could not go till I had told you this. Mary knows, for I have spoken to her about it, that what I have said to you applies to her as well.' She again paused. 'One other thing I should like. It would be well that the marriage should take place as shortly as possible after I am away. You need not mind what the world may say about a marriage following so hard after a funeral—the one is almost as solemn as the other.' There was a longer pause, while Mary wept silently. 'I have known you long, and I have the utmost confidence in you. I say that I have watched your love for Mary and rejoiced in it. Oh! how my words, like my thoughts, repeat themselves. Take her, Bob, and may she prove as good a wife to you as she has been a daughter to me.'

Mary looked up to Bob through her tears, and he fondly clasped her in his arms. Mrs Alton saw it all; a satisfied smile took possession of her face, and she turned her eyes away.

A short time, and the silence of the room was unbroken but for the long-drawn breathing of the sufferer. It was plain to these watchers that but a little while would elapse, before Ashfield Hall would be entered by a Visitor, seen and welcomed only by one, but felt by all. The night passed slowly and sadly, but at last the morning broke, and the watchers were roused by hearing laughter and joking from the adjacent rooms. Trevor went

out, and his spirit sank within him when he ascertained the cause. Workmen were busy throughout the house removing articles of furniture down-
stairs to the scene of auction, and above the noises
they made, their voices and laughter clashed painfully on his ear. He remonstrated with them, and
spoke of Mrs Alton who lay so near; but while
some heeded, others kept up the sport, and one remarked, ' I know if the sale had been in my 'ouse,
my old 'ooman 'ud ha' been glad to get hout an' sit
on the kerb.' This occasioned an outburst of laughter, and the noise was not allayed.

As the morning advanced, a crowd began to
assemble, composed partly of intending buyers and
City furniture-brokers; but there was a great pre-
ponderance of that curiously-minded class who
dodge about our City sale-rooms for no purpose,
bidding but never buying, whose eternal happiness we verily believe would be consummated
were they to find that Heaven is a place where
brokers ne'er break up and auctions have no end.
At noon the auctioneer ascended, and the sale began. Trevor had determined to furnish his house
from the furniture of the Hall, and commissioned
Mr Beeds to attend on his behalf. That gentleman
had also a note enumerating several articles of
value—household gods—that Trevor wished to retain. For these articles the bidding ran generally
very high, but they were eventually knocked down
to Mr Beeds, amid the muttered curses of disappointed brokers.

Old Willie, the gardener, stood sadly by. Poor old man, his heart was well-nigh breaking as he saw article after article, dear to the family, handed up by a greasy attendant, and made the subject of coarse auctioneering wit. His flowers, too—those of them which had been the object of his fondest care, growing in the front of the house, were either trampled by the mob, or ruthlessly torn from the soil. This was most galling to him; and in his anger he hoped that God would forgive him if he ever likened flowers to men again!

It was a sad scene. We believe that an auction-sale of household furniture, be the cause what it may, will make any reflective mind sad. Is it not painful to see articles, of probably more interest than value, round which the associations of old age and childhood cling, and between which, though they be insensate, age seems to have formed a relationship, separated for ever and made the subject of vulgar ribaldry, until they are handed over to the eager clutches of some bargain-hunting Jew? But this auction would doubly interest and pain those who knew the story of its cause.

But we must leave this scene for another equally painful. Let us go up the uncarpeted stair and enter the still room of the sufferer. But even here can be heard the derisive shouts of the mob and the hoarse cry of 'Going, going, gone!'

Mary knelt by the bedside of her mother, and Trevor stood by, earnestly looking on the pale face, expectant, and waiting for the change.

Mrs Alton lay calmly in that dying state which
the poet describes in lines beautiful as they are
true,

'Our fears our hopes belied,
We thought her dying when she slept,
And sleeping when she died.'

Mrs Alton continued in this state for some time,
now seeming dead, now only sleeping, while the
expression of her face was eagerly watched by the
two silent mourners.   Her eyes were sunken, her
cheeks haggard and pale; but now and then a smile
would lighten up her features, and her lips would
part as some dreamy thought struggled for utterance.   But are we not all familiar with the
characteristics of approaching death?   Do not our
memories go back to some such hallowed· scene?
Do we not remember the darkened room, and feel
ourselves again bound by that unseen presence?
Do we not recollect the retrospects and vague anticipations that moved our minds in that still
chamber?   Ah, yes.   And, though years have
passed, we can yet call up before us vividly, the
thin, pale, but sweet face that was the centre of
our tear-dimmed gaze!

Think ye of the Valley, for the last grains are
falling in the glass; hold firm the hand, for the
spirit gropeth in the dark; weep that ye shall hear
the kind voice no more; close up the vacant eyes,
it is a last service; and rejoice ye, with exceeding
joy, that your friend's life is hid with Christ in
God!

Mary, for a while, could not believe that her mother was dead; she waited, but in vain; and at last she flung herself on the breast that had nourished her, and cried wildly and long. Trevor turned his face to the wall and strove to hide his grief.

There was a strange discord heard in that dark room. Mary, within, moaned wildly; while, from without, came the clamour of the mob, and the croaking cry of 'Going! going! gone!'

CHAPTER IX.

HONESTY REWARDED.

THREE days afterwards, the green sod of the old church-yard at Ashfield was turned to receive the remains of Mrs Alton. The work-people gathered to the funeral in great numbers; and as the grand old service was read, many a stern feature was relaxed, and many a heart mourned the loss of an earnest friend. As a last mark of respect, all the shops in the village were closed; many an old widow stood by, as the cortege passed, with stricken heart and weeping eyes; and in the few words that were spoken, might have been heard how it was recorded in many a home that 'this woman was full of good works and alms-deeds which she did.'

On hearing of Mrs Alton's death, Maud Clayton had started immediately for Ashfield ; and
she found Mary in the rectory, for the clergyman,
at this time, manifested to Mary many a kindness
which was worthy of his calling. Maud's advent
was to her like a blink of sunshine through a
dark cloud. She had had other companions about
the place, but they fought shy of her company
now. In Maud, however, she found a friend in
whom, she knew, she could trust; one who, in
the hour of mirth, was ever ready to show forth
her joy, but who, in the times of mourning and distress, could approve herself a sweet solace and a
sure support.

Trevor was fast preparing a home for Mary in
London, and in the mean time Maud persuaded
her to go with her to Mrs Clayton's, where she
and that good lady did all they could for her
comfort. During that period Mary realized the
value of a true friend, and there grew up between
herself and Maud a strong and enduring relationship, which was pleasant in life, and which death
could not divide.

Faithful to the dying injunction of Mrs Alton,
the arrangements for the marriage were hurried
on, so that, in less than a month, Mary was taken
from Mrs Clayton's house to the altar, and Trevor
and she returned to their own home.

The new style of life tended to rouse Mary's
spirits, and the changed surroundings kept her

mind at work, so that she was sustained from lapsing into melancholy.

Indeed, considering all the circumstances, Mary and Bob were very happy in their new home. And, certainly, if, a man's love and strong devotion could bring happiness to a woman, that was Mary's lot. Nothing could be more pleasant than the unremitting attentions he paid her, and he was amply rewarded by an unmistakable appreciation of all he did for her comfort. But Mary was a delicate wife. The excitement consequent on the terrible trials and misfortunes which had come so quickly upon her, and with such a dreadful energy, told visibly on her constitution; but she did not complain, for she tried to bear up firmly. During the day, when Trevor was at business, Maud Clayton was very often beside her, cheering her up in those hours which otherwise might have been filled with monotony. We cannot but respect Maud for acting thus, for when she contemplated their homely happiness, no doubt she sometimes thought of the lot that might have been hers, and likely enough she linked the present with the long-past days at Tewton, when Bob delighted to speak of her as his little wife; but these thoughts bred no envy within her now, and her love and regard for them as individuals, was not the less strong that it was now bestowed upon them as one.

It was a glorious time for Prinkle when the

Messrs Hendry were winding up the concern of
Alton and Gregory. Master David made a companion of him, drove him about in cabs, took him
to places of amusement in the evenings, and
feasted him like a lord. The faithful note-book
he had kept was of immense service to his new
masters, and not less acceptable was the verbal
information which he so freely gave. Prinkle
was jubilant, and frequently he went home to
Nell in quite an ecstasy of delight.

'The fact is, Nell,' he would say, 'I believe if all
these cab journeys of mine were placed together and
stuck on their end, I would be in Hivin by this time!'

Nor did Prinkle in his hour of triumph forget
his humble friend Victor Cole, for that laconic individual was now roosting in a subordinate position
in the counting-house, at the salary of £40 a-
year. Dame Cole was a proud old woman; and
though she still moaned and groaned about the
old 'un, she broke out in wild glorification when
she came to speak of her honest boy, so broad and
tall! On the head of his new appointment
Victor managed to get credit for a new suit of
clothes; and he inspired respect among his fellow-
clerks, by letting drop, casually, the fact that his
uncle was a large landed-proprietor in Ireland,
while he had other relations extensively engaged
in hop-growing down in East Kent. Yet Victor
never had a relation that he knew of, except an
old uncle—a huckster—who was eternally dun-
ning his mother for debt.

Prinkle was not exactly sure whether he should be made a partner or no; Mr Hendry had never hinted at this; nor till the doors of Alton and Gregory's warehouse were closed for ever, was the subject of salary mentioned. He, however, saw that all the best positions in the place were now filled up, and he could not but think that a higher situation than any of these — perhaps that of junior partner or general manager—was in reserve for him. But time would show.

At the end of a week, during which Mr David Hendry, Junior, had maintained a systematic reserve, Peter's presence was requested in the private room. Our friend felt that the moment of his greatness had come at last, and he obeyed the summons in a state of great excitement.

Master David was seated at his consulting-table, but he offered no salutation in return for the low obeisance Peter made.

'Well, Prinkle,' he began — but these two words sent a shock through Peter's frame like that of electricity: it was the first time he had been addressed as *Prinkle*. But he recovered himself with a start, and answered,

'Yes, sir!'

'I'm sorry that I quite forgot to arrange with my father before he went back to Manchester, about your employment here; but we have had some correspondence on the subject, and we've agreed to keep you on.'

At this outburst of magnanimity, Prinkle's

eyes started wide open, and they glared like a
couple of flaming orbs.

'That is to say, if you have no objection. Eh?'

Peter nodded mechanically, but to what a
depth did his heart sink!

'The truth is, we've no particular need of a new
hand, for we had made other selections before we
ever heard of you. However, I suppose we'll be
able to find something for you to do, by and by;
In the mean time, I want you to assist generally
in the different departments as you may be required.' Peter's face was undergoing a variety of
contortions, but Master David continued without
taking any notice of the effect his words produced.
'With regard to the matter of salary, although I
have not consulted with my father on this point, I
suppose ninety or ninety-five pounds a-year will
be sufficient to commence with.'

Peter held up his hands. 'Great Hivins!'
was the only ejaculation he made.

'Come, come, Prinkle, I cannot allow you to
make use of such expressions here. Whatever
latitude you enjoyed in your last place, you must
remember that this is a very different warehouse;
and I hope to maintain a higher moral tone, from
the master down to the meanest servant in this
establishment! What do you mean?'

'Mean!' cried Prinkle. 'Mean! I mean to
say that it would be divilish difficult to maintain
a moral tone in face of such a preposition!'

'I insist, sir, that you have done with expletives. It is positively shocking!'

'Shocking, sir! Demit, sir! Shocking! I should rather think it is, sir! What the divil do you take me for? Do you think I'm a cow, or—or a bale of goods,—or—or something else that has no feelin's? Is it moral for to take me from a place where I had a hundred and ten pounds a-year, and after all the service I've been to you, to offer me ninety-five! Moral, sir! Good God, it's divilish!'

'Silence, Prinkle! You are beside yourself!'

'Perhaps I am, and I couldn't be beside a more ill-used individual!'

Hendry waited till he calmed down a little, and then continued.

'Of course you must recollect how we engaged that fellow Victor Cole for whom you pleaded so vigorously, at a much higher salary than he is worth; and besides—'

'I never mentioned no salary for Victor Cole, and I believe you're not the one to give him more nor he's worth!'

'And, besides,' pursued Master David quietly, without giving heed to the interruption, 'you must know that we have no means of verifying your statement about your last salary.'

'Great goodness, sir, I wonder the floor doesn't open and swallow you up! Do you think, after all the sacrifice I've made, that I would go and tell a lie now?'

'Perhaps,' he smiled maliciously, 'Perhaps you did not think you were making a sacrifice. Perhaps you had ulterior hopes.'

'Well, sir, I don't know what "alterior" means, but I think I know what *you* mean ; and it's cursedly shabby for you to make the 'sinuation. Ever since I could speak I've used my tongue honestly, and ever since I could work I've worked honestly; and that's a bigger boast than many a one in your position could make ! '

'Hah ! Well, Prinkle, I see that you are not reasonable to-day. You had better go back to your work, and I'll write to my father about the position of affairs. If he is willing to give you £110, I shall make no objection, but I'll retain my own thoughts on the subject.'

'And I wish you joy of them, sir ! But I wouldn't be you for a million pounds ! '

'Very well, Prinkle, go to your work peaceably ; but remember,' he said, rising to his feet, 'if ever you speak to me again in the same tone as you have adopted now, I shall immediately kick you out of the place without word or warning ! '

The sharp, angry manner in which Master David spoke the last sentence, awed Prinkle considerably, and he slunk away. It would be no easy task to describe the terrible state of the poor man's heart when he knew that his dearest hopes were shattered and crushed ; but he felt his degradation.

Of course the elder Hendry agreed to the

£110, and in doing so he administered a sharp
rebuke to his son for having hesitated in the
matter, but he did not know of the treatment
Prinkle had received. Besides that, he wrote a
long letter to Peter thanking him for the disinterested service he had rendered during the last
month or two, and wound up by promising to
further his prospects in every way he could. This
letter was a source of unbounded delight to the
poor fellow, and it again opened up to his mind
hopes bright and glorious. But he had yet to
learn with bitterness, that promises—the greater
they are, are the less likely to be performed.

Meanwhile his life was sufficiently miserable ;
for the boys soon discovered his weakness and got
much amusement from his passionate flights ; true,
he had no Gregory to torment him, but his young
master, beardless puppy that he was, did his utmost to render it unbearable.

Master David Hendry was a fool at the best,
overflowing with vanity, and callous in his tem-
perament ; and having been placed so suddenly at the head of this large establishment in
London, he was intoxicated with his newly-found
power. He did his best to pick a quarrel where
he could ; and, taking advantage of his position, he
bullied his subordinates as only a mean man could.
None of his employés loved him, none respected,
but all feared him. Still he was a religious man,
and unwontedly pious ; and we doubt not that his
righteous soul would have been shocked at the low

moral tone of his establishment, had he overheard
a tithe of the curses that were hissed at him at
every turn.

But does Hendry, Junior, stand alone in this?
No! you will find his prototype in almost every
warehouse in the land.

'Slaves cannot breathe in England!' It is a
wretched lie! For a worse form of slavery exists
within these shores than was ever denounced by a
Brougham or depicted by a Stowe. Twist the fact
as you may, it is still a fact. Extortionate labour
and relentless tyranny are practised by our
Christian men, and 'the poor clerk' is a by-word
which provokes a laugh among our merchant
princes, and our traffickers who are the honourable
of the earth! But the system is fruitful of dire results, for it is turning our warehouses and our
counting-houses into little better than hot-beds of
embezzlement and of fraud.

'Go to now, ye rich men, weep and howl for
your miseries that shall come upon you. Your
riches are corrupted, and your garments are moth-
eaten. Your gold and silver is cankered; and
the rust of them shall be a witness against you,
and shall eat your flesh as it were fire.'

Most heartily do we recommend our commercial
men to read, in the light of their present lives, the
old Book from which the foregoing is an extract;
and we would ask them to note well how those
who oppress the hireling in his wages, are classed

with the filthy and the most dastardly of the earth !

One would have thought that whatever failings Master David Hendry had, the want of common honesty should not have been numbered amongst them. Yet Prinkle was not three months in the place before he had earned the intense hatred of his master by refusing to comply with orders the honesty of which he questioned.

A box had been returned by a customer in Bristol, containing a number of pieces that were considered ' not up to sample.' In fixing the address card, this customer had stupidly used nails which had penetrated the lid and damaged several yards of the shirting. Prinkle showed the damaged piece to Master David, and inquired what was to be done ?

' How many yards are torn ? ' he asked.

' Five and a half, sir.'

' Dear me, it is very careless. But the piece is quite up to sample, and besides, we must make him pay for the trouble he has given. Debit him back with ten.'

Prinkle was not sure that he heard aright.

' But there is only five and a half yards damaged, sir.'

' I hear you, Prinkle ; but the fellow must pay for our trouble. Debit him with ten.'

Peter could not understand this, and reiterated strongly,

'But, sir, there's only five and a half damaged.'

'Debit him with ten, I say!'

'But, sir; what if he should want to see the piece?'

'But, sir! But, sir! Do as I bid you! I suppose it will be easy enough to damage other five!'

'Yes, sir,' replied Prinkle with fervour; 'it will be easy enough, but it is not honest, and I won't do it! I'm sure Mr Alton would not have—'

'Hold your tongue about Alton! What has he got to do with it, I wonder! We all know what he was, and I won't have him held up as an example here! Do what I tell you, and debit ten yards.'

But Prinkle persisted in the disagreeable reference. 'I'm sure, Mr David, when I was in Mr Alton's ware—'

'Silence, I tell you, about that man and his warehouse! I won't have any such examples here!' And he struck the table with his fist. But Prinkle's temper was fairly up.

'Mister David,' he screamed, 'I will *not* do what you tell me! If you send me about my bizness, it may be a concentration to Mr Alton's friends to know that he wasn't the only swindler in London! *You* may sin your soul for five yards of flannel at 1s. 10½d. a-yard, but I tell you *I* won't; no, I'm d—blist!' and he threw the piece on the table, with a bang that made books and

papers jump. Young Hendry at once seized him
by the collar of the coat, and in another instant
he was kicked out of the private room.

This disturbed Prinkle's relationships with
David Hendry, Junior, for all time to come, and
from the ceaseless tormentings of the boys he had
no appeal. His life with Hendry & Son was that
of a dog, and his honesty was rewarded with
sorrow upon sorrow. Nell's spirit was well-nigh
broken by the tale of distress which her husband
poured forth each night when he came home; her
life was filled with the bitterness of affliction ;
and many a longing desire arose within her, as in
days before, for that time when the wicked should
cease from troubling, and the weary should be at
rest.

CHAPTER X.

BREATH !

MR WOODROW, still retaining Rachel as housekeeper, ever since his sojourn at Sandhaven had
resided in a quiet way on the outskirts of the
City. Although he had ceased long ago from
taking an active part in the concerns of the firm
which still bore his name, he continued to draw
a revenue from the business sufficient to supply
the wants of his little household. The manner

of his life at Sandhaven had not been without
its effect; you could see it in the increased whiteness of his hair and in the absence of that elasticity
which was wont to characterize every movement
he made.   For a while after he returned, it was as
if a sullen cloud of unpleasant recollections had
settled upon him; he manifested signs of vexed
impatience each time that reference was made to
the place or any of his associates there, for he
heartily despised himself for the part he had
played.   His manner was fretful in the extreme;
all company save that of Rachel, and Trevor at
times, was evidently obnoxious to him; and in the
long strolls he took, on the bright mornings when
Rachel was at his side, he was even then moody
and incommunicative.   Yet Rachel bore with
him bravely; attending to all his wants with an
alertness and cheerfulness that did her credit in
such trying circumstances; and no fault of his
effaced from her recollection for a single moment
the kindness he had extended to her when she
was in her terrible distress.   But when trials
came upon Trevor in the shape of Mr Alton's
disgrace, all Mr Woodrow's energies seemed to
revive.   Many a time he took a trip into the
City, ostensibly for the purpose of beguiling an
hour or two amid by-gone associations, while in
reality it was to get a quiet chat with his friend,
if so be that he might drop a word of consolation
into the cup of his affliction.   Then something
of his old brightness revived when Trevor took

Mary to his home, and it was a moment of great
joy to him when he received her for the first time
at the door of his little cottage. There was something of the old stateliness left in him yet, for he
stood up straight and took her two hands in his
own; while, in contemplating the beauty of the
young wife for a minute or so silently, as if the
dreams of other days were rising before him then,
the muscles of his face seemed to quiver and grow
warm with love, and he said, simply and affectionately,

'Welcome, Mary, my child!'

Yes, there was a stronger bond between him
and Trevor than that which exists between friend
and friend; and it was a mightier impulse than
that of mere good-will, which made him salute
Mary so tenderly as he did. Mr Woodrow admired
Rachel greatly and gratefully for the way in
which she studied his comfort, and for the complete
self-abnegation she made, 'all,' as he often told her,
'for the good of an old man;' but highly as he regarded her, his feeling towards Mary was warmer
and deeper, for he cherished her with an affection
that brought to his mind many a memory of his
own youth.

It is pleasant for an old man to feel as if he
were living his life over again while he is watching
the affections and aspirations of the young around
him. The timid glance, the dimpled cheek, the
strong hopes, and the fervent eye; these are limned
in many a picture of the past, familiar as the haunts

of boyhood, and the more pleasant to look upon that they are seen through the mellow light of years.

Mr Woodrow had not been attacked anew by his old trouble, but he was quite aware that his frame was fast becoming frail, and he often remarked that he was quickly going down the hill. It would be difficult to imagine what his prospects were, if he had any that stretched beyond the bounds of natural life, denying as he did the immortality of the soul. Trevor frequently tried to approach him on this subject, but when he did so . he immediately became reticent and sad.

Mr Twentyman Beeds, who, by the way, was now on very intimate terms with Mr Woodrow, often tried to cope with his doubts, but without any measure of success. But strange to say, Mr Prinkle was the only one with whom he seemed to delight to talk on this subject. Perhaps he derived pleasure from the quaintness of Peter's style; certainly he listened to all his arguments with patience, and he was amused, if not convinced. When Prinkle came to see him, it was sure to become the subject of conversation ; they never tired of it.

One time they were sitting together in the parlour, when Prinkle, in his own way, made an appeal to Mr Woodrow's feelings.

'Have you never no yearning in your heart for another life beyond this ?'

'Perhaps I have, Mr Prinkle ; but in conceding

that, my argument loses nothing. You know perfectly well that the wish is often father to the thought.'

'Very true, sir; very true.'

'And realities stand by themselves, not on desires. If I had been spoken to on these subjects when my heart was young and more easy to be guided by leading-strings, in all probability I should have been of your way of thinking. But it is too late; I am too old now.'

'Ah,' cried Prinkle, with an argumentative wink, 'I believe that half the sighs of this life are contained in the words " too late." Besides, you must not question those things with the head, you should look at them with the heart.'

'But my head is as good as my heart.'

'Very likely, sir; very likely, and perhaps a great deal better,' he replied, with a smirk of complacency. 'Very likely you're like the image that Nebuchadnezzar saw in his dream; its head was of pure gold, its breast of silver, its thighs of brass, its legs of iron, and its feet of the miry clay; very likely,' he laughed, 'the far'er down—the worse you get!'

Mr Woodrow enjoyed this heartily, and after much more argumentation, Peter brought the conversation to a close by asking,

'Do you mean to say that you don't believe there's any existence after death ?'

'I do. But do you mean to say that there is ?'

'Of course I do,' he replied with a chuckle.

' And if your idea is correct, I've got one consolation;—you'll never have the opportunity of crowing over me, and telling me that you knew you was right!'

From conversations such as that, Mr Woodrow derived much amusement, and Prinkle was at all times a welcome visitor.

There were very few incidents that relieved the monotony of his life; he received almost no letters, and these were left, tossing about, open to the eye of Rachel. But one morning the postman handed in a missive bearing the Australian stamp. Mr Woodrow regarded it with fear and agitation in his face, crushed it into his pocket, and shut himself up in his room alone. Rachel had noticed his agitation, but wisely restrained herself from asking questions, or from watching his movements. However, as two hours had passed since he shut himself up, and she had heard no movement in his room, she became solicitous, and tapped at his door. There was no answer. Having knocked again with as little success, she opened the door gently. There was no change in the room, but Mr Woodrow lay stretched upon the bed with his face downwards. To her mind there was something so strange in this that she uttered a faint cry, which was suddenly repressed when she saw her master struggle slowly to his feet. But what a change was in the man! He seemed shrunken and decrepit. His face was like that of a man of eighty, and his clothes hung loosely on his frame. They gazed upon each other silently for a minute, while he rested with his hand on the bedside.

'Don't ask me, Rachel,' he faltered. 'Not now. I may speak of it again.'

But Mr Woodrow put away the letter, and never after this referred to the matter. However, from many little things, and especially from his persisting in wearing black clothes although he seldom crossed the door-step, Rachel divined that he mourned the loss of a near friend.

He never recovered from the shock, but as Summer gave place to Autumn, and Autumn to Winter, Mr Woodrow knew that his strength was falling away with the year. Fits of despondency came upon him often and again, while at other times he would chat with the calmness of a philosopher on his prospects of death.

Prinkle came to see him frequently still; but there was now a truce to their arguments about an after life, Mr Woodrow finding that he could get no enlightenment from the evidences which his old clerk stored up, and feeling that the solution of the difficulty was coming too near to be made the subject of amusement or jest.

'Rachel dear,' he said, one day when they were seated by the parlour-fire together, 'you might fetch me a glass of water; I wish to chat with you.'

She did so.

'Now,' he begged further, 'you might kindly

leave your work for a while—our conversation may be long. I am very feeble, and I might speak the more easily if I saw that you were listening closely to all my words.'

Rachel cheerfully laid aside her sewing as requested, and composed herself beside him in the attitude of attention.

'Rachel dear,' he began, tenderly and feebly, 'I am an old man, my strength is failing fast, and I have been thinking, for some time, that I have seen my last Christmas—'

'Oh! don't say that, sir; please,' she said, interrupting him sorrowfully; but Mr Woodrow raised his hand for silence, and continued.

'It is true, Rachel, and I am thankful for it. I have lived long enough to enjoy life, and if I remain much longer I shall be a burden to myself and to others. I have no relations that the world knows anything of, my friends are few, and I shall die a poor, but I hope, a contented man. I can number all the true friends I ever had, on the fingers of one hand, and therefore I die with the less regret. You and Mr Trevor have been my two best friends, and I should have liked him to be present while I communicate what I am about to do. Those with whom I was associated when in business, and those who have been my companions since, know as little about where I came from and what I was, as I know about where I am now going or what I am to be. So I think it is my duty that I should reveal a few things regarding

myself before I disappear altogether. I have se-
lected you, Rachel dear, for this communication,
because we have been good friends, and something
more than Fate seems to have linked our lives.'
A shudder crept over her, and her eyes fell. ' I
was born at Wyecaster, in Northumberland, fifty-
eight years ago ; and you know as much about my
mother as I do. She must have died when I was
very young, and I might have been without one
altogether for aught that my father would tell me
regarding her. My godfather was Sir George
Gartly of Garth. I remember him well—a stern,
inexorable old man. Are you attending, Rachel ? '

'Yes, yes,' she replied, raising her eyes to his.
' I am.'

' Well, Sir George had no children, and in the
natural course of events his estates would have
fallen into the hands of his nephew as heir. But
it so happened that this nephew—Philip Gartly
—had earned the displeasure of his uncle by a
long course of indiscretion. Sir George tried to
persuade him into better ways, but without success. At last he threatened that if there was not
a stop to his scandalous manner of life he would
disinherit him altogether. For a time this threat
had its effect on Philip, but before many months
had passed he was as bad as ever. Sir George,
on learning this, was furious, and determined
having nothing more to do with him, and sent for
me. At that time he signified to me that I should
make Garth my home, and if I conducted myself

as a gentleman, he would make me his heir. I did—' but Mr Woodrow stopped suddenly and swept his hand across his face as if in pain. Rachel rose, but he motioned her back to her seat. 'Well,' he continued, falteringly, 'in the world's eyes I behaved as a gentleman; but, Rachel, before God, I was the veriest wretch! Yes, yes, do not interrupt me. Three of us knew it. The grave holds one; the other is a waif—I am the last—and the grave will soon hold me!'

'Perhaps, sir,' said Rachel, trying to soothe him, 'you are unwell now; had you not better stop?'

'Rachel, will you hear me out? It may be the last favour I shall ever ask,' he implored. 'I have had a strange life: there has been a strange —a something wanting in it all: but if you bear with me I shall recover presently, and I shall have the more peace. Well, I never saw the will, but he—Sir George—had told me more than once that one had been made bequeathing the bulk of his estate to me. More than that, when he lay on his death-bed, he called me to his side and coun- selled me how to act as a country gentleman. I was therefore more than astonished when he died, that no will was forthcoming. Search was made in every corner; and, what was more extraordinary, his lawyer—a man Richards—denied knowing anything about one having been made. I had my suspicions of this fellow, and they were confirmed when I found that he had quietly left the place,, taking with him his daughter—a little girl, and all his papers. No one could ever find out anything about him; he was searched for, but in vain; and his whereabouts have remained a mystery to this day.'

As Mr Woodrow uttered the last few sentences Rachel's eyes were fixed upon his. She seemed to drink in his words with avidity, and her eyes gathered light till they glared unnaturally.

'What!' she exclaimed, rising and coming near him so that her face was close to his. 'Garth! Wyecaster! Richards! Were these the names?'

'Rachel, Rachel,' he cried apprehensively, 'be calm. I am an old man. Rachel, for the sake of all that is left of me, if you know my secret, do not deal harshly with me!'

But he had mistaken the cause of her excitement.

'Tell me, sir,' she cried again, as her voice gathered a wild force, 'were these the names?'

'Yes Rachel dear,' he replied piteously, 'but you are beside yourself.'

'And a little girl?'

'Yes, Rachel, yes.'

It was enough. Her passion broke. With a great cry she threw up her hands, clasping them above her head.

'I know, I know, I know!' she cried; and she sank back upon her chair with a hysterical laugh, and covered her face with her hands.

Mr Woodrow was greatly troubled, but he tottered over to where she sat and tried gently to remove her hands.

'Rachel dear, what is it you know? Be calm, Rachel.'

Rachel did not reply, but still covering her face she rocked herself backward and forward, crying loudly all the while, 'I know, I know, I know!'

Mr Woodrow, in a state of great excitement, implored her to tell him what she knew, hung over her, and called her by her name. But Rachel was out of the present and back in the past. She remembered all these names, Garth, Wyecaster, Richards: the days of her early childhood came back to her like the fragments of a forgotten dream. The horrors of her youth, spent as it was in a wretched den among musty parchments, where her father lived in an atmosphere of greed and fear, came up before her in a terrible array: the memory of her short wifehood, her fiery trials, and her still-born child, was there; and there, too, in her mind, was the dastardly parent with his unnatural curse standing like a spectre among the years. Truly, the Alpine avalanche is not to be compared with the terrific emotion which a little word or a single thought may awaken in the human breast.

The old man was fearful for the woman, and he caught her by the arm and implored her; but Rachel was beside herself for the time.

With a cry she sprang from her seat, threw
Mr Woodrow rudely from her, and rushed out of
the house into the cold, frosty air. What with
excitement and increasing frailty the old man had
no strength to bear such usage, and he fell across
the arms of his chair in a fainting condition.
The keen atmosphere acted upon Rachel and her
senses returned. With a dread of having done
something fearful she quickly re-entered the
house, and there she found her old friend, lying
where he had fallen, as if dead. With a cry of
agony she flew towards him, dashed water on his
temples, chafed his hands, and conjured him to
speak. By and by his eyes were opened, and he
muttered words upon words; but there was little
of sanity in these uneasy orbs, and his speech was
but the gibberish of a child.

While this was going on, happily Nell came
on a visit to Rachel, and with this assistance Mr
Woodrow was laid on his bed. A doctor was
called immediately, and he examined the old man.
He hurriedly put a few questions to Rachel about
a former illness, which were answered clearly.
Then there was another short examination, and he
shook his head when it was over.

'I presume neither of you are relations of
his?'

'Neither of us,' replied Nell, for Rachel was
overcome.

'Then, if there is any one who, you think,
would like to see him in life, send word for them

at once. He may speak again, and he may
not; but he cannot live beyond 48 hours. For
your own satisfaction, however, you ought to send
for his former medical attendant, the more especially if he is a personal friend. But what you
intend doing, do at once, for his time is short.'

In a few hours Trevor was by the bedside,
and Prinkle came a little later on.

Mr Woodrow lay all night in a troubled sleep,
often crying out in his dreams with the voice of
a child, 'I know, I know, I know.'

Rachel related to Trevor the story he had told
her, but was silent as to the intelligence she might
yet be the means of throwing on Mr Woodrow's
early disappointment.

By the afternoon the old man had fallen into
a deep sleep, and Dr Binks, who had arrived early
in the morning, gave it as his opinion that he
would never awake.

'I am sorry,' said Binks, 'that I cannot remain longer, but there is no need of me here, and
my time is not my own.'

Evening came, but there was no change ap-
parent. Nell, who had never left, was rejoined
by her husband after business was over. Mary,
too, would have been there had she been allowed,
but Trevor had too much solicitude for his delicate
wife to trust her in the cold air and excitement.

No one went to bed; and Trevor remained with
the others, determined to see the last of his friend.

About three o'clock in the morning, contrary

to the expectations of every one, Mr Woodrow
awoke from his sleep, seemingly as reasonable as
ever, although in the last stage of weakness. He
tried to raise himself on his elbow, but failed.
Rachel bolstered him up, and after a while, looking round on the group, he said, faintly and
wearily,

'I must have slept for a long time—something
like a year—Have I not?'

'Not so long, Mr Woodrow,' said Trevor, bending over him and affecting a smile, for his friend
smiled too. 'Hardly a year.'

'Ah, I see it all. You have come to see old
Woodrow die!'

'I hope not, sir,' said Trevor, taking his hand.
'I hope not, Mr Woodrow!'

'Whether you hope for my death or no, you
expect it: and hope and expectation are much
akin. Where is Bowles?' he cried, in a rough,
broken voice. 'It was he—the scoundrel—who
poisoned Peter's mind!'

Trevor saw he was wandering and tried to
recall him.

'This is not Sandhaven, Mr Woodrow. It is
your own home.'

'Ah, I see. We've left Sandhaven—a long
time ago. Isn't it Trevor?'

'Yes, sir, yes.' And he tried to soothe
him.

'Where's Rachel? Oh, here is the dear
woman. I say, Trevor, *she* has a soul! and

Prinkle and Nell, all here, all souls; but, Trevor, not I. You see I know you all!'

'Of course you do, Mr Woodrow.'

'Yes—' he muttered slowly. 'Trevor, Rachel, Nell, Prinkle—good company. Old song, Trevor, jolly companions every one!'

At this extraordinary reference, each restrained a smile, but Prinkle was too honest, and laughed outright.

'That's Peter's laugh — poor Peter. Good, simple Peter Prinkle. But we should not laugh, people say, when men are dying.'

His eyes then began to wander about the apartment, and no one spoke for a while. At length he broke the silence; and he spoke slowly, with his eyes fixed on Trevor.

'I wish I could believe it, Bob.'

'Believe what, sir?'

'Ah—Bob!' and he heaved a long sigh.

'What is it, sir?' he asked kindly.

'I am a fool to speak as I have done, while my forty and eight hours are ebbing fast. I heard him, Bob, when you were not there. The doctor —I mean.'

'Calm yourself, sir. Do not say so much at a time, for you are weak.'

And indeed he was weak, for it was some time before he again tried to speak.

'Yes, yes, Bob,' he muttered, 'I wish I could believe it.'

'Tell me what, sir. Say what you would like to believe.'

At this the dying man heaved his breast with a igreat sigh, and cried with a strong voice that echoed through the house,

'That I might go to her, since she shall not return to me!'

In saying these words he tried to rise from his pillow, but his strength failed him, and he fell back in his place.

A large vein rose swollen and blue upon his long-stretched neck, and his mouth opened wide.

'Water, water,' cried Rachel, as she ran.

'Breath!' gasped Mr Woodrow. It was his last word, for a convulsion shook his frame and he was dead.

CHAPTER XI.

NEWS FROM A FAR COUNTRY.

THE only mourners who followed the remains of Mr Woodrow to the grave, were Robert Trevor, Prinkle, and Mr Beeds, the lawyer. The last-named gentleman had taken Mrs Alton's death very much to heart; he was growing old; and by the silent way he conducted himself at Mr Woodrow's funeral, it was evident that his thoughts were brought to a very near contemplation of the realities of life. After the service was over, and the grave closed, they returned to the house for the purpose of hearing the will read.

It is an interesting scene when the relatives of some one deceased are assembled after the obsequies, to hear read the last will and testament of the one who has gone. What anticipations are crowded into that company; what jealousies and calculating of chances as in a game! As item after item is read, what hopes are born, what expectations crushed! Envy is there to grumble at the better fortune of another, while Chagrin and Malice join in a mutual commiseration. And often, when the will has been read and all is over, there are those who leave the house muttering a curse on the memory of the one over whose grave they have just breathed the hypocritical sigh! But there was no such scene as that in Mr Woodrow's little parlour; a genuine grief clouded every face, and no stimulants were used to keep up the mask of sorrow.

The will was short but quaint, and the little lawyer, who knew more of Mr Woodrow's life than his friends were aware of, had to stop oftener than once to wipe off a certain dimness that clouded his spectacles. The document treated of Sir George Gartly's lost will, which the deceased had still believed to be extant; and on the assumption that the Northumberland estate was his by right, he bequeathed the same to Trevor in the event of the will being found. Out of his realized effects the sum of one hundred and fifty pounds was to be paid down to Rachel, and the remainder was to go to Robert Trevor. Further, in the event of the estate coming into Bob's hand, an annuity of one hundred pounds was to be settled on his 'trusted and faithful friend, Rachel Rubens.'

Trevor thought that there was little chance of the lost will being found, indeed he entertained doubts as to its ever having existed. However he thought, with Mr Beeds, that another search ought to be made; and a few days later, the old lawyer, frail though he was, started with a professional man for the North, to make the necessary pre-liminary inquiries.

Rachel heard the resolutions made, but said nothing, although she determined to make a search in her own quiet way. The name of Richards was most familiar to her, for she re-membered that a vast number of letters in her father's possession were enclosed in wrappers bearing that name and the designation of North-umberland. She recollected, too, a man of the name of Gartly who was in the habit of visiting her father in his dirty little den in the City. These two men were constantly quarrelling about money; but she remembered well that her father invari-ably succeeded in extorting what money he de-manded, by some threat which he held over the stranger's head. Rachel strung her recollections together, and made out to her satisfaction that her father's real name was not Rubens, but Richards; that he was not a Jew; and that in the stolen will lay the power which he exercised when he wished to extort money from the man Gartly, who without doubt was the usurper of Mr Woodrow's lawful rights. Her belief was confirmed by an incident that occurred a few days later in Trevor's house. She was seated with Mary, and they were talking over the affairs of the late Mr Woodrow.

'By-the-bye,' said Mary, rising, ' since you are interested in that Northumberland estate, perhaps you would like to see the photograph of Philip Gartly, the present occupant.' And she rummaged in a portfolio which lay on the table.

'Here it is. What do you think of it? He is not a bad-looking man. Why, what is wrong? You are pale ; you are ill, Rachel.' And she ran and brought a glass of water which the agitated woman drank eagerly.

'Are you ill?'

'No, no; it was merely a pain that shot through me here.' And Rachel laid her hand on her heart as she took the photograph from Mary.

She held it with both hands, and gazed on it as if her eyes fed on each feature.

'That is the man,' she said, as if speaking to herself. ' That is the man ! '

'What man, Rachel?'

'That is the man!' she cried exultantly.

'What do you mean, Rachel? Do you know the man?'

'Oh, nothing, nothing. But I must go.' And without another word she drew her shawl more tightly around her, and glided past Mrs Trevor to the door.

Mary was bewildered at her sudden departure, and when she looked out at the window, she saw her disappearing hurriedly round the corner.

Of course Mary narrated this incident to her husband, and it was the more inexplicable to him when he found immediately afterwards that Rachel had gathered together all the odds and ends that belonged to her in Mr Woodrow's house, and had quietly taken her departure, no one knew whither. This was still the more extraordinary that she had left without making the slightest inquiry about the legacy of one hundred and fifty pounds. As soon as the effects were realized, Mr Beeds advertised for her in the papers, but no reply came, and the affair continued wrapped in mystery.

The investigations in Northumberland resulted, as every one expected, in nothing. Most of those who had been acquainted with Richards at the time he absconded, were in their graves long ago, and those who were left could throw no new light on his departure; so that the lawyer and his professional man returned from the scene of their inquiries, weary and baffled. This, however, occasioned no great disappointment to Trevor, who

had never allowed himself to become elated with
any prospects of success ; besides, his business was
flourishing, and his home-life was enviable; for
Mary and he were bound up in each other with a
love which does not always exist between man and
wife. Perhaps Mr Beeds felt the disappointment
more than he, for the natural enthusiasm which
characterized every effort he made on behalf of
another, received a check which damped his spirits
and made him moody. Besides, he had no happy
home to fall back upon ; the cheering influences of
which might have mollified the disappointments
and dispelled the cares of the day. His was an
empty home; the voice that had once filled his heart
and it with joy, had become silent long ago, and the
form he had regarded with reverence and love, was
nothing now but a shadowy remembrance of a joy
that once had been. The flowers of his compan-
ionship had dropped off one by one; the man whom
he had known longest, and who had stood nearest
to his heart, was an alien from his country, a dis-
honoured man, and little better than an outlaw.
For his efforts after the welfare of others, he was
rewarded by a declining business: his professional engagements were becoming scantier and
scantier every day : he trusted too much to the
honesty of others, and his debtors trafficked with
the goodness of his heart. Disappointment following disappointment, and ingratitude crowning
ingratitude, might have dwarfed the sympathies
of other men ; but Mr Beeds did not allow a single

reproach to escape his lips; he had an excuse for each delinquent; although, inwardly, he had hoped for better things. Thus, burying his disappointments in his heart, he wandered about like a frail old man, careless but kindly, till, as his housekeeper expressed it, his spirit seemed to have come to such a pass that it must either mend or break.

It was only natural in Trevor, though his affection for Katherine had long died out, that at Mr Woodrow's death he should take some interest in the papers which that gentleman had left, from the idea that he might solve more clearly the mystery which had surrounded his parentage.

But not one letter of hers did he find; every vestige of her handwriting had been destroyed; and the only paper which bore on her history was that which caused Mr Woodrow so much pain a short time before his death. The letter, which dated from ——, near Melbourne, was written in a bold, round hand,—more like a man's than a woman's,—and read as follows:—

'SIR,

'You are unknown to me, and I to you. My object in addressing you is to fulfil the dying request of one, who, although a stranger to me, I have reason to believe was once near and dear to you. It was by the merest accident that her case became known to me. I know not what her history was: evidently it had been a painful one: but, as she chose to be reticent with regard to the past, I did not trouble her. Enough for me that she was in a state of destitution, that she had seen better days. I received her into my house, five months ago, and in it she lingered on, in great distress, till she died, on the 10th of the present month. Yesterday my husband and my little boy . stood by her grave till the earth closed over her. I do not know, nor do I ask, what interest you had in this woman, whose very name is unknown to me, but it may be a consolation for you to learn that, for a few days before her death, she seemed to have a foretaste of that peace which I hope and believe she now enjoys to the full. Although she never spoke of it, my own experience led me to see that she had been deeply wronged, but with her last breath she forgave all, even as God had forgiven her. Now, sir, the little I know of this woman's history reads like a page of my own life. I know not whether she ever tasted the bitter draught, the dregs of which I was made to drink; but my heart is now lifted to my Redeemer in grateful thanks, too rich for words, that He has put it in my power to be the willing means of lessening the sorrow, and brightening the path, of one of my own frail sex as she descended into the gates of death.

'Sir, I am, respectfully yours,
'LIZZIE GORDON.'

Trevor did not manifest any great grief on

learning of his mother's death; he was too much
bound up in Mary for that; nor did the letter in
which the intelligence was conveyed, strike him as
anything else than the production of some female
fanatic. Had Mr Twentyman Beeds seen that
letter, how it would have pleased him! How he
would have rejoiced over that signature—Lizzie
Gordon—thinking that he had not lived in vain!
But the sympathies of Mr Beeds ranged far and
wide, while Trevor's centred in his wife and extended no farther than his home.

It may be wondered why Mr Beeds had never
heard from the old couple whose daughter he had
saved from ruin. But such was the case, and he
could give no reason for it.

CHAPTER XII.

NOVEL-READING.

MAUD CLAYTON sat in the drawing-room of her
aunt's house, busily tatting; while that formidable,
good-natured relation of hers lay stretched at her
full length and breadth upon a couch, reading a
book in yellow covers. Aunt Clayton yawned and
threw the book on a table near her.

'Finished at last; and it is the most unmitigated trash ever given to a reader!'

'You are surely late in finding that out. Why
did you continue reading it?'

'Just because I bought it,' replied the aunt.

'But why did you buy it?'

'Oh, I suppose, merely from curiosity.'

'Now, aunt; I've caught you at last. Don't, after this, tease me by saying I have such a stock of woman's reasons when you are so well supplied. "Just because" and "merely from curiosity" do not betray any extraordinary reasoning powers.'

'Maud, hold your tongue. Remember I am your superior in age.'

'Well, aunt,' she replied in a tone of pleasant banter, 'I must commend the elegance of your first injunction, while the last is not difficult to fulfil, seeing that a pair of ordinary eyes, and not a retentive memory, are necessary to the remembering that between us there does exist a considerable difference in age.'

'Why, girl, you talk like a book,' laughed the aunt.

'Which is but a questionable compliment considering the criticism you have just delivered on that.'

'It is a true one, however. Heigh-ho! each novel I read is to be my last, but somehow I always lay my hands on another.'

'And pray, does that not argue a power in these books, which you are loath to acknowledge?'

'No. It argues that which I shall be frank to acknowledge—a weakness in myself.'

'There, I think, you mistake yourself. Your

weakness lies, not in the way you gratify your appetite for reading works of fiction, but in your failing to acknowledge the entertainment you receive. *I* am fond of novels—of course there are novels and novels—but I refer to those which afford a channel to the flow of those ideas of life which most of us possess though few can express. I believe the majority of mankind *think*, and desire a higher life than they can possibly live in the midst of a world's turmoil and each day's disappointments; and it is a good thing that our aspirations should have healthy scope even though it be in a work of fiction.'

'Very true, Maud; but how seldom now-a-days is there a novel published which one can really enjoy. For instance, if I were to form my judgment of society from this book which I have just finished, I would believe that all women were mere simpering, sensual nonentities, and that the ten commandments had no other position in the world beyond that assigned to them on church walls.'

'I have not read the book,' replied Maud, 'nor shall I, if that is its tone. I wonder you don't write one, aunt; you have seen a good deal of the world.'

'I never tried, but I am convinced that any individual's life, properly written, would make a good novel.'

'I am not so sure that it would. Many of our lives would prove but poor, aimless histories. But

if our ideal life were written, then there might be
a book worth the reading. If an author were to
write of life as he finds it, depicting the foibles,
eccentricities, and absurdities of high life, or the
squalor, wretchedness, and redeeming wit of low
life, his book would be a clever satire or a touching tale at the best. But if a man writes from
the ideal, giving reality to his own aspirations in
the history of his hero, he adds to the world a life
which may be well worthy our emulation, and in
the tracing of which we shall feel ourselves en-
nobled by the desires and strivings which it
may create. I remember, when I was a girl,—and
I believe that my experience then was that of
nine children out of ten,—how much I enjoyed
your stories about the little boy who was born in
a stable, how He was lost, and found in the temple
answering the arguments of wise men; how
afterwards He healed the sick, raised the dead,
and how He died; yet at that time I never
thought of Jesus as other than an ideal character
—far away and above this life of ours—but I
tried, for all that, to live after the ideal with
which these stories filled me.'

'I did not know, Maud, that you had been a
little sceptic.'

'No, aunt, I was not a sceptic; but His life
was so different from what I saw around me every
day, that I never thought of Him as of others.
Of course, I merely state that fact to show what
aspirations an ideal may awaken.'

'But when did you begin to think otherwise?'

'How do you mean?'

'When did you begin to realize the—the reality of that life?'

Maud hesitated for a moment, for her reply necessitated the mention of a name which seldom escaped her lips, and never without a tremor and a tear.

'It was Frank—Frank Grierly. You remember what a fine voice he had as a boy. We were sitting in one of his father's fields, talking of serious things—for he never talked like a child—when, without warning, he burst into singing—

> " I think when I read the sweet story of old,
> When Jesus was here among men—"

He sang the hymn through, but these two lines struck me. It seemed as if scales had fallen from my eyes, and with more light I got more love.'

Maud turned her face from her aunt, and her tatting rested on her knee.

Mrs Clayton mused awhile on the thoughts that Frank's name awakened, until she saw that her niece was still brooding, and she thought to rouse her.

But Maud turned from her reverie as if she had never been in one.

'Do you know, aunt, I commenced a novel long ago?'

.' Indeed!'

'Did you not know?'

'No ; but I am not surprised. Long dresses produce a peculiar effect on girls; for when they are first assumed, the mind begins to create shapes in the future, and build *awfully* nice castles in the air. Everything new seems to them *so* new, and every sensation *so* jolly, that each commits her feelings to paper, it may be in the shape of poetry or a novel. Are you continuing yours ? '

'Oh, no. I gave it up years ago.'

'Why so ? ' inquired the aunt.

'Because I tried to create a heroine and failed. I found that a heroine must be allowed to speak as little as possible consistent with the story. If she says much, she is sure to commit herself and talk trash. If her conversation should embrace topics of interest and subjects deeper than dress, the reader might think her masculine or unnatural, and the soft ideal creature of the author is not comprehended.'

Maud laid aside her tatting and wandered to the window, where she stood fingering the cords, now looking towards her aunt and then into the street.

'Then,' she continued, ' the taste of the public is depraved, and if you don't write to suit your readers you may as well not write at all. If you would depict a heroine in these days, she must have a smattering of slang and be mistress of innumerable pretty wickednesses, or you won't succeed.'

'I wonder,' said Mrs Clayton, 'how *our* conversation would look in a novel.'

Maud laughed right out at the idea.

'You would be set down,' she said, 'as an old vinegary reviewer, and I as a premature bluestocking.'

'Very likely,' laughed Mrs Clayton, as she rose from the couch and came to the window.

'By-the-bye, Maud; I wonder if that estate will ever come into Robert Trevor's hands. He does not look as if he were sanguine of success.'

'Ah! I forgot to tell you that Mr Beeds has returned quite baffled. Mary told me so yesterday. She promised to call to-day if she were feeling well, but I do not think she'll be here now, so I'll take a run out and call on her.'

'Poor, dear girl,' said Mrs Clayton, shaking her head. 'I hope nothing happens, for she is far from strong. Yes, Maud, you should go, for I know that she wearies her life out when Bob is away.'

But Maud did not move just then, for she stood vacantly gazing down on the street, as if she were thinking of something about which she hesitated to speak. At last she seemed to muster courage.

'It is a queer thought,' she said, 'but I often wonder what Bob would do were Mary taken away. She cannot live long; and when I think of the terrible trial it would be to him were anything to

happen now, you can have no idea of the pain it
gives me.'

'It would, indeed, be a severe trial. But you
should not allow yourself to think of these things
and grieve over them.'

'I cannot help it, aunt,' she pleaded.

'Well, Maud, your feeling is very natural;
and it does credit to the goodness of your heart
that, since you were a little girl, your desire for
the welfare of Robert Trevor has never veered by
the shadow of a line.'

'Whether it does me credit or no,' she replied
with the slightest falter, 'it is a fact; and I can
tell you, for I may say anything to you, aunt,
that there is nothing a woman could do, in honour,
that I would not do for that man.'

'I believe you, Maud, and it is nobly said.
But I often wonder—and I know you will tell
me if I ask—why it is that you invariably shun
him? You always leave Mary before he returns
at night, and you seldom mention his name.'

Maud tried to hide the tear that trickled on
her cheek, but she had to clear her voice before
she replied.

'Well, aunt, there is not another woman on
earth to whom I would answer that question, but
I am always happier when I open my heart to you.
Ever since I first knew what sympathy was, I
have cared for Robert Trevor; and I care for him
now as I care for his wife: but while there is a
response in her heart to mine, there seems to be

none in his. He is so much bound up in Mary that he is even callous to me. Perhaps it should be so; but I cannot help feeling that he might show a little warmth of friendship towards me, if it were only for the sake of past days.'

Maud maintained command of her voice to the last word, but as soon as she had finished, she passed out of the room, leaving her aunt alone.

'Heigh-ho,' sighed Mrs Clayton,—

> ' The pale moon may wax and wane,
> And the red blood rust on the steel,
> Flowers melt to tears on the frozen pane,
> But the heart of a maid is leal !'

CHAPTER XIII.

A SEARCH FOR THE STOLEN WILL.

RACHEL, having been established in her convictions by the photograph she had seen in Trevor's house, determined to gain possession of the will in such a manner as would preclude her father from being charged with the crime of its concealment. She saw that to save him she must keep her own counsel, and confide in no one. In order to work out her discovery in her own quiet way, she broke off all connection with her friends, for the time, bundled up her little stock of clothing, and took her departure unknown to any—not even Nell.

After leaving Mrs Trevor so abruptly, she went to Mr Woodrow's cottage and got her things together; she then wandered about the City till after dark, when she turned into the narrow street in which her parent resided. She had not visited the place since the time she was thrust out from under her father's roof; and as she passed and repassed the door, she shivered at the remembrance of the unnatural curse with which she had been driven into the night.

Suddenly the door was opened and shut, and a man left the house and hurried along the street, keeping within the shadows of the dingy walls. Rachel saw that it was her father's servant, and she knew the nature of the man with whom she had to deal. She hurried after him, and called him by his name.

'Bill.'

Bill turned round sharply; it was an unusual thing for any one to accost him in the street; but when he saw that it was Rachel, he was astounded.

'Well, I'm curst if it ain't Rachel. I'll be bound!'

And by way of expressing his amazement, he stuck his hands deep in his breeches pockets, and fetched his shoulders up about his ears.

'How is father, Bill?' she asked softly; but Bill delayed answering, till he had slowly withdrawn his right hand and effected a meeting between his forefinger and the tip of his nose.

'You're agoin' to pump; but it ain't no good,'

he said slowly. 'I ain't agoin' to tell secrets on nobody, mum. I's a paid secretary, and I's agoin' to uphold the dignity of the hoffice!'

'You are quite right, Bill, and if I were in your place I wouldn't tell either. Here's a reward for virtue;' and Bill's eyebrows disappeared under his cap with astonishment when she placed a crown-piece in his hand.

'S' help me, Rachel; 'ow is it you've come by the blunt? You ain't agone an' changed your ways o' livin', I 'opes?'

But Rachel knew how to work him; so she turned the side of her face and looked up at him out of the corner of her eye.

'You are agoing to pump, Bill, but it's no good.'

Bill knew that he had got a Roland for his Oliver, and by and by he became interested in the girl. After a little sparring, Rachel was able to draw out of him that her father was restless and unwell, and that Bill was on the way to the apothecary's for some medicine.

'Is he very ill?' she inquired.

'Wich he is, and no doubts; but he just takes a little of the doctor's stuff as 'll make him snooze. But he ain't agoin' to die, 'owsomedever, as he'll serve the devil a mighty sight better 'ere than in th' other place!'

Rachel shuddered as he spoke.

'I should like to see him.'

'Wich you shan't, by no manner o' means.

The old man's 'ouse ain't no 'ome for you. If he
caught you there he'd crack your precious skull,
and mine too—if he could. So it ain't no use
tryin'.'

Rachel saw plainly that she would not be
allowed to visit her father that night, at any rate;
so she did not press Bill further.

Her plan was that she should enter the house
when the old man was asleep, for he never left
the place, and see if she might get a peep into
his private papers, and so, perhaps, lay her hand
on the missing will. Night after night, for the
space of three months, did she come to that street
meeting Bill, but on no account would he allow
her an entrance to the house. At last she thought
of a different plan, and that was to take Bill into
her confidence. Meeting her so frequently he
began to conceive a liking for the woman : Rachel
noticed this, and encouraged it; but still she had
more wisdom than to act on the mere strength of
what might only be a man's whim. Little by
little she hinted at the magnificent opening she
could make for Bill; contrasted his present servi-
tude and poverty with the freedom and opulence
he might yet enjoy; till his curiosity was in-
flamed, and he began to question her, and press
her to speak more plainly. But Rachel waited
till she knew her time had come. Then she laid
the whole story before him; pictured the ingratitude of her father, the criminality of Philip
Gartly, and their unjust treatment of the proper

heir; plied him with promises of a happy future, and held out prospects of a great reward, till Bill was dazzled. Yet he would not enter into the plot; not for lack of desire, but he was a coward. The part he had to play was a critical one, and it was some time before Rachel got his promise to try it. At last she succeeded; and the night came on which the attempt was to be made.

They met, and having procured an extra dose of sleeping-stuff in a packet by itself, they returned to the house. Bill entered, leaving Rachel to wait in the street. Old Rubens, as he continued to be called, was waiting for Bill at the foot of the narrow staircase.

'Bill, you dog,' he cried, shaking his withered fist, 'if you keep me waiting like this again I'll poison you! What d'ye mean by keeping me here, shivering alone till I hear the creak of the door?'

'Master, the street was busy and the shop was full.'

'Oh, you dog—I know yer lies. Give it me, and go up!'

Bill handed the usual packet to the old man, and walked up-stairs before him to the room above.

As Rubens proceeded to examine the medicine, Bill went over to the table on which stood a jug of water; and, as his master bent over the one packet, he adroitly dropped the contents of the other into the stone jug. Rubens, having satisfied himself with regard to the stuff, loosened his gown and stretched himself on his low bed.

'Fetch me the water, you thief.'

And Bill came to the bedside with a large-sized tumbler, and stood before Rubens with the jug in his hand. The old man then emptied his packet into the tumbler and commanded Bill to fill up with water.

'Lots of water, you dog—More—give me lots of water!'

But Bill hesitated to pour, for he feared lest he might deprive his master of life. The nature of the drug, however, demanded a good supply of water.

'More water!' growled the man. And Bill filled it up with an unsteady hand.

'Ah, you rascal, you would poison me; I know yer tricks!'

This was a usual saying of the old man's, nevertheless Bill trembled like a leaf.

'As God is my witness, master, I would not poison you!'

But Rubens laughed at his agitation, and took the contents of the tumbler at a draught.

'Ha, ha,' he laughed, 'rather a cool thing, Bill, to call down your Judge and make a witness of Him!' and so saying he fell back on his pillow and drew the bed-clothes over his head.

In a short time, which seemed an age to Bill, Rubens gave audible demonstrations that he slept: otherwise all the house was still.

The attendant waited anxiously, his heart throbbing with excitement, till the City bells tolled Twelve; and when he rose to admit Rachel, his legs tottered under him. He surveyed the old man for a minute, then slipped his hand under the pillow for the keys. As he did so the sleeper stirred, and he started back from the bed, his heart striking wildly against his side. After waiting for some time longer, he made another effort to gain the keys. He succeeded this time, without disturbing his master. He then slipped stealthily down-stairs, and the increased excitement swayed him from side to side like a drunken man. The moment he opened, Rachel swept past him into the house, and the door was shut.

She was not a whit less excited than he was; for, besides the anxiety of the moment, she had to contend with the bitter remembrance of that unnatural act which was perpetrated on her by her father, the last time she stood on his threshold.

Neither of them spoke, for Rachel stood with her hand on her heart, gasping for breath. At length she took the keys from Bill, and with shaky hand tried one after another at the lock of an iron chest that stood on the floor. After some difficulty she got the safe opened, and she knelt beside it to examine the papers it contained. Bill stood behind her, listening for the slightest movement in the apartment above, trembling in every limb, and starting at each gust of wind that shook the street-door.

Rachel rummaged through the whole chest, but found no trace of the will; and, as she was closing it, the iron lid fell with a noise that resounded through the little house. Bill became as pale as death, and impatiently muttered a curse on her carelessness.

Another chest was opened, and the first paper she lifted bore the name of Sir George Gartly, of Garth; but it was not the will.

'It is in this chest, I am sure,' she whispered; and Bill came close behind her and eagerly watched the search.

Suddenly she snatched up a document, and read, 'The last will and testament of—' but the remainder of the writing swam before her excited vision, and she gasped, 'I've found it! I've found it!'

Her excitement had reached its climax. She hurriedly tore open the front of her dress, and was in the act of placing it in her bosom, when they heard the creaking of the door at the foot of the narrow stair behind them. Both turned at once, and were paralyzed at seeing, in the dim light, the old man standing on the lowest step, his fists clenched, and his whole frame in a fury.

With the yell of a demon, he sprang upon his daughter and fixed his sharp nails on her throat. The two fell with a crash on the floor, Rubens uppermost, and the dark blood trickled from the woman's neck!

CHAPTER XIV.

THE DESERTED HALL.

'Howsoever these things be, a long farewell to Locksley Hall!
Now for me the woods may wither, now for me the roof-tree fall.'
TENNYSON.

SINCE the time immediately after Mrs Alton's death, when Mary availed herself of the hospitality of the old rector, Ashfield Hall had remained tenantless. It was thought that Mr David Hendry, Junior, might have some inclination to take up his quarters there, but, whether on the score of convenience or economy, he kept to his furnished apartments in London. The elder Mr Hendry, immediately on entering in the possession of Mr Alton's estate, had paid off all the mortgages which the straitened circumstances of that gentleman had necessitated his giving over his property; the house in Esther Square was sold; the warehouse shut up and the stock transferred; and, as was freely whispered at the time, he pocketed a large sum of money over and above the amount of which he had been defrauded. Mr Beeds did what he could in the interest of Mary, but, as may readily be imagined, he had to drop many claims to save the worse exposure and pain which a weary lagging in the law-courts would certainly have entailed.

At first, Ashfield Hall was advertised to be let, but as no one came forward who was willing to take it at the rent demanded, Mr Hendry withdrew the advertisement and offered it for sale. But the winter had passed, and there was no purchaser; not from a want of applicants, but that Mr Hendry had set a price upon it, many thousands of pounds above any offer he had yet received. In these circumstances the fine old place fell a prey to the draughts and damps of a tenantless house. The bills which had been stuck on the doors and windows announcing the sale of furniture, were still there, hanging in tatters and flapping in the wind. The gardens lying to the front, which were at one time the pride and care of Willie Scott, were trampled and overgrown with weeds; not a flower was left; and even the adjacent shrubbery, broken and abused, still bore witness to the unthinking barbarity of the auction-mob. The brave old trees were there, it is true, but they looked down upon an aspect of desertion and neglect; and you would have thought that they were giving vent to their feelings while the wind sighed through their branches with many a sorrowful cadence.

It was a cold grey morning in early March, when the soil was soaked with rain, and the aspect of Ashfield Hall was at its worst, that a man emerged stealthily from the thick shrubbery behind, and looked about to see if any one was there. Seeing no one, he picked his steps across the spongy sward, eschewing the gravel walk, till he stood on the doorstep of the coachman's house. He was tall, seemingly more so from his thinness; and he

wore a long black surtout buttoned tightly up to
his throat, with the collar raised about his neck
as if to make the most of a garment which was far
from sufficient for such a morning of cold and wet.
His soft felt hat, which was also of black, was
brought forward slouchingly on his brow, in such
a way that it was evident he wished to keep his
features hid.

Clearly he had no idea that the place was deserted, for when he found that the tapping he
made with his knuckle brought no one to the door,
he raised the knocker and brought it down with a
noise that echoed through the empty house. The
noise was greater than he had expected, for he
started and looked round; but when he had waited
for a little and there was still no answer, he stepped
back on the gravel. Hitherto he had kept his head
bent down, but he raised it now; and when he saw
for the first time that the shutters were all closed
in the windows, he uttered a sharp cry, for he then
knew that Ashfield Hall was tenantless! Having
no further cause to conceal himself, he passed round
by the front, among grass-grown walks with weeds
on every side; and when he looked up at the picture of desolation, with its straw-strewn terraces,
broken windows, and fluttering posters, you could
see, as the rain pattered on the upturned face, that
the features, agonized and pinched though they
were, were those of no other than Mr John Alton!
Not satisfied with what he saw, he walked up to
the main entrance and rang the door-bell; but there

was no answer,—indeed it was a strange infatuation
that made him ring,—and there, on the identical
spot where a thousand times he had met with an
affectionate greeting from the lips of lovely
daughter or of gladsome wife, he read that the
furniture of Ashfield Hall, as forming part of the
sequestrated estate of John Alton, was sold by
auction on the premises only five months before!

Mr Alton was filled with deep suspense, for he
wished to know what had taken place in his family
since he left England, and in that suspense he was
well rewarded for his protracted silence. He
could not go to the village; he had shunned it
already; for in coming to Ashfield Hall he had
made his way through fields and country roads
from a neighbouring town. He thought of the
lodge. Was it possible old Willie might still be
there? And so he hurried towards it, not by the
direct way of the carriage-drive, but along the
foot-path at the side of the stream. But when he
came to the place, he saw that no one was there,
that the great gate was shut, and that the grass
had begun to grow up about it. When he again
came back to the House he did not venture on the
deserted lawn, but struck down, and crossed the
river, and climbed up a narrow path on the other
side. This led him on to the public road, and he
turned to take a last look at Ashfield Hall. There
it was, seemingly very near to him, across the deep
valley which lay between. The sun was out from
behind the clouds, and the rain cleared off; and as

there was no one passing, John Alton paused for awhile in contemplation of the scene.

But, while he was standing, an old man, bowed by the weight of infirmity and years, and leaning on a staff, tottered up to him unnoticed. The back of the tall stranger was towards him, but when he got a glimpse of the face he threw up his withered hand and exclaimed, 'Maister Alton! God bless me—it's you!'

Mr Alton turned and was shocked at the great change in his old gardener, but he merely said, 'Dear me, Willie!' and held out his hand.

He shook it warmly. 'Bless you, sir, bless you: I ken't you wad come back! But come into the house wi' me; it's just roun' the corner; and we'll ha'e a crack ower the auld times.'

Mr Alton still remained silent, but accompanied Willie along the road till they stopped before a romantic little cottage, with a rustic porch in front covered with luxuriant fuchsias.

'You see, sir,' said Willie as they entered, laying down his staff on the window-sill. 'There's been many a change since you left us. The wee bit lassie that used to mak' ready my meat, is planted awa'; and I'm left my lane. I've been changed wi' the lave, and I'm ower auld for a hard day's wark.'

'Is your leg still troubling you, Willie?'

'Hoots, ay. But I've nae fear but it'll last me.'

'You must take care of it: you are an old man.

I see, however, that your gardening instincts have
not left you.   These plots in front are finely arranged; you'll have a splendid blow in summer.'

'Yes, sir,' said Willie, rising to look out.
'There's some o' my auld frien's there.   I thocht
it was a pity to leave them to perish.'

'By-the-bye,' he said, 'how were you enabled to take this cottage?   When did you quit
the lodge?' for he did not wish to make Willie
believe that he knew so little about his family, and
he wanted to draw him on to the subject so that
he might deduce what he could.

'Weel, sir,' said Willie, 'wi' the aid o'
Providence, and an auld stocking, I had laid by a
gude wheen o' bawbees, so that, when the time o'
need cam', I was able to buy the place.   I'm provided for, in this world and the next.   There's a
sma' balance in the bank, and I've put it in my
will that they should carry me up to Clydesdale,
and lay me beside the gude-wife.'   And he repeated thoughtfully, 'I'd like to sleep in Clydesdale, and beside the gude-wife.'

But Mr Alton was impatient, and wondered
that Willie should not speak of his family; and
he was framing a question, when the old man
asked,

'Have you seen Mrs Trevor, lately?'

The question took him so much by surprise
that he started; and he saw that it were useless to
feign any longer.

'No, Willie,' he said, resting his elbow on his

knee and covering his face. 'I have seen none of my family. I came to Ashfield this morning, knowing nothing. And my heart was grieved to find—' but he fairly broke, and Willie finished the sentence for him.

'—That your house is left unto you desolate! Oh, ay, Mr Alton, there's been many a change!'

'Yes, Willie, I see there have been changes, but I know not to what extent. What of my family, Willie?—tell me of them.'

The old man started, and pushed back his chair in a corner. 'Wae's me,' he muttered, 'that you should 'a' come to me! Yes, yes,' he faltered, 'there's been many a change.'

'What of my family, Willie?—are they alive? —tell me.'

'Ah, sir, you dinna ken the warst,' he cried, bursting into tears. 'A' that's left o' your wife's a memory that all must love, and a name written on the cauld stane that stauns abune her grave!'

Mr Alton covered his face with his hands. 'It is too much,' he cried, 'too much;' and for a while there was nothing heard but the sobs of the two men.

'I know I was bad,' he cried again, 'but God knows I never meant to be a murderer!'

'Na, na, Mr Alton. Dinna ca' yersel ony bad names. There's Ane abune that can mak' the crooked straight, that wadna ca' you a bad name, but wad freely forgie you if you only asked Him.'

'I know it, Willie, I know it: but I've been a wicked man!'

'Dinna misca' yersel, sir; dinna misca' yersel! In His hand there is good in every ill.'

'Yes,' he cried like a distracted being. 'But there is no good in me!'

'Ah, man! lift your thoughts from yourself to God. Is there anything too great for Him? Do you know that from the rottenness of filth he puts the stripe on the carnation and the blush upon the grape?'

'Yes, Willie; but my wife, my wife!'

'Weep not for her, but for yourself. My wife has gane the same gate as yours this many a day, but I would not ask her back. No!—and she was God's best gift to me.'

By and by, Mr Alton sobbed himself into rest. He remained with Willie throughout the day and over the night, and got from the old gardener's lips the sad history of change. Next morning, before the village was astir, the broken man stood by the grave of his wife; but we shall leave him in the church-yard, nor shall we draw the veil that hides communion with the dead.

CHAPTER XV.

SHE PASSETH AWAY.

'The moonbeam now,
That falls upon her unsubstantial frame,
Scarce finds obstruction ; and upon her bones,
Barren as leafless boughs in winter time,'
Her infant fastens his little hands, as oft,
Forgetful, she leaves him awhile unheld.
But look, she passes not away in gloom ;
A light from far illumes her face, a light
That comes beyond the moon, beyond the sun—
The light of truth divine, the glorious hope
Of resurrection at the promised morn,
And meetings then which ne'er shall part again.'

POLLOK.

In the course of time, Mary presented her husband with a little girl. But she was ill able to stand the exhaustion of confinement, and the malady which had threatened her for the last few months, was progressing with rapid stride.

It is a sad fascination which makes us contemplate the decline of a beautiful woman. The transparent glory of the cheek, the languid lifting of the hand, and the listless movement of the frame, compel us to raise our thoughts to that land whose light brightens in the eye, the nearer she is drawn towards its celestial gates.

Trevor was beginning to look apprehensively upon his wife, but still he consoled himself by thinking that her sickness was not unto death.

On the long cold nights they would sit by their bedroom fire, Trevor on the one side and Mary on the other, a white shawl drawn around her, and their little cherub asleep in a cradle between them. Bob looked down on the sweet little thing with all the love for a first-born welling in his heart; but as the young mother smiled on the first-fruits of their love, a tear glistened in her eye and rolled down her delicate cheek. Mary was a heavenly-minded creature, and her thoughts were already clinging around that goal which she was to attain so soon. Gradually she was slipping away; silently but surely, even as the sand falleth in the glass.

A husband is slow to believe in any approaching change, but the dread reality was brought home to Trevor's heart when his young wife was no longer able to quit her bed. Many were the tears he shed in secret, and great was the anguish which he strove to hide.

Maud was now a constant attendant on Mary, and in that still chamber the true nobility of her character shone forth. The clergyman, too, was a frequent visitor; and Mary derived much comfort from his message of Peace.

Often on the long dark nights, prostrated on her bed, when all the house was still, and no eye saw nor ear heard, save one, her bosom swelled with glorious anticipation, and her lips moved with the thought—

' Nearer, my God, to Thee,
Even though it be a cross that lifteth me ! '

She had often spoken of a desire she entertained
for seeing her father before she died. This was
soon gratified, for the old gardener had at last
prevailed upon Mr Alton to visit his daughter.

The meeting was touching ; beyond the power
of pen to describe. The misguided man, shorn of
his integrity, fairly broke down, and his humility
was complete. Mary had nothing for him but
words of kindness; but her forgiving smile lighted
up no cheerfulness in his heart; all pleasure in life
had gone from him ; and his misery was the in-
effable misery of a man—good at heart—who has
lived to shed tears over the grave of his own good
name. Sweetly did Mary speak to him of the last
days of her mother, trying to infuse into his spirit
something of that hope which, in Mrs Alton, had
risen clear and strong in the midst of shattered
fortune and the loss of friends.

Long nights of watching were repeated, bells
were muffled, and the exhausted watchers glided
noiselessly about the room. Mary knew that she
was dying ; and although she grieved deeply that
she must leave the friends whom she loved so well,
she was borne up by the assured hope that she
was about to enter upon a glorious immortality.
There could be no doubt as to the future of that
sweet soul : already her features were illumed by
the light of that other life.

A day came, and at her request she was set in

an easy-chair by the fire. Maud was by her side,
and Bob stood leaning his elbow on the mantel-
piece, gazing sadly on his wife. Mr Alton sat
back from the others in a corner of the room,
cross-legged, with his hand over his mouth, looking
over-sorrowfully upon his daughter.

Mary did not speak, but her eyes wandered
about, now turned on the time-piece, and then
with a sad smile to the familiar faces around her.
The little clock rang out the hour, and Mary
seemed startled, and the hectic spot burned brightly on her cheek.

'Five o'clock,' she said. 'It is the last time
that I shall hear it'

'Don't speak in that way, Mary; it makes us
sad,' implored Bob, with a voice full of suffering.

'Why should it?' and her eyes wandered to
the time-piece. Again smiling on Bob, she said,
'Why don't you come closer to me, dear? I like
so well when you are near me.'

Bob drew in a chair beside her, and sat with
her thin white hand in his.

'You should not grieve; it will soon be over.'

Trevor strained his tearful eyes upon her, but
did not reply.

She continued in a sweet, low voice—'For the
last three nights mamma has visited me on my bed,
and we have had sweet communion. Last night
she said she would come no more, that I should
go to her.' And she again looked wistfully on the
hour. 'I am sorry, sorry to leave you all; but

oh! I am grieved for my child.' And her breast heaved with a heavy sigh. She turned her hopeful eyes, full on her husband. ' We shall meet again, Bob.'

' I hope so, dear.'

' Say that we shall.'

' We shall, Mary; we shall,' and he clasped her hand fervently to his heart and kissed her lips. A deeper glow burned on her cheek, and she looked upon her husband with eyes full of love.

A tap was heard at the door, and Maud rose to answer it. After passing a few words in a whisper with the maid, she returned and communicated the message in an undertone to Bob.

' Willie Scott!' said Mary, her eyes brightening up as she caught the import of the message. ' Has he come?'

' He is in the kitchen, dear,' replied Bob.

' Bring him in. I should like to see the old man once more.'

Maud went out, and Mary's eyes again wandered vacantly around the room. Ere the door was shut, a cloud had fallen on her face, and she thought no more of her visitor.

However, as the old gardener tottered in, her face brightened up again, and she greeted him with a sweet smile.

' You have come to see me, Willie: I thought you would come. I am dropping off like one of your flowers.'

'Yes; and it's the drappin' aff o' a bonny
rose that'll leave a sweet-scented memory ahint
it!'

'Give me your hand, Willie. It was kind—
very kind of you to come. But we have been
good friends.'

'Ay, ay,' cried the old man, as his voice faltered
and broke. 'We have been gude frien's—but the
best o' frien's maun pairt.'

She still held his hand, and although Willie
wept, and shook on his staff, there was no tear in
Mary's eye.

'Good-bye, Willie.'

'God bless you, my bonny bairn. When thou
passest through the valley thou need'st fear no
evil, for His rod and staff shall comfort thee.
Hech, my!' he cried, fairly giving vent to his
good-will. 'I wish I could gang wi' you mysel'!'

Mary smiled as she disengaged his hand, and
her eyes closed. Willie fell back among the
others, and no one broke the silence.

Her lips quivered and seemed to move with
her thoughts. At last she inquired for her child,
and Maud rose and brought the babe.

'Bring her near to me, Maud, that I may kiss
her.'

Maud held the child to its mother, and a pallor
came upon her countenance as she kissed it.

'Ah!' she sighed, gazing on the blue, unconscious eyes, 'what will become of her!' And she
pressed her lips to it again.

'Leave her to my charge, Mary,' said Maud with enthusiasm. 'I shall be a mother to her. You have known me, Mary, and can trust me; leave her to me, and I shall bring her up for your sake! She shall know so much about her good mother from what I tell her, that she will almost remember you! Do, Mary: leave her to me.' And Maud pressed the little thing to her breast, as if it had been of her own flesh and blood. Mary saw this, and smiled.

'But think of the trouble, Maud: you do not know what you ask.'

'Trouble! Why, I feel that I could live for her alone! Give her to me, Mary,' she pleaded, kneeling with the child before her. 'I will bring her up in such a way that, when we all meet again, there shall be no reproach between us!'

Mary laid her hand upon Maud's head.

'It is not that I fear any harm for the child in your hands; but remember, Maud, that you may have a husband of your own, and children of your own, and my child might become a burden to you.'

Maud again kissed the child, as if ravished by it, and a tear started in her eye as she looked up full on Mary.

'No man, however good, although I might even wish him for a husband, shall ever step between me and this child! Mary,' she faltered; but her voice was deep and rich, 'I have known what it is to love a man, but it is not—it cannot be, a holier thing than love for a motherless child.'

Mary saw that she was in earnest, and, bending down, she imprinted a kiss on the noble brow.

'Take her, Maud,' she faltered, 'and speak to her often of her mother in Heaven.'

'Oh, I shall do that,' she cried, as if beside herself with joy. 'I shall do that; and she will learn to love one whom she never knew.'

The young mother then bent over her child, till Maud took it away. Mary now felt happier in the prospect of death, for she saw by her husband's looks how grateful he was to their friend.

Maud Clayton took the child to another room, and wept and smiled over it, kissing it fondly, and pressing it to her breast. She felt that she had something to live for now, and the whole wealth of her love was lavished on Mary's child. She could hardly leave it, and for the space of an hour she remained with her little charge.

A tap was heard at the door, and a voice whispered, 'Come.'

Maud hastily kissed the child, and glided off on tiptoe to Mary's room.

Her heart sank within her as she entered. The servants were there; and all were upon their feet, except Trevor, who hung over his wife.

Mr Alton also was near her ; for she had called for him; and he stood holding her by the hand, while his tears fell freely and fast.

It was plain to all that she was dying, and although every one had expected death and were waiting for the change, all hearts were beating more fiercely, and faces were blanched, when it was known that Death was in the room.

A light that was not of earth, lit up Mary's eyes before that life passed from them, and a sweet smile flickered on her face and died away.

Trevor saw this with an agony in his haggard face impossible to describe. He gazed upon the dead face for a while, as if it were hard—hard to believe; and then he clasped her to his breast, exclaiming with loud complaint—

'Mary, Mary, my own wife! Why are you taken from me?'

There was not a dry eye in that room, and Maud felt her soul lifted within her, with a sympathetic yearning for Trevor in his agony of love.

In a little while there was a voice heard, and all heads were bowed. It was that of Willie: and, as he prayed, he murmured, 'All flesh is grass, and the glory of man as the flower of the grass; the grass withereth, and the flower thereof falleth away.'

But oh! how difficult did the mourners feel to join in the conclusion of his simple prayer—'The Lord gave, and the Lord hath taken away; blessed be the name of the Lord.'

CHAPTER XVI.

THE INSULT.

'A shrivell'd, lifeless, vacant form,
   It lies on my abandon'd breast;
And mocks the heart, which yet is warm,
   With cold and silent rest.

'I weep—my tears revive it not;
   I sigh—it breathes no more on me;
Its mute and uncomplaining lot
   Is such as mine should be.'—SHELLEY.

FOUR days afterwards, Trevor returned from the grave of his wife, a grief-stricken man: returned to what? An empty home, a vacant chair, and a companionless couch. Many, we doubt not, will appreciate the desolation that reigned in his heart, and measure the depth of his grief by what they themselves have experienced, fully understanding his refusing to be comforted because one was not. What cared he for the world, now that his wife was dead? What had he to live for? You will say, his child; but he could hardly bear the sight of her, it served to open up his wound afresh and make his distraction worse than ever.

Such was the change that had been wrought in him, his friends became anxious for his welfare; tried every expedient to cheer or soothe, but all of no avail.

'Trevor, man,' said the old lawyer, when he had sought him out one day, laying his hand kindly on his shoulder. 'You must break from this. Strive rather to think of your wife's present happiness, than ponder over your own misery and bereavement. Man, man, I have come through all this myself. I had a wife, kind as your wife, and as loving towards me as yours to you. But she was taken from me. God knows how I grieved for her, with a sorrow that experience, not words, may fathom. Often was I tempted to fly in the face of Him who had given her to me and had taken her away. And I tell you, that for years there was but one step between me and a course of dissipation. I tried to bear up in spite of everything, but again and again I fell, till the time came when I knew you first. You remember it, Robert. It was you who brought me into contact with that poor girl whom we rescued from an evil life. It was then that the whisper of Religion came to me, speaking peace to my weary heart; and from that time to this I have believed, and nothing shall ever shake my faith, that the best half of man's happiness on earth is derived from a devout submission to the will of God.'

Trevor shook himself from the kindly hand with impatience.

'What would you have me do, sir?' he cried, with knit brow and flashing eyes. 'What would you have me do? Would you have me tear my wife's image from its throne in my heart, and fill up the void with an uncertain, hankering belief in a few stale platitudes about the will of God?

If there is a God, sir, what has he done for
me?'

'Robert, He gave you her whom you have
loved most.'

'Ay, sir, and he took her away,' he replied
with bitterness.

'True, my friend,' he answered still kindly,
'when a finite mind, like yours or mine, contem-
plates a present ill, such as the loss of a wife,
it sees in it nothing but evil, provocative of despair; but if our minds were infinite, we might be
able to recognize in present evil the germs of
ultimate good.'

'But,' he cried, with exasperation, 'our minds
are not infinite, and what can we do?'

'*Submit* to the Infinite,' Mr Beeds replied, with
his head reverently bowed.

Trevor laughed a ghastly laugh.

'Belief! Belief! Blind belief! What next?'

'Nothing next. For simple belief, ridicule it
as you may, is the First and Last of man's
happiness.'

'Would you make a child of me?'

'Yes. A child in faith. In fortitude a man!'

Trevor was stung by the last reply.

'You would taunt me,' he cried.

'I would not!' Mr Beeds replied, with a
rising voice. 'I would admonish you. My experience of life is greater than yours; my trials
have been—not less. I would tell you of the
way by which I rose from them, and you reward

me with a sneer! The time was, when my reason
was as proud as yours, but it got subdued. I was
brought to my knees, and I thank God for that!
In my search after Truth, I became, as did a
greater mind than either yours or mine, like
"an infant crying in the night, and with no
language but a cry." But the answer came, and
Truth dawned upon me in the darkness of my
life. I leave you now, but I would warn you before
I go. If, in trials such as this, you do not raise
yourself above Self, which I believe to be the very
devil of this world, you shall drift before each
storm, helpless and anchorless; and when you are
wrecked you may remember me, when I would
have pointed you to One who has proved, in my
experience, a refuge from the storm, a covert
from the tempest, and the shadow of a great rock
in a weary land. I am an old man, I say,—much
older than my years; I have always tried to act
towards you openly and justly; we have been
something like friends since the first night' you
entered Mr Alton's house—it was I who carried
you in, sir, in these arms—and, perhaps, if I have
presumed to admonish you now that you are a
grown man, you may cast your memory back on
one or two incidents of your boyhood and think
that I have not arrogated to myself a position to
which I have no right. Good-bye, sir, and I hope
you will think over some of the things I have
said, and accept my advice in the spirit in which
I have offered it.'

So saying, Mr Beeds turned from Trevor and passed out.

But such visits as these did Bob no good; they only served to bring him to bay, and his morbid spirit was rather irritated than subdued. As time wore on he gave less and less heed to business, until he seldom went to the office at all. He had not the heart to work, but sank into a deeper dejection day by day; and often he wished fervently, as he moped idly about the house, that he might lie where his heart was—in the grave with Mary. If he had gone to work with a will, this dejection would soon have passed from him, but he could not work, but tried to drown his sorrow in a way that he should not, so that, before two months had passed, he walked with an unsteady gait, an unnatural excitement burned in the hollow of his cheeks, and his eyes were streaked with red. His friends had all noticed the change in his appearance, but none grieved over it so much as Maud. Many were the expedients she tried to win him back to a better life, but all in vain. Giving little heed to business, that began to dwindle away; and his wretchedness was rapidly becoming complete. Commercial losses were already draining his resources, and yet he must have the means to live. At noon, without having broken fast—not that meat was not offered him—but he had no heart to eat—he would leave his desolate home, carelessly attired, to seek—not the houses of his friends—but the more exciting haunts of infatu-

ation and vice. His friends were not congenial to
him now; they served to remind him of the sorrow
that was gnawing at his heart; and he strove to
kill that, in the mad infatuation of the gaming-
table, and strangle memory in the fierce whirl of
intoxication. His sorrow did not allow him to
wait until this fatal fascination should gradually
assert its power and draw him deeper down, but
drove him, at once, into the very vortex of
dissipation.

We cannot peep into one of these haunts of
vice, whose excitement deadens almost every better
feeling, without thinking that, among those who
frequent them, there are men who are not, at
heart, the depraved wretches they seem; and in
whose lives, if we could read them, we might trace
the tale of misery to a different source than that
of lust for gold or wine. We by no means wish
to palliate such offences against morality, or plead
extenuating circumstances on behalf of Trevor.
Far from that, we blame him the more for trying
to tear from his heart the image of one whose
memory ought to have been a light unto his feet,
and a lamp unto his path.

Maud set herself earnestly to see what she
could do for Trevor; she placed his child before
him, tried to raise his heart from Mary's grave to
a contemplation of Mary's happiness; but in all
her efforts she was sorely tried and hopelessly
baffled. Her visits, which were received coldly,
were never returned. His demeanour was even

harsh at times. His nature became seared and callous, and, on account of these repeated visits, he imputed motives to Maud which were absolutely incompatible with a disinterested spirit.

Men are the most thankless and conceited of all animals, and Trevor manifested these qualities in an extraordinary degree, when he believed that Maud kept his child, more in hopes of a living husband than out of regard for a dead friend. But he had not yet mooted this insinuation in her presence. The fact was, he was angry with her. Immediately after his wife's death, Maud had extended to him all the great sympathy of which a heart like hers was capable; but when she saw that his grief was running into all sorts of evil disorders, she had chided with him gently, and made indirect appeals to his manliness. Trevor had never betrayed any gratitude for the consolations she tried to hold out to him, but took them as a matter of course, as if he had a right to expect them at her hand; but as soon as she adopted a different tone, and mingled with her sympathies the merest touch of rebuke, he resented this as an unkindness and an impertinence.

But Maud, in spite of former receptions, determined to make one more trial; and this happened about twelve months after Mary's death.

Trevor had sold off all his furniture, and had gone into furnished lodgings; and it was only natural that Maud should think twice before following him thither. In spite of the way he had treated her former visits, he looked upon their discontinuance as another evidence of the hollow-heartedness of one's friends ; and like not a few individuals we know, he had set his mind to hate the world, yet chide with it for not showing a proper regard for him, and enough of sympathy in his misfortunes.

It was about twelve o'clock in the day, he had tasted no food, and had only taken a little drop of brandy to keep up his system, when Maud was ushered into his presence by his landlady, who immediately withdrew. He rose as she entered, made no forward motion towards her, but grasped the back of his chair with his hand, and rested his one knee on the seat.

Maud was startled by his appearance, for his long hair was hanging in dishevelled masses on his brow, and his eyes were glistening and weak, but she advanced cheerfully and offered her hand.

But he only looked at her silently.

' Do you refuse to shake hands with me, Bob?'

He slowly took her hand, and spoke lazily.

'I suppose I may shake hands with you; but I assure you, Miss Clayton, this visit was not anticipated by me.'

At this, Maud drew back her hand as if it had been burned ; a whiteness chased the beautiful colour from her cheek, and she surveyed him haughtily for the moment, as her pale lip curled slightly. ' Nor,' she replied slowly, but distinctly, with pride in every word, 'did I anticipate such a reception ! '

Trevor was taken aback by the manner in which she spoke, and he asked her to be seated.

' No,' she answered, with a cold, mechanical smile. 'It is somewhat against my nature to remain where I am not made welcome. Why you should have assumed this demeanour towards me I do not know, but I certainly expected to be treated differently by the father of Mary Alton's child ? '

This taunt had the effect of rallying his evil nature.

' If you are tired of the child,' he said, ' you can return her to me. Remember, I cannot reward you for keeping her.'

Maud drew herself up to her full height, and replied with dignity,

' I have more regard for a promise made to a dead mother, than to deliver up her child to one, from whose course of life she would learn to regard the memory of her who bore her, as a disaster and a scourge ! And,' she added scornfully, ' do you think I could expect a reward from you ? '

' Oh ! you know that best yourself, Miss Clayton,' he replied, raising his other knee on to the chair, leaning forward on its back, and nodding with an insinuating sneer.

' What do you mean, sir ? ' she cried, as a suspicion flashed across her.

' Oh ! I see you know.' Nodding and smiling as before.

A cold shiver ran over her, and she looked at him with a deadly pallor in her face.

'Are you mad?' she shrieked, starting back with her gloved hand clenched.

'Oh, no; I am not mad,' he replied jauntily, in a way which showed that her suspicion was no mistake.

Maud threw her shoulders forward, stared at him wildly, but stood motionless for a moment. Then she drew herself upright, and spoke in a voice which showed that she had conquered her passion.

'I cannot go without saying that I am pained to observe that Robert Trevor has lost the manly spirit which once characterized him; and it is out of respect for a memory which seems dead in him, that I do not reply in the language which his unjust, unmanly, insinuation deserves. More than this, as a lady, I cannot say or do.'

So saying, she bowed coldly and passed out of the room.

Trevor remained for a minute in the position in which he was, and then sank upon the chair. Her words had withered him, and his better nature rose within him to curse the foolishness of his craven heart.

'Wretch!' he cried; 'how I have yearned for her coming, and how, like a petulant child, I have dashed from the extended hand the draught that was to assuage my thirst!'

Hearing the noise, his landlady became apprehensive and opened the door. She had always been afraid that his intemperate habits would lead to the worst, but she tried to calm him.

'Let me alone,' he cried. 'I tell you I am mad.'

' 'Oh, Mr Trevor,' she pleaded, not at all awed by his manner. 'Calmness is the only thing for it. Keep calm, sir!'

'*It!* *It!* What's *it?*' he cried. But the landlady only shook her head.

There was enough of significance, however, in that, for him to get one glimpse of the chasm over which he stood. The increased shaking of his hands, and the increased twitching of his lips, had filled him with dread for some time past; but this was the first real look he had got of the inevitable goal of a furiously intemperate course.

'No, it has not yet come to that!' he replied with resolution. 'And, God help me! it never will.'

'Amen, sir,' was the only answer which Mrs Lilywhite made; and seeing that he was calmer now, she left the room.

Bob came out of the throes of his excitement, helpless as a child. His limbs were so weak that it was with difficulty he stood upright, and a cold sweat broke upon his brow.

'No,' he said to himself, 'it will never come to that.' And something like a prayer burst from his lips as he leaned his elbow on the mantel-piece, and wept for the first time since he had lowered his dead wife into that lone grave at Ashfield. Then he felt a desire to see his child, to touch those baby lips on which Mary had left her last kiss; and, not least, to wipe away that foul outrage which he had just cast on the face of dignity and love. He felt that he must see Maud, and at once. And with this intention he passed out, and wended his way along the streets.

Maud's love got a severe wrench, and her heart was wounded. When she came into the street a giddiness took possession of her, and she at once hailed a cab and drove home.

As she entered the house she met the nurse with the baby. Her heart was full of suffering, and a tear started to her eye as she kissed it; but she rushed hastily past to her own room, where, after bathing her temples, she threw herself on her bed.

Mrs Clayton was in the country, and it was perhaps as well; for Maud could never have had the heart to hold up Trevor to her in such an unholy light. She would bear this trial herself, and bury its sorrow in her heart.

It cost Trevor an effort to go up to the street door and ring; but he did it. On asking for Miss Clayton he was told that she could see no one, and the servant, who did not recognize Robert Trevor in his present ill-conditioned appearance, slammed the door rather hastily in his face.

This refusal of admittance stung him to the quick, for he looked upon it as having come direct

from Maud, who, in fact, knew nothing of it; so he
retraced his steps, angry and chagrined, with the
slouch of a beaten hound.

'What need I care, if she does not?' he said
to himself, as he wandered — he scarce knew
whither. 'It was my last chance, and, mercy on
me! it is not my fault whatever comes next.' As
he uttered these words he stumbled down a couple
of steps into a gin-shop, in a narrow street into
which he had turned. Even there he felt something battling against his desire, but he conquered
it with an angry cry for drink.

'Did you give your order, sir?'

'Yes.' And he struck the counter with his
desperate fist.

'Half a pint of brandy,' he demanded.

The man gave him the spirits in a tumbler,
which he raised to the light, at the full stretch of
his arm. He tasted, and laid it down again. And
with a harsh voice of bravado, he shouted some
snatches from a poem which he could once repeat.

> 'Every heart, when sifted well,
> Is a clot of warmer dust,
> Mix'd with cunning sparks of Hell!
> *   *   *   *
> Bring me spices, bring me wine;
> I remember, when I think,
> That my youth was half divine!'

And with a desperate gulp he drained the glass,
and smashed it on the floor. The man demanded
payment for the broken vessel, and he tossed him

a shilling, and reeled out of the place with a loud, insensate laugh.

. Now he was in the middle of the street, now on the pavement jostling the passers-by, or rubbing his shoulder against the walls. Many turned round, apprehensive that danger might befall him; but on he reeled, caring for no one, with his coat buttoned tightly up and his hat drawn forward on his brow. He was in the last stage of consciousness; but even at a juncture such as this, his mind would grasp at the memory of his wife. It was a disease with him now, for he often started during such drunken reveries, and stared into vacancy, thinking that he saw the reproving spectre pass before him. He saw it there; there as he stood in the middle of a crossing. Passers-by had scarcely time to pause and wonder at the shrunken, miserable wretch, who was standing stock-still, glaring at some object which no eye saw save his, ere a furiously-driven cab whirled round the corner, the shaft of which came in contact with his shoulder and struck him violently to the ground. For a moment he could be seen to curl up as the wheel passed over his breast; but already a crowd was around him; and in a few minutes, amid the shrieks of women, his apparently lifeless form was lifted into the vehicle and carried away.

CHAPTER XVII.

THE REVENGE.

ROBERT TREVOR will not easily be forgiven for the outrage which he had perpetrated on Maud. When she returned from his lodgings she threw herself upon her bed, and began to wonder if, in the pure simplicity of her actions, she had ever done anything unwittingly which might have been misconstrued by the most ungenerous mind. But her memory could lay hold of no such thing.

If she had only known of his having come to make what reparation he could, it would have greatly relieved her ; but of that she knew nothing, and she was tortured to think that she should have been deemed so mean. And if ever she had an inclination towards Trevor, she felt that that was dead in her for all time to come.

Wretched man, it must have been a wonderful conceit which made him think for a moment that Maud, noble and beautiful as she was, would sink her nobility and sacrifice herself to one so drunken and depraved ! But wherefore should we wonder, knowing that ingratitude and conceit, every day, make men play such unnatural tricks ?

Next morning, Maud sat by the parlour fire, in her dressing-gown, with Trevor's child on her knee. She prattled to the little thing like a mother, poked her finger into the laughing cheeks, and

laughed with her and kissed her again. In spite
of her seeming happiness, however, a grieved expression might have been seen in her eyes, and her
cheeks were paler than usual. In some women
these expressions might have betokened only a
little grief, but in Maud they told of suffering
made more painful by its suppression.

The nurse having taken the child, Maud composed herself on a low seat before the fire, and
placed her feet on the fender, folding her arms.
Her vision seemed to pierce the fire, and extend
into the far distance. She was thinking of the
times at Tewton, and of the companions with whom
she had romped in the old exuberant days. Many
of them were in distant lands, and some were dead.
Would *they* have subjected her to such treatment
as this? No: her heart cried 'No.' Yet, she
thought again, none of them have been tried as
Robert has. Misfortune makes the misanthrope,
and anything is possible after that. But Frank
Grierly in no conceivable circumstance could have
descended so low. And Mary, was she cognizant
of all this? That was the most painful thought
of all. She took from her neck a little cross that
sparkled in the light. It was pleasant to have the
token there with her now, for she remembered the
words of the giver: 'I wish you to wear it, when
I am far away, as a token of the respect with
which I shall never cease to regard you.' The
words seemed to thrill her yet. She needed some
such expression of respect, and it was not the less

welcome that it came from honest Joe. But Maud never allowed her thoughts to wander away with young Alton. She looked back upon him as an extraordinary character; yet she wished sometimes that she had known him longer and better, but when her desire went beyond that, she would check herself and become confused. She rose and contemplated her face in the mirror.

'Ah, Maud,' she said, 'and you were trying to catch a widower by keeping his child! Fie, fie, what a trick!'

But, had you stood behind her then, you should have seen how her reflection repelled the charge. The fact was, she could not get yesterday's scene out of her mind; she tried to laugh at it, but the ugly, gaunt insinuation still rose before her.

As a last resource she caught up the morning newspaper that lay on the table. But scarcely had she opened it when she was startled by the following paragraph—

'Serious street accident.—Yesterday, in Newton Street, West, about 2 o'clock, a gentleman was struck to the ground and driven over by a cab. He was at once taken to St Simeon's hospital, where it was found that he had received serious internal injuries. He was too weak to articulate, but his name—Robert Trevor—was ascertained from cards found in his possession. Eye-witnesses affirm that the gentleman was intoxicated. Be that as it may, we may state that serious apprehensions of a fatal result are entertained.'

As Maud read these lines she started as if she had been struck, and the paper fell from her hands. Then she caught it up and read the paragraph again. Now that she knew Trevor was in suffering, all her contempt for him was gone, her better feelings were revived, and she only thought of what service she might render him, even if it were to smooth his pillow and be kind to him in his last hours.

Without thinking of what she was about, she hurriedly dressed herself, got a cab, and drove to the hospital. When she arrived she asked for the superintendent, whom she knew, and in a short time she was admitted to the ward in which Trevor lay unconscious. The change in his appearance was so great that it was with difficulty she could recognize him. His glazed eyes were but half shut, his mouth agape, and his lips were drawn back and parched, leaving his teeth bare. When he breathed, his whole body was lifted, and he literally writhed for breath.

Maud could hardly look upon the spectacle of pain, and her feelings were those of love and pity only. She thought not of his harsh and callous words, but the story of his life passed before her; and she remembered the soft-hearted boy, the ardent lover, the devoted husband, the midnight watcher, and the wretched man.

Before leaving the hospital, she was reassured by the surgeon who attended Bob that there were no internal injuries to speak of, and that, if his system had not been previously vitiated, he would in all likelihood have been on his feet already. If there was any cause for apprehension in the case, it was from what effect the shock might have on his nervous system.

As Maud was about to step into her cab, a female who had been standing by the entrance, with an old shawl drawn tightly around her, stepped forward and detained her by the arm.

'Is he dead?' she inquired eagerly.

'What!' cried Maud. 'It is Rachel! Where have you been?'

'Is he dead?' she inquired again in a low voice.

'He is not. But, Rachel, what is the meaning of this?   Where have you been?'

Rachel did not heed the question, but asked, 'Is he dying then?'

'I hope not.   But he is still insensible; and the doctors cannot say much till that is past.'

Rachel, on hearing this, placed her hand on her brow, sighed deeply, and kept looking on the ground.

'I hope he lives,' she muttered.

Maud took her by the arm.

'Will you tell me what is the meaning of this, Rachel?   Can I assist you?'

'Oh,' she exclaimed with an abstracted air, 'I should like him to know.'

'To know what, Rachel?'

'May I trust you?' she inquired, 'raising her large intelligent eyes full on Maud.

'In anything honourable you may.'

'Then I will. I have found the document which should place Robert Trevor in possession of the unentailed estates of the late Sir George Gartly, of Garth.'

Maud was bewildered.

'Come,' she said. 'Come with me, Rachel. I am alone in the house, and you can tell me more of this.'

The two then stepped into the cab, and it rattled away along the street. When they arrived at the house, Maud got the whole story from Rachel, how she had recovered the will.

At the critical juncture which has already been described, Bill, who was standing by, rushed forward and felled the old man with a blow, so that he rolled over on the floor insensible. Rachel, who quickly recovered, secured the will, and then lent her father what assistance she could. But Rubens did not soon recover. The great excitement of the moment, and the stroke which he received at the hand of Bill, acted on his previous illness, and for many days he remained insensible. Although after a while he recovered his consciousness, he was never able to walk about the house, but required to be assisted from his bed to his chair. Rachel placed the will in security, but was determined not to make known its discovery until after her father's death, which she thought might take place at any moment. But the old reprobate was tough, and, though he had struggled

with Death for many months, he was, at the time
when Rachel met Maud, still to the fore.

It may appear unnatural to some, but Rachel
had no particular desire for the prolongation of her
father's life ; not that she wearied to be put in
possession of her annuity, but because she was
acting a criminal part in keeping the will con-
cealed. Bill waited for Rubens' death more impatiently than she, and for a different reason : he
remembered his promised reward.

One day, after looking for some time on the
old man who lay asleep, he shrugged his shoulders
with a grim smile.

'I say, Rachel; hadn't we better call in a
doctor ? I never know'd a man live so long, attended by one o' them chaps.'

Rachel shook her head and smiled.

'Well, ain't it a blasted shame that an honest
cove,' and he turned his thumb towards himself,
' is kept out of his property 'cos the old 'un won't
cock his toes ? It ain't no use of shaking yer
head, for it's as true's a bit of gospel. It's a
shame, me girl, and it shows a good heart in me
that I don't just give him a squeeze here and do it.'
And Bill coolly drew his finger across the old man's
throat.

Rachel started in a passion.

'Bill, if you hint at murder again—merely by
a breath, I'll have you exposed at all hazards !'

'Murder,' muttered the old man, starting from
his sleep. 'Who talks of murder ? Girl, would

you murder me in my sleep? I am your father!'

'No, no, father. Nobody would do that.'

'But I would have murdered you,' he hissed, raising his clenched fingers as if he would do it yet.

'Hush, father,' she replied, soothing him. 'Remember you are dying: you should not speak in that way.'

'I am what, girl? I am dying—I am strong! See—' and he made a great effort to raise himself, but fell back exhausted.

'Dying—dying,' he muttered slowly, closing his eyes. Then he cried abruptly, addressing his daughter, 'Where do we go, girl, when we die?'

Rachel answered not, but retreated from his bedside.

'Where do we go when we die, Bill? *That* is the question!' he shouted fiercely.

'Wich it is, and no doubt; but nobody ever told it to me, and I can't tell you for certain, though I've a wery good guess,' and he winked knowingly with his right eye.

'We must go to—There is no Hell,' he cried, in a harsh, broken voice.

'I don't know whether there be a Hell or no, but we're wery likely subjects to go to Heaven, ain't we?'

'We must. Hell is a lie!'

'It's just this, guv'nor,' replied Bill, smiling through his grim philosophy. 'You may go to Heaven if you like, but I wouldn't go there in a compliment if I was to keep company with the likes of you!'

'Hush, hush,' said Rachel, stepping forward; 'this is painful.'

'Painful—painful,' repeated the old man, and he closed his eyes again.

CHAPTER XVIII.

WILL SHE MARRY HIM?

THUS Rachel laid the whole story of the recovered will before Miss Clayton, and when it was told, the latter could easily comprehend the anxiety manifested by the woman at the entrance to the Hospital.

On the following day Mrs Clayton returned to town, and she was greatly shocked when she heard of the accident that had befallen Bob. Contrary to her wont, Maud did not take her aunt fully into her confidence, for she was so ashamed of the way in which her old friend had conducted himself towards her, that she thought it better to repress that part of the story, quite as much out of regard for her aunt's feelings as for her own. Nor did she speak of the long-lost will.

'Dear me,' said Mrs Clayton, 'it is pitiful how some men are brought so low. Who would have thought that little Bob, with his happy laughter and winning ways, should ever come to such a pass? Well—well!'

'It is very painful,' rejoined Maud, 'but we must not lose hope altogether. There must be something good in Robert Trevor's heart, for the man who was capable of such love as was his for Mary, cannot be beyond the influence of good.'

'I hope so, Maud, but yet—well, well, it's a sad world at the best.'

Shortly before one o'clock, Miss Clayton appeared in the drawing-room in presence of her aunt, dressed and ready to go out.

'Dear me, Maud, going out again! You make yourself a perfect slave to these poor children of yours.'

'But I'm not going after the children now.'

'Indeed—where?'

'To St Simeon's Hospital.'

'What!' cried Mrs Clayton, starting from her seat. 'To see Robert Trevor? Not one step, Maud. You must think better of this.'

'I am sorry, aunt, but—'

'No, no; you must not think of it. You cannot go. Are you infatuated with that man?'

It was very seldom that Mrs Clayton spoke severely, and her niece felt it the more on that account; but she was hurt by the unkindness of the last insinuation. She remained firm, but her cheek quivered.

'No, aunt,' she answered meekly, 'I am infatuated by no man.'

'It is very like it, I must say! First, you bring home his child—I made no objection to that, for it was a good and Christian thing to do—and then you go after him to the Hospital! It is folly; you must not!'

Maud still restrained herself, and her aunt continued,

'Do you think it is right, that a young girl like you should be found in the Hospital, by any man's bedside? What would the world say?'

'I care not,' she answered; and when she raised her eyes, they were full of tears.

'But you must care! If Robert Trevor chooses to fritter away his good name, it is no reason why you should. He is a worthless creature.'

'Oh, aunt, aunt, do not say that!' she exclaimed, bursting into tears, and taking her hand. 'Do not say that! You know that you loved him when he was a little boy; and you know that he was cast upon the world when there was not a soul to care for him so far as his higher welfare was concerned, and yet he was kept from evil! When he came to manhood, a wife was given him on whom he lavished such a wealth of love as might have gladdened any woman's heart, but, in the prime of life and hope, she was taken from him! Could you have seen his anguish over that dead wife, as I now see it, you would have a kind word for him at least. Bear with me, aunt: I do not wish to play upon your affection. But, was it not you who taught me that God loves those whom He chastens most; that we should try to recognize His hand in the afflictions which come upon us?

And if God's hand may not be recognized in such
a death as Mary Alton's, where shall we look for
it? Oh, aunt, aunt, if it was His hand that af-
flicted Robert Trevor, surely, surely, he is not
worthless, but cared for!'

Mrs Clayton was visibly affected, for, as she
said many a time, with all his faults, she liked
Bob. She sat herself in her chair, and drew Maud
close to her.

'Tell me, Maud,' she inquired softly, 'have
you carefully thought over the step you are about
to take?'

'I have, aunt,' she answered. 'Carefully and
prayerfully.'

'That being the case,' she said, freely using
her handkerchief, 'I have nothing to say against
your going, and you have my warmest and best
wishes.'

Maud bent and kissed the upturned brow.
'Thank you, dear aunt.'

'Heigh-ho!' sighed Mrs Clayton, rising and
putting away her handkerchief. 'What an old fool
I have been, to be sure. But, mind you, girl, it
was all for your good I said it.'

'I never doubted it, aunt,' she said, smiling.

'And, after all, I may not be very far wrong,
for tongues *will* wag. However, you are old
enough to judge for yourself, and I must say that
I have never had any reason to question your
judgment. If Bob is able to receive it, give him
my earnest love.'

Maud put her arms round her neck, and kissed
her twice ; and in a little while, Mrs Clayton came
to herself in a mood for pleasant banter.

'You'll see what the world will say. They'll
say that you are making a dead set for a husband.'

Maud knew that this was not said to deter her
from going, but her aunt's words went deeper than
she cared to show.

'Aunt,' she replied, drawing herself up, 'any
charitable action may be misconstrued, and imputed to the meanest motives, but I shall not allow
that to hinder me from doing what I consider to
be my duty. This may be a turning-point in
Robert's reckless life. He is my oldest friend ;
and if I can be the means of saving him from ruin,
I shall not fail to attempt it, merely from the
consideration that there is scandal among silly
women, or because the world may say this or that !
So, good-bye, auntie ; and I'll take your good
wishes with me.'

And so she passed lightly from the room,
leaving her aunt alone.

'Well, well,' mused the old lady. '"Never
noble man but made ignoble talk," and, I suppose,
the same thing holds good with women too.'

When Maud arrived at the Hospital, she was
greatly gratified to learn that there was a marked
improvement in Bob's condition.

'Last evening,' she was told, 'when he awoke,
he asked if any one had called to see him, and
when we informed him that you had been, he was

much pleased, and wanted to know if you were likely to come again. He is asleep now, but you may go in and sit near him till he awakes.'

So Maud went in, and found him sleeping. He was very pale, but breathed regularly, and his fingers worked nervously above the bed-clothes.

By and by she sat herself by his bedside, and kept wondering what reception should be offered her when he awoke. The light was streaming past the drawn blinds, and she fixed her eyes on that, thinking — thinking, till she was lost in meditation.

The fingers worked more nervously, as if he were dreaming ; the bosom rose with a gentle heave ; his eyes opened, and he was awake. For a little while he kept his eyes on Maud, but she was still thinking—thinking, and he did not speak.

After a minute or so, a smile passed across his emaciated features, and he laid his hand gently upon her wrist. Maud started when she felt the fevered touch, but when she saw the languid smile upon his face, the blood ran crimson to her cheeks.

' Maud ! '

' Bob ! '

And the two looked upon each other silently.

' You turned me from the door, Maud, when I came to seek forgiveness,' he said reproachfully, but in subdued tones, as an exhausted expression played upon his features.

' I ! when ? ' she ejaculated softly, in astonishment.

'Do you remember my cold words, Maud? It was not I who spoke them, for I was mad.'

Maud's bosom heaved as she peered deeply into those large, pleading eyes, as if she could see truth there at last, and her only answer was a tear.

Bob held her by the hand. 'Nearer, Maud, nearer.' And she bent over the pale, exhausted face.

'Do you forgive me, Maud?' he muttered deeply, in the old rich tones.

But she could not speak, for the sympathy that welled largely from her heart choked her utterance, and she only bent the closer over him, keeping her breath for a moment, as a kiss fell upon his brow.

Bob's eyes closed again, and he let go her hand as a happy expression settled on his face.

When she contemplated this, her thoughts fled away back to their youthful days in the country; and even in these harder lines of manhood, she traced the familiar features of the tender-hearted boy. When she rose to leave him, it seemed as if he were still asleep, and she paused over her dear old friend. As the memories of other days crowded in upon her mind, a bright tear rose to her eye and fell upon the thin pale cheek before her. Surely the Angel of Love, which is God, stood over the bedside to guide that tear; for it touched upon the only green spot in conscious Trevor's heart, passed into his soul, and turned the tide of ruin there!

Maud was quite overcome; and when she

came into the room to her aunt, on her return home, she had not yet recovered. With much simplicity she portrayed the deep contrition of Bob for his past courses, but she carefully kept out all reference to the ugly scene in his lodgings. Mrs Clayton was touched with what she heard.

'Come near to me, Maud,' she said. And her niece came to her where she was reclining, and knelt, with her arms in her aunt's lap.

'Maud, do you think it is possible Bob may change ? '

'I do,' she cried. 'I have prayed for it so earnestly, and I know that the object of my prayer is just. He *will* change.'

'Maud,' she said again, in serious tones. 'When you were speaking of him now, it was as if you still regarded him as your old boy-friend in Tewton. You always cared for him : do you love him still ? '

Maud was silent for a moment, as she hid her head in her lap, but when she raised it, the tears were streaming down her face.

'Yes, aunt, I love him—I do.'

'Maud, would you marry him ? '

But when she answered this question, her eyes opened wide; and there was a beautifully-honest expression in her countenance, free from the slightest approach to contempt, when she spoke solemnly and slow,

'No, aunt. I love him. But marry him I never shall ! '

And Mrs Clayton thought what a queer girl was her niece, but she did not upbraid her for her curiously-framed but frankly-spoken answer ; for she imagined that there might be a fine nobility in Maud's nature, which even she could not comprehend.

CHAPTER XIX.

'OUR DEAR BROTHER HERE DEPARTED.'

OLD Richards struggled on for some time between life and death. But one dark night, when all the house was quiet, and there was nothing to disturb the silence but the snoring of Bill, the last struggle came in which death had the mastery. There were a few convulsive clutchings at the bedclothes, a hoarse gurgling in the throat, and the eyes rolled and set in darkness.

When Bill awoke next morning, he was astonished at seeing the old man lie so quiet, for he had never seen a dead body before. He got up and went over to the bed in which his master lay, and, putting his hand on his breast, he moved him slightly.

'Wake up, old man. Wot makes you stare like that, and never wink ? Wake up ! ' and he shook him again.

But still there was no answer, and when he

gazed on the quiet frame, he began to comprehend that the old man was dead. When this dawned on his intelligence, his limbs quaked beneath him, and from the dead face he turned apprehensively at every creak of the floor. There was a coarse towel hanging near him, and he took it from its peg; but before throwing it over the vacant eyes he scratched his ugly head, gravely reflecting,

'Wonder wot he saw last?' and with a shiver, 'Wot's he seein' now?'

This last reflection seemed to trouble Bill, for he hastily threw the towel over the face; and when he took the key from under the pillow, he kept as far back as possible, as if he were afraid that even yet the old man might rise, ghost-like, in his wrath. But, when he had locked the door, he breathed more freely as he hurried along the street. Still the reflection forced itself back upon him—'Wot's he seein' now? Guess I'll know some day,' he answered to himself, working his big hand under his cap.

Rachel's lodgings were close by, for she had come to this locality to be near her father in the event of anything serious taking place. Bill met her coming to the house, but before he had said a word, she knew from his scared look that all was over.

'When was it, Bill?' she asked.

'Sometime through the night,' he said, 'but can't tell when. His eyes was stuck straight, an' all glazed over, w'en I got up, an hour ago.'

Rachel asked no more, but they hurried back together. Of course, the body lay in the same position, although Bill averred that it must have stirred during his absence; for it was, he said, not nearly so neatly covered, now, as when he left it. And, shaking his head with considerable apprehension, he told Rachel that he would remain down-stairs while she set about the business she had to do, for Bill was aware that she had already made preparations against this day.

With dry eyes and steady hands, Rachel nerved herself to her task; so that, in less than an hour-and-thirty-minutes, the old reprobate who had steeped his hand in fraud and infamy to serve his greed;—who, in the uncertain hope of hush-money, had made the attempt to blast the reputation of one he had never seen; who, with an insatiable lust for revenge, had at first tempted an honest man— though a weakling—into the committal of a great crime, and had ever after tortured him with the threat of exposure; who, in violation of all paternal instinct, had struck his only daughter and cursed her from his door, driving her at midnight into the bitter rain; who had abjured his faith to cloak his crimes; who had lived through all these years of guilty seclusion, a curse to himself and a shame to humanity, Rubens—Richards—the old reprobate, was laid out at last for Christian Burial! Two days afterwards, he was carried to his grave by hireling hands; and in reading over it the beautiful service of the Church, the parson spoke of him as 'our dear brother here departed;' but when he murmured in nasal tones, 'In sure and certain hope of the resurrection to eternal life,' Bill, who was standing near, looked up at the church porch, and wondered why the chubby little angel over the archway did not wink his eye or cock his finger to his nose!

When all was past, Rachel took the long-lost will from its seclusion, and with a light heart she hastened to the office of Mr Twentyman Beeds. The old lawyer was greatly delighted when he read it over, for he saw that its provisions were quite in keeping with the ideas entertained of it by the late Mr Woodrow. There was no time to be lost, and he took a cab at once, and rode away to Trevor's lodgings. Mrs Lilywhite said that since his accident Mr Trevor had not returned to his rooms, but she thought that in all likelihood he might be found at Mrs Clayton's. Mr Beeds immediately acted upon this hint, and in a few minutes the cab was drawn up at Mrs Clayton's door.

'How opportune,' said that lady, when she received him in her parlour, 'for Bob has only now expressed a wish to see you. I am glad you have come, for he was so anxious to claim your friendship again that I believe he would have gone in search of you, in spite of our telling him that he is yet too weak to venture out.'

'That is well,' said the lawyer, but he did not hint with regard to the will.

'Yes, Mr Beeds; and you can have no idea
what a changed man he is.   His one desire since
he was taken here from the hospital seems to be
to make what reparation he can to those friends
whom he outraged, and whose counsel he disregarded.'

'That is most gratifying,' he answered, 'for
when one's repentance takes this form, it is sure
to be deep, and there is no pride to mar it.'

'I wonder,' said Mrs Clayton, after a bit, 'if
anything can be done for him.   His business is
quite ruined, and I can see that this depresses
him.   For one who has been his own master, and
who has lived in affluence, the idea of commencing
the world again, is certainly a hard one.'

'Yes, yes,' chuckled the lawyer, rubbing his
fingers on his shaven chin.   'It must be.   It must
be a hard one.'   But he laughed in such an extraordinary way that Mrs Clayton was puzzled.

'I beg your pardon, Mrs Clayton,' he said,
rising, 'but is there any obstacle to my seeing Mr
Trevor, now?'

'Certainly not, sir,' she answered, laying her
hand on the bell.   'My niece is with him in the
drawing-room, but you can easily see him alone.'
And she kept staring at the lawyer, for she was
taken aback by his abruptness.

'Thank you, thank you.'   And he kept rubbing his hands, and bowing his plump little body.

'Jane,' she said to the maid, 'would you
kindly inform Miss Clayton that I wish to see her.'

And in another minute Maud came into the room. On seeing the lawyer she blushed slightly, and her eyes brightened up; for she had received a note from Rachel the day before, and she knew the errand on which he had come.

The usual greetings passed between them, and Mrs Clayton said to her niece,

'Maud, be so good as to conduct Mr Beeds up-stairs. He wishes to see Mr Trevor, alone.'

The lawyer thanked her, but as soon as they were outside the door, Maud stopped and put her hand in his arm.

'Mr Beeds, do you wish to see him about that will?'

The lawyer answered her, but he was curious. 'How came you to know of it?'

'I'll tell you more about that again; but I had a letter from Rachel yesterday, informing me of her father's death.' And she was excited when she spoke. 'But, Mr Beeds,' you must be careful, for he is still very weak and it may hurt him. *Do* be careful!' Mr Beeds smiled at the affection of the girl, but made all sorts of promises; and when he was ushered into the drawing-room, Maud retired.

Trevor lifted his eyes with pleasure, and rose to meet him, and they grasped each other's hands. His face was thin and white; he was dressed in black; and when he rose, Mr Beeds saw that he was suffering from great weakness.

'Keep your seat, Bob,' he said, laying his hand

on his shoulder. 'Keep your seat, and we shall chat quietly.'

'Mr Beeds, I am glad you have come. This has been a dreadful time, but, thank God! it is over now.'

The lawyer stuck on his spectacles, nor did he wait to clean them, for these were tell-tale eyes of his.

'I hope so, Bob. Your experience has been a sharp one.'

'Indeed it has,' he answered, and he bent forward where he sat, with his hand on his brow. He then faltered out some words of regret for the way in which he had treated the lawyer when he came to him in his distress, but Mr Beeds stopped him, and bade him be of good cheer.

'Better let that theme drop, Bob. We shall be good friends yet.'

And after a while, when they had talked over matters, and Trevor had opened up his heart with all frankness, he rose to his feet uneasily, as if he were about to ask his advice on some subject; but he sat down again without speaking. Mr Beeds observed this, and thought to draw him out.

'Your business must be in a very backward state,' he said. 'Do you intend to return to it?'

Bob's eyes glistened with satisfaction, and he unburdened his heart.

'Well, Mr Beeds, I am glad you have mentioned this. My business is ruined, and I have no money to take it up again. What am I to do?

I am a changed man, whatever comes of it; but
the world is before me. What *shall* I do?'

The lawyer fumbled with his hand in his breast-
pocket, but he feared to fetch forth the secret, lest
it might overpower him in his present distress.

'You remember Mr Woodrow's will?'

'I do.'

'Do you think there is no chance of that other
will which it refers to, being brought to light?'

'Oh! Mr Beeds!' he cried wearily, 'why
do you mention this? There is no hope from that
quarter. Do not buoy me up with hopes which,
during these last two days, I have tried to crush!
I want realities now; I have had enough of such
false hopes. Give me something I may rely upon,
even if it be only your sympathy.'

'But, Bob,—indeed, you know, I would not
offer—'

'Yes, yes, I know you do not mean it. But
that will has been a devil's whisper in my ears for
the last two days! You see, Mr Beeds, I believe
in the devil now; I have been snatched from him,
but I know he has been dangling that light before
me to lead me on to the morass again!'

'Ah!' said the lawyer with a cheery laugh,
'see that you don't be too hard on the devil!
Perhaps you have mistaken some other voice for
his. Such things have occurred before now!'

'Well, well, sir, you know what I mean.'
And in spite of his inclination, Bob's weakness
made him fractious. 'I know you have been a

good friend to me, and I would be greatly your debtor if you would do one thing for me.'

'Name it,' said the lawyer.

And Bob thereupon began to express a hope that something might yet be recovered from his business, if the books were carefully examined.

'Will you do this for me, Mr Beeds? Something may be saved from the wreck.'

The lawyer could keep his secret no longer, and he rose from his seat and again put his hand in his pocket and grasped the will. But he did not bring it out.

'Mr Trevor. You had better leave that business to rot on the shores where it was wrecked. I have not come to you empty-handed. Now, you are not to be astonished and hurt yourself, for you are still weak. There is a certain estate which wants to be looked after, very badly; and I want you to take it in hand. The estate is in Northumberland. The owner is a client of mine. I thought it would suit you, so I have the appointment ready and signed. I have it in my pocket. There it is.' And he placed the long-lost will of Sir George Gartly in Trevor's hands.

As soon as Bob saw what it was, the document fell from his feeble hand, and he covered his face and burst into sobs. Mr Beeds jumped about like a man dementate, shed tears copiously, and whistled like a bird.

'It is too much—too much!' cried Bob. But the lawyer came to himself again.

'Not too much, Mr Trevor! When you were at your lowest there were kind hearts to care for you, and though you were cast down you were not forsaken.' And the old lawyer was very serious when he continued. ' It is not for me to express my ideas of the dispensations of Providence; but it has happened frequently in the history of man, that God has reduced His creature to the lowest depths of despondency, to make him a willing instrument of His power. That document conveys to you a great power. But I would not have you look upon it merely as an accession of wealth, but rather I would have you regard it as the key to a larger sphere of usefulness ; and by the example you may show, and by the beneficence of your life, I hope you will render to God some return for this kindness, and that you will yet learn to thank Him for the fiery trials through which you have passed.'

CHAPTER XX.

MR BEEDS TAKES HIS REST AMONG FLOWERS OF HIS OWN GATHERING.

THE recovery of this will of Sir George Gartly had a wonderful effect on the drooping spirits of Mr Twentyman Beeds, and he set about the task of putting Trevor into his new property with great delight. From numerous letters found in the

strong boxes of old Richards, there was abundant
evidence to show that Philip Gartly was cognizant
of the existence of a will, and, therefore, all along,
had been art and part in its concealment. That
man was terribly taken aback when Mr Beeds
placed the matter before him, and, rather than face
a prosecution for his crime, he was not slow to accept the alternative of leaving the country. There
were grand rejoicings all over the estate, for the
tenants had no love for their late landlord, on account of the way in which he had lorded over their
interests, and they received their new master with
great style and ceremony.

In a few months Trevor became a pronounced
favourite among the county-people, and also
among the peasantry, for he dispensed his favours
with an unstinting hand. Nor was he unmindful
of his old friends; for Rachel, besides receiving
her annuity, was taken back to the land of her
nativity, where she lived in a free house. Old
Willie Scott was persuaded to journey Northwards,
and Trevor provided him with a neat little cottage
in the bosom of a glen, where he indulged his
floral propensities, and philosophized at his leisure.
Bill got his reward as promised by Rachel, but he
also was taken North, and received employment
from the new landlord. The strange thoughts
that first entered his mind on the morning after
Richards' death, made him change his ways of
living, and all through life he never forgot the
reflection which rose within him when he con-

templated the dead, fixed stare—'Wot's he seein' now?'

Mr Twentyman Beeds returned to London, and the lively spirits which had kept him up for the last few months, began to subside, and he slipped back into his old weary way.

The offices and domicile of Mr Beeds were contained in one tenement, of which he was the proprietor; or rather, only one-third of it still belonged to him, for the remaining two-thirds had been placed under mortgage.

The time was when it was all his own; but that was in the halcyon days, before the crows' feet were about his eyes, when there were pleasant and profitable associates around him, and he had a stout heart within. Now, his circumstances were reduced. The prime vigour of manhood had given place to the frailness of premature age; his associates had left him, or he had survived their honour; and the stout heart, which was wont to be ready, at all times, in the service of kindness, was becoming sad and weary, now that it was inured to the ingratitude of the world. As his business failed him, he reduced his establishment accordingly, and now, at the time of which we write, he had only two dependents left; the one, an old housekeeper who looked after the few wants of the household; the other, a quaint little urchin who mounted guard in the office each morning at 9 o'clock—not that there was any office-work to be done, for he spent his time in making paper-boats and paper-hats, or in modelling babies in sealing-wax, for the edification of Betsy the housekeeper.

If the day was fine, Mr Beeds went out shortly after ten, and generally remained out till the afternoon, when he would return to dine. What he did when he was out, no one knew, but his times of going and returning were regularly kept, unless the weather marred his unknown arrangements.

'Hi, Betsy,' cried little Tim, the urchin, one forenoon as he discerned the attenuated features of Betsy peering through the glass door in the back of the office. 'Come in, Betsy, an' I'll show you the beautifullest himage of a wax boy as ever you saw. Ain't it pretty?' he asked, as she came beside him, looking up in her face for approval. 'Ain't it pretty, Betsy?'

'Why, Tim; lor' bless yer, you're a reg'lar sculpture—it *is* pretty, to be sure.'

'Ev I had wax enough, I'd make a whole family o' boys. I'm proud of my boys! I say, Betsy,' he whispered, nudging her elbow, 'wot's for dinner?'

'Chops, Tim.'

'And tomato sauce?'

Betsy nodded, and smiled. The boy twisted his body and looked up to her slyly, while he concentrated his face into a wink.

'You're a fishing, Betsy. Hever since I told you the story of Mr Pickvick, you've been havin' chops and tomato sauce hevery blessed day!'

'You go along, Tim.'

'But I won't go along, Betsy. It's a shame for a wigorous maiden like you to bear down on sich a weak old man and try to captivate him with chops! Chops is played out! Why don't you try on duck and green peas?'

'Lor' bless yer, Tim, master would be put out o' countenance if he saw duck and green peas for dinner—it ain't a solemn dish. Chops is solemn, and more in keeping with master's nature.'

'Yes, Miss Betsy, dinner comes to be a solemn business if you've got the same dish served up to you for three blessed months without wariation. I ain't agoing to stand it no longer, and I'm going to look out for another place. Hi, Betsy. Cut! Here's the gent as was here in the morning.'

Tim had seen the gent from the window, and as Betsy beat a hasty retreat, he got up on his high stool and appeared to be busy 'backing' letters. In a few moments the gent bounced in at the door.

'Has Mr Beeds come yet, young man?' inquired a thin, shrill voice.

'No, Mr Wrinkle—'

'Prinkle, please, *not* Wrinkle,' he demanded peremptorily.

'I beg your pardon, Mr *Prinkle*, but I said when you called this morning that Mr Beeds would not return till two, and it is only twelve now.'

'You said noon, you young scoundrel!'

'Well, sir, if I said noon, you said Wrinkle—and I ain't a young scoundrel—there!'

'By Jingo,' cried Mr Prinkle, with exaspera-tion, 'if I was at your ears you would get it.'

'P'raps I would; but you'd require to perform a pretty steeple-chase over them desks and stools before you'd get at them!'

Peter was amused.

'Where did you learn your manners, boy?'

'I never learned any,' he replied promptly, 'I picked 'em up.'

And the pompous gent, not wishing to prolong a sparring match with one who was artful as he was small, intimated that he would return at two, and bobbed out at the door.

As soon as he was gone, Betsy came back on tiptoe, and with a very long face.

'Who's he, Tim?'

'Blist if I know! But I'd like wery much to take him off in wax. Ain't he a rum cove, Betsy?'

Betsy ventured to assert, 'He's a wulture.'

''Cos why, Betsy?'

''Cos why!' she cried with indignation, ''Cos why—there's nobody but wultures comes here now. It's a case of more furniture to be took away and sold—*I* know,' she blurted with her apron on her eyes. '*I* know—they're all wultures!'

'Well, well,' said Tim, 'it's a cussed shame, too, the way as they go and bleed the guv'nor.

It's all owin' to his havin' a large heart. When a man has a big heart, all the rogues in creation think as how they ought to get a bit of it. But it'll come to an end some day. Have you any furniture in the third room to the right, Betsy?'

'Not a stick, Tim—it's cleared out too.'

Tim sagely shook his head. ''Strikes me, he'll be offering to pay my wages one o' them days with the parlour time-piece. He wants some 'un to keep him right, Betsy. Why don't you marry 'im right off, against his will? It would do him good.'

'Ah, Tim,' she whined, 'if I could only see my way, I'm sure and certain it would do him good.'

'Wouldn't you sweep down on the wultures, Betsy?'

'That I would, Tim. That I would.'

But Betsy was beside herself with grief, and she sobbed right out.

Truly the old housekeeper had a good heart towards her master, and these desires which she frequently expressed with regard to her position in the house of Mr Beeds, were more the outcome of her earnest care, than the result of any matrimonial design which she entertained. She had now been in his service for upwards of twenty years: she had been with him since the day of his great grief; she had served him during the palmy days of his prosperity; and she had witnessed the gradual withdrawal of his friends, the reduction of his establishment, and the corresponding decline of light-heartedness which once characterized him. But Betsy often wished that she could come down on the wultures, by which term she designated those persons who subsisted on the charity of her master, and for whose benefit one room after another had been divested of its furniture, till there was barely sufficient left for his own comfortable accommodation.

'Well, Betsy,' Mr Beeds would say when she ventured on an expostulation, 'we need not care so long as there is enough left to keep us going. I have no need of a great house, and I may as well give my goods away while I live, as leave them at the disposal of others when I die.' And besides that, he had given Betsy to understand that ample provision was made for her in the event of his death. Of course, Betsy was grateful for this assurance, but it never reconciled her to the 'wultures.'

Shortly after Mr Prinkle went out, there was another arrival in the office, and Betsy made the same quick exit as before.

There were three of them: a tall, broad-shouldered man with face and hands brown as mahogany,—an evidence that he had just returned from foreign parts. The woman who accompanied him was slim but comely, as if nature had cast her in a finer mould than that of the strong, but somewhat uncouth, man. With them was a blithe-faced, curly-headed boy, in whom you might readily have recognized a distinct likeness to both of his protectors.

The woman asked if they might see Mr Beeds.

' Mr Beeds won't be home for 'alf an hour yet,' replied Tim, promptly, having taken stock of them as they entered; 'but if you like to wait, I shall ask the housemaid to show you up-stairs.'

He was thanked; and the woman held a short conversation with her husband, the result of which was that they determined to wait for Mr Beeds.

Accordingly they were shown up-stairs, but Tim had no sooner settled down to his desk, than the curly-headed little fellow appeared with his nose flattened against the glass in the door at the back of the office, apparently waiting an invitation to enter. The invitation was given and accepted.

' Come 'ere, my little chap. Wot a curly 'ead you've got, to be sure! I'll take you off in wax.'

' No you shan't,' returned the little fellow, stoutly enough. ' You shan't. I'm not very big, but my father is, and he'll fight you.'

' Where d'ye come from?' asked Tim, curiously.

' We've come from Australia. But I am a Scotchman, and we are going home to Scotland.'

' From Australia! That's the place, ain't it, where people walk on their 'eads?'

' No they don't,' he answered contemptuously, ' and I think it's foolish of you to say so.'

' Well, you are a rum little chap, to be sure! '

But Tim was interrupted in this observation

by the appearance of his master, much earlier than
was expected.

The old man had had a smart walk, and, immediately on entering, he rested at the counter and
bent his white head on his hands. On lifting his
eyes he was evidently astonished at the presence
of the little stranger, for he cried, 'Halloa!
whom have we here?' And he came in, and took
the boy by the hand.

Passing his fingers through the curly hair, he
said, 'What a fine boy you are! What is your
name?'

The little fellow smiled radiantly as he looked
up at the kind old man.

'My name is Gordon. They call me Lawyer
Gordon, but my right name is Twentyman!'

The lawyer started, and shook in every limb,
and held him so that the boy was frightened.
The wrinkles of his old face seemed to smooth
away under the bright influence of his recollection.

'Gordon!—Gordon!' he muttered. 'Where
do you come from, my boy?'

'We have come from Australia. My father
and mother are with me. They are waiting for
you up-stairs.'

Mr Beeds tried to restrain his agitation, but he
made a frantic rush up-stairs, dragging the astonished boy behind him.

Tim was beside himself with amazement, but
he had hardly time to express himself, ere Betsy

glided in, with her hands raised on either side of her elongated features.

'Tim, Tim!' she whispered mysteriously. 'They're 'll be no more dinners. It's the last day! The sky's a falling in! Oh, mercy, mercy! master's agoin' mad!'

'Wot is it, Betsy? Who are they?' he asked.

'The Lor' knows,' she cried. 'But master met the woman on the stair, and they fell to on each other's necks, a kissin' an' cryin'. Lor'! Lor'! I never see'd the like!'

But Betsy was brought to her senses when she heard her master's footstep, and she vanished silently.

'Tim, Tim. Run away home. Quick,—never mind these letters—I'll put them right. Come back to-morrow as usual.'

Tim got his hat with alacrity and scampered out, and when Mr Beeds had locked the door behind him, he came back and sat himself at a desk, giving vent to the full flood of his tears!

Then Lizzie was not ungrateful after all; and her long silence was not that of forgetfulness! How his old heart warmed within him when he thought of this! And his gratitude went up to Him to whom all gratitude is due, that He had brought back in prosperity her, whom in saving from ruin long ago, he had learned to love!

They made a lively evening of it in Mr Beeds's house. The old lawyer sat by the fire with the child upon his knee, and ever when the boy spoke to him, it was 'Grandfather.'

'Mrs Gordon,' said the lawyer, with a cheery laugh, 'I require no other evidence of your affection for me, than that you have named your boy— Twentyman. But it is an infliction which the child scarcely deserved.'

'Ah,' laughed the husband. 'That was my idea, but Lizzie jumped at it.'

'Well, well, it was very good of you both. I am a happy old man.'

And, indeed, the radiant pleasure of his face in no way belied his words.

'But,' said Lizzie, perhaps somewhat abruptly, 'we want you to go North with us and stay. My husband has saved a lot of money ; we intend buying a farm, and you shall find a comfortable home with us.'

'What!' ejaculated the lawyer. 'Leave London! And I—an old man!'

'That is the very reason,' rejoined Lizzie, softly. And she went on to tell him, how that, ever since the death of the old folks, they had looked forward to this.

Mr Beeds, of course, laughed at the idea, but when the night wore on, and they had talked over the proposal, he was far from ridiculing it. It opened up such a bright prospect for the friendless old man, that, the more he thought of it, the more he was charmed. But before he had given his consent, the door-bell rang violently, and Betsy

rushed in to inform her master that a very excited
gentleman waited him below. Mr Beeds offered
a hasty apology to his guests, and hurried down-
stairs, where he met Mr Prinkle in the hall.

'Great Goodness, Mr Beeds, I am glad you
are in! It is the third time I have been here to-
day. You were out, the first time; and when I
came again, the office-door was locked. I don't
know what to say to you, sir, for I am in great
distress. But it is not for myself, it is for another,
and you are the only friend I've got.'

'Dear me!' exclaimed Mr Beeds. 'Is it anything serious?'

'Serious, sir! it's of the last moment. Per-
haps you remember me telling you about a lad—
Victor Cole—for whom I got a situation in the
Hendrys' counting-house?'

'Well?'

'Well, sir, he's made a mess of it. He has
embezzled a lot of money, and I want to know if
they can come upon me for it?'

'Certainly not, Mr Prinkle.'

'But, sir, it was I who recommended him!'

'Well, it matters not.'

'But, sir, Mr David Hendry says I must make
it good.'

'Surely you are mistaken.'

'As sure, sir, as I am a living man!'

And Peter drew himself up, and laid his hand
solemnly on his breast. But Mr Beeds was still
incredulous.

'What did he say to you, Mr Prinkle?'

'Say to me! He called me into the private room, where Victor was crying like to choke hisself; and says he — "Prinkle, here's a young scoundrel, whom we have caught stealing. We took him into this office on your recommendation, and you are therefore liable for his misconduct." "I, sir?" I said. "Yes, you," he repeated. "The amount is £23 11s. 7d., and seeing that you are not everybody, I am willing to receive it in small instalments, once a-month, when your salary is paid."'

'Did David Hendry make such a proposal as that?'

'Proposal, sir! It was a threat; and he means to carry it out. Oh, Mr Beeds, if you could understand all the pain and suffering through which I have come in the service of that man, you would know the agony of these tears!' And he sat himself on one of the lobby chairs and wept piteously.

Mr Beeds was indignant, and promised to do what he could for him.

'Where can I see this Victor Cole?'

'In his mother's house, sir. She is like to break her heart.'

'Is he there, now?'

'Yes, sir, yes. I have just come from there, and if you went with me now, I am sure you would save the poor woman's life! Victor is the only son of his mother, and she is a widow.'

Perhaps it was this last sentence of Prinkle's which made the lawyer determine at once, calling up as it did a bright episode in the life of one whom he ever sought to serve. He looked at his watch for a moment, and telling Peter he would return immediately, he ran up-stairs and made an apology to his guests. When he came down again, he threw on his top-coat and his hat, and they hurried out.

In less than an hour, they stopped at the door of the widow, and Prinkle entered first.

Victor was sitting in his shirt-sleeves by the fire, with his head buried in his hands, and his mother lay on a low bed near him, manifestly overwhelmed with grief.

The misguided youth raised his haggard face at the approach of Mr Beeds, but immediately turned it away.

The lawyer went over to the bed and took the hand of the old woman.

'This is a sad business,' he said.

'Ah, sir!' she cried. 'I have seen many trials since the day of my birth, but this beats 'em all! In the ways o' the world, gentlemen, I ain't a proud woman, 'cos I've little of its gear, but I own I was proud of my son, an' I thought as God had raised 'im up to be the stay of my widowhood and old age! Oh, sir! it's a great heart-break—an' I'm all broke!'

This was a wild, piteous cry; and in our memory there comes up another, like a bright refrain to a plaintive song, when, months and months ago, the old lady rapturously kissed her son's brow and exclaimed, 'If my Victor waren't honest, I should die, I know ! '

'Tell me all about it,' he said kindly, going over to Victor, and laying his hand on his shoulder.

' Oh, sir, I don't want to make no excuses for myself. I did it—that's all.'

' Did you mean to steal ? '

' Steal!' he cried, springing to his feet. ' Steal! I steal ! As God is my witness, I never wronged a man by a penny-piece ! '

'Dear me !' said Mr Beeds, looking about, as if for an explanation. 'What is the meaning of this? '

' I'll tell you,' he cried, placing his hand under the breast of his shirt as if striving to restrain himself. ' By the kindness of Mr Prinkle here, I was recommended to the younger David Hendry, who engaged me at the salary of forty pounds a-year, to do every manner of work, clean and un-clean. I did what was given me to do, with all faithfulness; and although my master worried and bullied me, I never answered him in his own kind. He stung me with his sneers, and worried me with his fault-finding, till I sulked before him like a dog. Forty pounds a-year!' he cried : ' Sooner than endure again what I have done through these months, I'd bare my back to forty stripes a-day ! My duty was to collect accounts, and often I returned at nights with a thousand pounds in my pocket. One day—and it was a sad day for me—when I was making up my statement,

I found I was ten pounds short of the accounts I had collected. In no way can I account for that. I went back to all the places I had been, but the cashiers told me as their cash had balanced correctly. I searched the office, and could not find it; and I reckon as I had dropped a ten-pound note. I told my master of it—he did not doubt my word, but he told me as I must pay for my carelessness, and I should receive no salary till the sum was cleared off. And, in the face of that, I was sent out for accounts as usual, bringing in my hundreds—my master all the while expecting me to exist for three months on nothing! If he had swopped me at once for carelessness, I could not have blamed him,—but he treated me as if he had said—"Go and steal!" I had saved some thirty shillings, and as long as that lasted, we managed to get along. But when there was not a penny in the house to buy bread, what was I to do? Think of it yourself, sir, and imagine the temptation.' Here was I, returning to the office with a pocket-full of notes, and after that, to go home to a fireless hearth and a starving mother! It was too much for human nature. I began to think what I should do, and there was an account of twenty-three pounds and odds which I lifted; but I did not give it up, for I planned to keep it over till I should be receiving my salary again, when I would make it up in full and hand it in. But it so came out that I had retained the money, and David Hendry charged me with embezzlement. As sure as Death, sir, I meant to pay it back! I have squandered none of it. I only took from it what was necessary to keep us in life ; and to show you that what I say is true, there are twenty-two pounds and three shillings of it lying in that chest! I need not tell you that my mother knew nothing of this. I kept it a complete secret.' And then the tears gushed from his eyes again ; but he swept his face with the back of his hand, and rejoined : 'Do you call that stealing, sir? Mr David said it was ; but that was in his own place, when I was powerless, and in terror that I might be sent to jail. But,' he exclaimed, rising to his full height, and lifting his ponderous fist, ' were he to say it here, before God, sir! I should stand accused of a graver crime ! '

'This is terrible,' said Mr Beeds, wringing his hands. 'It is infamous ! '

' It is, sir,' answered Victor, opening the chest, ' but it is true ; and there is the money. It has been there for two months. You see I was careful of it,' he smiled bitterly, ' for during that time we have lived on eight and twenty shillings! '

'Did you not give this explanation to Mr Hendry ? Does he know that the money is here ? '

' I made explanation to neither man nor boy, and no one knew the money was there, till now. I might have told it to Mr Prinkle to set him at ease, for Hendry has threatened to keep it off him ; but as soon as I was charged, my senses was clean gone, and I was too excited to explain anything.'

'Dear me!' said Mr Beeds, and he sat himself by the fire.

The old lady had hardly yet recovered from the effect of her son's speech, but she now struggled from her bed. Coming to Victor, she flung her arms about his neck.

'*My* Victor—*my* Victor,' she cried, 'so broad and tall—and he is my own honest son!'

'You go along, mother, I've blubbered enough for a life-time—there! Let Mr Prinkle take back the money to-morrow, and I'm sure and certain Mr Hendry won't try to prosecute me.'

'There may be a doubt about that,' said Mr Beeds.

'None in the world, sir,' replied Victor. 'If he could gratify his malice without exposing his criminal narrowness, I should have been laid by the heels ere now!'

'Very likely, very likely,' muttered Mr Beeds, taking out his purse. 'But it might be well to make restoration in full, so, Mr Prinkle, there are twenty-eight shillings to make up the amount. Of course,' he said, turning to Victor with a laugh, 'you understand that you are my debtor; but your own time will suit me.'

'Thank you,' cried Victor, firmly grasping the lawyer's hand. 'I thank you, sir. I'll pay you back, in full, with my first savings. I'll get out of this Hell of a City, for I'm sick of its round of lies and meanness! And if hard, honest toil will keep

a man in life, I'll throw my coat, and earn my
bread by the sweat of my brow !'

Before the lawyer left them, he gave another
sum of money to Victor, as a loan, to pay off any
expense they might incur by removing to the
country ; and the old woman wet his hand with
the tears of her gratitude, when she called down
the widow's blessing on his head.

'May God bless you, sir ; and when it pleases
Him to take you to 'imself, He'll remind you of
the good deed you've done this day, for He who
did not despise the widow's mite, will hearken to
the widow's prayer!'

It was a long distance to walk, but Mr Beeds
trudged cheerily back to his own house. And
when he entered it, he did so with a lighter heart
than had been his for many a day, for now he had
other associates around his hearth than the gaunt
spectres of the past. The bright happiness of
Lizzie, the solid earnestness and good sense of her
husband, and the sprightly manner of their little
boy, acted upon his nature so that he seemed to
live in the old days again ; and when this genial
fellowship was enjoyed by him day after day and
night after night for the space of two full weeks,
he felt as if his old heart would droop and die when
the separation came. But Lizzie won the day, and
the lawyer passed his word to go North with them.
He desired them to go on at once, and promised to
follow, so soon as he had set his affairs in order ;
but neither Lizzie nor her husband would hear of

this, but determined to wait and take him with them. In another week Mr Beeds got Tim a situation, where, let us hope, he had more substantial work than that of modelling wax babies, or of amusing himself with the idiosyncrasies of an old maid. Betsy was provided for by an annuity, but while she was thankful for this, she could not help thinking that 'her master 'ad been clean took off by the wultures!'—for so she expressed it. Yet another week, and Mr Beeds was in Scotland.

If you should happen to journey so far as Inverness, and if you have an hour to spend when the morning is fair and bright, you ought to take a quiet stroll along the north bank of the river, past the Cathedral, up to the Islands of the Ness. And if in your peregrination you should meet with an old man of cheerful countenance, with hair of silver grey, attired in professional black and his neck girt with a spotless tie, you may hazard a guess that this is Mr Beeds, hale, hearty, and strong. It was on a seat in one of these islands, with the swift river washing past us at our feet, with the grand old town in the foreground, and in the distance the dreamy Black-Isle shadowing the Moray Firth, that we sat with the old man in the autumn of '74, and listened to the story of his life. Grasping our hand, while in his eye there was a trace of his inability to hide the workings of his heart, he said,

'Good-bye. I have never any inclination to return to London. I am resting among flowers of

my own gathering. And,' he added, raising his
hand in the direction of Tomnahurich with its
wooded slopes and quiet cemetery, 'when my time
comes, I shall be laid up there.'

CHAPTER XXI.

THE FLICKERING UP OF AN OLD FLAME.

'And thus, whate'er our onward way,
    The lights and shadows cast
Upon the dawning of our day,
    Are with us to the last.

'But oh! the morning breaks no more,
    As once on us it burst,
For future springs can ne'er restore
    The freshness of the first.'—ANON.

'WELL, Georgina, if he never gave her the
chance, it was no fault of hers,' said Jane.

'Of course,' exclaimed Georgina. 'All the
world knows that!'

'I wish to goodness,' cried John, from the sofa,
'that you girls would stop talking nonsense, and
let me read.'

'Whether John remain here or not, he can
please himself, but his sisters must be allowed to
speak if they choose.'

'All right! Go on. Who cares?'

'And such a fine property too! How galling
it must be for her!'

'After all the fuss she made about him—of course it must.'

'I wonder if he ever comes to see her when he is in London.'

'Never. Oh, never, you may be sure! His taking his daughter away to live with him, was as much as to say, " We shall part." And now that the bait is away, I don't think he'll care to come back to the trap!'

'I wonder, Georgina, that she can lift up her head after all the work she made with him,— taking his daughter to live with her, and then visiting him in the hospital—the bold monkey! If I had been her aunt I should have boxed her ears!'

' Yes, of course, if *she* had not been in the plot as well. But I believe she was, Jane, and quite as anxious to catch him. Do you think she would have received him into her house for any other reason? No, thank you, Mrs Clayton knew what she was about. I am certain she must have known that the property would come to him, or she never would have acted as she has done.'

'Very likely—*most* likely—but I never thought of that. The fact is, I take so very little to do with other people's affairs that that phase of it was never present to my mind. Although, I confess, I had my eyes on Maud all along, ever, I think, since her party.'

' Oh, we all noticed it there—but that's an old story.'

'And you remember, too, how she tried to play off Frank Grierly against Trevor, but it was no use!'

'You girls,' cried John, stepping up to them, and interrupting angrily, 'would make a fellow swear! If either of you possessed a tithe of Maud Clayton's dignity and self-respect, you would not speak as you have done. Do you think she would demean herself by marrying such a selfish and incapable wretch as Trevor has proved himself to be?'

'Oh! who knows?' exclaimed Jane.

'It is none of your business, John.'

'Nor is it yours! You girls are most infernally ungenerous to any of your sex who seem to live in a clearer atmosphere than your own! There is as much love in the tip of Maud's little finger as there is in both your hearts! In picking Trevor out of the gutter, in spite of your scandal and your calumnies, she acted nobly to the friend of her childhood; and if she were to marry him—which I don't think she would, though he asked and asked her till doomsday—I could not pass an opinion on her determination, for she is the best judge of her own actions, not I. But if it would be any satisfaction to you, I may tell you that Robert Trevor was in Mrs Clayton's house yesterday, and the day before yesterday, and he and Maud went off together for a drive to-day. There now, offer me your thanks, for I've given you fresh food for scandal!'

Jane and Georgina burst into tears, and called

their brother an unfeeling monster, and rushed from the room.

But who, you will ask, are Jane, Georgina, and John?

They are our next-door neighbours; they are our friends across the way; Jane and Georgina are always *so* happy to meet us; they are incessantly telling us we are looking *so* well; and although their affection has the strength of a watery gruel, it does not possess its comforting influence. John lifts his hat to us when we pass, and occasionally stops us at the corner of the street to say that the weather is good, or bad, as may be. In every circle there is a Jane, a Georgina, and a John.

* * * * * *

Mrs Clayton and her niece were together in the drawing-room alone. The aunt tossed over to Maud a note which she had just received and had read aloud, and she watched closely the expression on the face of her niece as she read it for herself.

'Well, what do you think of that?'

'Nothing particular,' said Maud, blushing slightly, nevertheless. 'It is quite natural, if he has a few days to spend in London, that he should come here. Don't you think so?'

'Oh, yes,' she laughed, 'it seems quite natural; but, Maud, I'm afraid it must come to it!'

Her niece made no false show of failing to comprehend her, for she answered calmly,

'I'm sure I shall be very sorry if that is his

errand, for to cause Robert Trevor pain would be the last thing I would willingly do.'

'But why, Maud? why should you look at it in that light? You cannot fail to see that, ever since the great change came over him, he has re-garded you with the warmest affection.'

'That may be quite true,' she answered pen-sively; 'but yet—'

'Well?'

'It cannot be.'

Mrs Clayton roused herself, and sat up on the couch.

'I tell you, Maud, you might do worse.'

'Perhaps so. That is very likely.'

'Now,' cried her aunt, good-humouredly enough, however. 'You are a tantalizing thing! I wish you would give me some reason for this decision of yours. Look at the influence you have exercised over him—how completely you have led him to turn over a new leaf!'

'Ay, ay,' she murmured slowly, as if to herself, and with a depth of meaning which her aunt could not appreciate. 'He has turned over a new leaf, but he has left his finger-marks on the last!'

'But you should forget that. It is hardly generous to remember it.'

'It may be possible to forgive, but there are some things beyond human nature to forget. And yet, I think I am not ungenerous. At least, it is against my will if I am.'

But Mrs Clayton had never been told of the

great trial through which Maud had passed, and consequently she had no means of knowing the depth of her words. But Maud brightened up, and turned the argument in another way.

'You remember, aunt, when I first went to the hospital to visit Bob, you tried to dissuade me from going, by asking, "What would the world say?" Now, if I were to marry him, the world would say I had cast my net to catch a husband.'

'Very true,' argued Mrs Clayton. 'But if you do not marry him, the world will laugh, and say that, even with all your pains, you failed to catch him.'

The thought of this fairly roused the spirit of Maud, and she rose from her seat.

'Let it laugh!' she cried, with a certain degree of bitterness, as the fire mantled upon her cheek. 'It has laughed before, and it can laugh again! If these silly women, whom you dignify with the name of the world, find an object of ridicule in me, they may, for aught I care! I'll not take time to despise them; they are not my friends; and the ridicule of disappointed women is not hard to bear! I hate that question—"What will the world say?" nor shall I degrade myself by ordering my procedure by what I might expect its uncharitable answer to be! If Robert Trevor should ask my hand in marriage, it will be a severe trial, I believe, to both of us; but I shall meet it calmly. And, whatever comes of it, I shall not change towards him; for, since the first day he called me his little

wife, and prattled love to me like a boy, he has, of
all men, held the first place in my affection, as he
is now the nearest to my heart ! '

Mrs Clayton did not try to protract this painful discussion, but told her niece, 'Whatever comes
of it, Maud, I wish you well.'

A few days later, Bob arrived at Mrs Clayton's,
and received a most cordial welcome from both.
Maud never tried to disguise her affection for him,
nor did she do so now, but treated him as one for
whose welfare she cared, and was never out of his
company for long.   Any one who did not know
her thoroughly, might have thought that her
manner towards him was that of one who would
have been far from loath to share his happiness,
but Trevor himself knew her better.   Ever since
that day when his waking eyes rested upon her in
the hospital, his heart had gone out to her with an
increasing love, but when he had gone North and
settled in his new home, that love had become a
yearning within him, and he longed that he might
yet be enabled to take her home with him, to fill
the blank at his fireside and in his heart.   At
times, when she seemed to regard him with a
warmer affection than usual, especially when he
referred to the loss he had sustained in Mary's
death, his eyes brightened up with renewed hope,
but so soon as he made any attempt to touch upon
the subject which was dear to him, he saw that she
discountenanced it by her restraint.   And yet he

often returned to it, picturing to her the vacant chair and the motherless child, for he was not blind to the affection which Maud still evinced on the mere mention of the young girl's name.

One day he made the proposal that they should go out to Ashfield together to visit the old place, and Maud made no objection, but accepted it frankly. On leaving the train they first traced their steps to the quiet churchyard. He had never been there since the day he had stood by the open grave, when his heart was torn by a contemplation of the fearful reality of his great bereavement. And now, standing on the same spot with Maud, with his whole soul yearning for the love of her by his side, and with the same sense of bereavement—although softened by years—upon him, he felt that the two great passions mingled, and flowed consistently together.

Maud was busy with her own thoughts, for when she contemplated the simple inscription on the stone, she recalled to her mind the whole story of Mary's life, and when the death-scene rose before her, her memory lingered there. She felt that Mary expected, nay, even desired, that in becoming a mother to her child she should also step into the vacant place in Trevor's home. And then there was the recollection of that fearful cry —'Mary, Mary, my own wife! Why are you taken from me?' These reflections softened Maud's nature, and for the moment, Trevor, though he

knew it not, was in possession of her love. A
word, then, would have brought it forth beyond
recall!

In coming out of the church-yard, he proposed
that they should stroll along the banks of the Ash
and view the mansion from the opposite side. It
was a beautiful summer's day, not a cloud passed
between them and the blue expanse of sky, the
birds were warbling cheerily, and the trees were
waving green. Maud felt the old fascination for
Trevor, and she consented. Trevor knew this, for
in that short hour during which they had wandered
along the Ash, under the big trees and through
the fragrant thickets, Maud did not try to restrain
her regard for him, but treated him frankly and
with confidence. Then, too, when he was assisting
her over the rustic stiles and palings, as she looked
down silently with those large, warm eyes of hers,
it seemed as if her heart had caught the flame.
By and by, when they came to that bend in the
valley from which a romantic view of the old
mansion was to be had, under a shade of leaves
and trees, through which the sun's rays fell like a
bright percolation, they seated themselves in a
nook of ferns and moss.

The scene was familiar to them both, but each
was impressed with that strange feeling which falls
upon us while we contemplate the scenes of other
days, knowing well that many of the actors are
separated from us, perhaps in other lands, or silent
in the grave. Each felt that it was a place for

meditation rather than for speech, and it was some
time ere the silence was broken. Their conversation began with the scene before them, but it soon
turned away back to the days of their childhood,
and they recalled many a happy memory of the
time. Then, coming back through the years, it
touched and dwelt on scenes, happy and sad, to
which they were both bound by ties of affection.
It was natural, in a retrospect such as this, when
their thoughts and emotions were the same, that
their hearts should become, in some degree, as-
similated, and restraint, in the same degree, relaxed. Trevor sat close to Maud, holding her
hand in his, and when he spoke in the old rich
tones that used to thrill her, he kept looking
warmly into her eyes as if every word had a
meaning of its own. Maud did not withdraw her
hand, but she kept her eyes intently on the ground,
and who shall blame her if her heart was not
utterly impervious to the love of other years?

'Have you scenes such as this in Northumberland?' she asked.

'There are many quite as beautiful, or even
more so, to an indifferent observer, but not to me.
Everything here is toned down by sombre memories, making the picture complete. I can dwell
on this with a deeper interest than that of admiration for scenery.'

'Does little Mary romp about much?' she
asked further.

'Little Mary,' he answered tenderly, but with

a shake of his head, 'romps about when she is allowed to, but she is not strong. She is very fond of the old gardener who was here—Willie Scott—and often it makes the tears come to my eyes, when she mounts on his knee and asks what becomes of the flowers. "Tell me about the Great Gardener?" she says—for Willie has taught her to look upon God tending His people as the gardener tends his flowers.'

Maud did not wish to carry the conversation further with regard to Mary, for she saw how it pained him.

'Willie,' she said, 'was always a most interesting old man.'

' 'Well, he is the same as ever. And I like him much, for his reflections about men and flowers are conceived in a charitable spirit which one seldom meets with in this world.'

'Have you found the world so very uncharitable?' she asked. And Bob sat up and caught her hand in a firmer grasp.

'I have, Maud!' he cried. 'When I was most in need of its charity, I got its contempt. When I required its comfort, it shunned me, and those persons whom I had wronged the least were the ones who cried the most loudly against me!'

'Ay,' muttered Maud, 'that's the old story.'

'But there was one exception, Maud,' and he held her firmly. She looked full upon him for the moment, and her eyes fell. 'There was one exception. And if I had got scorn and contempt at her hand I could not have blamed her, for I wronged her, the most of all, unworthily. But when every one shunned me, she visited me; when I was wretched, she soothed me. Maud, this was yourself! When I saw you, that morning in the hospital, and felt your hot tears drop upon my cheek, the cords of my love were fastened upon you, and by them I have been drawn from all my misery!'

All through this his rich tones faltered, and when he ceased, his hand fell upon her waist. Maud's bosom heaved like a wave, her cheek was flushed, and, as she gazed out upon nothing, a tear rose in her eye; but she answered not a word.

Trevor's excitement was intense, and he trembled for her reply. The pupils of his eyes were dilated, and the blood throbbed upon his cheeks, but still she was silent.

'Speak to me, Maud!' he cried. 'I know I have your love, but, tell me, will you be my wife?'

During her silence Maud had conquered herself, but when she turned fully and encountered his eager gaze, her mighty heart was well-nigh bursting, and her burning tears fell fast.

'Bob,' she began, in broken accents, pressing her hand on her breast, 'you have said truly that I love you.—But—' she faltered, 'I cannot be your wife. I could not—no, I could not—step into Mary's place. Somehow I still regard her, more as an absent, than as a dead friend. If I have seemed to favour expectations other than this, you will not judge me harshly ; it was only by a declaration such as this that I could define the true nature of my love. When I first saw this affection in you, my intention was to break up our friendship, but my heart revolted at the idea, and here I am! The ordeal is painful, but I trust that strength shall be given to us that we may bear the trial. Bob,' she said, calmly laying her hand on his arm, 'if you want a wife, seek another than in me; but do not disdain a love which made you its object when you were a little boy, which ever since has clung around you in sorrow and distress, and which is now as pure and true as the heart of the child which first gave it forth !'

Maud pressed her handkerchief on her eyes when she had finished, and for a while they sat in silence.

By and by, the shades of evening began to fall, and she rose and drew her dress around her, saying sadly—'Let us go.'

CHAPTER XXII.

THE LAMP IS SHATTERED, AND THE LIGHT IN THE DUST LIES DEAD.

'Man's inhumanity to man
Makes countless thousands mourn.'—BURNS.

IT may be remembered that, when Mr Alton offered Mr Prinkle a three-years' engagement, the terms were £110 for the first, and a rise of £20 on each of the two succeeding years. One might have expected that, whatever more the Messrs Hendry gave him, they would at least see to it that he should not suffer in a pecuniary way by the exposure he made, in their interest, of the nefarious practices of his former masters. But it was not so. For here was Mr Prinkle dragging out his third year, a victim to the brutality of his young master, a butt to the practical joking of a great warehouse, and without a single penny of an advance since he first entered the place. This was peculiarly galling to a sensitive nature such as his, and his spirits, always volatile, became a prey to nervousness and despondency. There were times, too, when he was maddened by a sense of injustice, when, for some petty mistake he had made, such as sending goods to the wrong address, Mr David Hendry would deduct a few paltry shillings from his pay.

'It must be done, you know, Prinkle. If you make mistakes you must just pay for them.

'But, Mr David—'

'Tut, tut, I have no time to speak. Take your money, or leave it.'

But when he had to inform Nell of scenes like this,—Nell, who had been the empress of his bright dreams, the lady of his hopes, for whom he had toiled for years and years against an adverse fortune,—it was then that you could see the dreadful pass to which he had come! In eye and feature, limb and tongue, his nerves were shattered; in voice and gesture there were the vagaries of insanity; with no bright prospects to dazzle him, no joys to beguile, you could see that hope itself was dying in his baffled breast!

But Prinkle recollected how that, when the younger Hendry demurred at giving him so much as £110 of salary, the elder at once conceded it, and wrote him a friendly letter. And he had yet another reason for believing Mr Hendry was favourably disposed toward him, and that he had not forgotten the services which he had rendered. Invariably, when that gentleman came from Manchester to visit the London warehouse, Prinkle was the first for whom he sought, and indeed he was the only one with whom he spoke on cordial terms. He would take him by the hand, and ask after his own welfare and his wife's; but a third party could easily observe how careful he was that his cordiality should carry him no further, or pre-

sent an opportunity for Prinkle to press for pre-
ferment.

When Peter began to think of this, his
hope flickered up again, and he determined to
write to Manchester and state his grievances.
This he did without consulting Nell, and two
days later his spirits were raised to an unwonted
height, when it was whispered in the warehouse
that the elder gentleman should visit them on the
following day. Although this visit had really no
connection with his letter, it was natural that
Prinkle should think it was wholly on his account.

That night he went home to Nell in great
spirits, and when he met her at the door, he kissed
her joyfully.

'Cheer up—cheer up, Nell!' he said, putting
his arm about her waist as they entered. 'I'm
going to get things set right at last—the days of
our mourning are ended!'

'But what is it, Peter?' she said with a smile.
'I am glad to see you so bright.'

'I should think you are!' he cried. 'And
if you only knew what a good friend Mr Hendry
has been to me—'

'Mr David?' she asked.

'No — Dash Mr David! It's his father!
You should have seen how he treated me when
that swindle was being exposed. How he used to
come into the warehouse on the mornings, smiling
so nice, and taking me so kindly by the hand.
Mind you, he didn't take any of the others by the

hand—he was quite different to them—and hoped
I was well! '

Nell thought to herself that this was an old
story, but she let her husband continue.

' I could not help liking him for it. "Good
morning, Mr Prinkle," he would say. Give
me your hand, Nell — just this way. "Good
morning, Mr Prinkle. How is your good wife ?
I hope she is very well." And he would smile so
nice. And then when he would turn away from
me, he didn't even look to none of the others, but
passed them haughtily. He's coming to-morrow,
Nell, and I'm sure he'll make it all right.' And
Peter squatted happily in the arm-chair.

' But what is he to make all right, dear ? ' she
asked meekly.

' Right — right,' he repeated, perhaps with
some degree of uncertainty when he came to think
of it. ' Why, by my exposure of Alton and
Gregory, I have put thousands of pounds in his
pocket, and yet Mr David has made me lose by my
honesty. There was the promised rise of £20 the
first year, and another rise on that, making forty
for this,—in all about £60. Of course Mr Hendry
doesn't know anything of that himself, but I wrote
and told him about it, and he is coming, on purpose to pay me the £60, and set me right for the
future ! Won't it be fine, Nell ! You shall be a
lady at last ! '

The smile passed from her countenance and a

cloud came in its place, but to hide this she knelt down for the purpose of drawing off her husband's boots.

'Why don't you congratulate me, Nell?' he asked, laying his hand softly on her shoulder.

'I don't know what it is, Peter dear, but I think we are as comfortable as we could be. We have enough for our wants, and I would rather remain as I am, a simple wife, than be made a fine lady.'

Prinkle was irritated.

'Is that the way you thank me for trying to make you what you once were? If you don't want to be a lady, I want my wife to be one, and not require her to pull off my boots when I'm tired!'

Nell heard this with pain, but she looked up sweetly.

'I did not mean to grieve you, Peter. I only wished to let you know that I am quite happy as I am.'

'Well, *I'm* not!'

'I thought you were,' she said. 'If you are not, I cannot be.' And Peter was slightly moved when she added, 'Let me be ever so fine a lady, I would not allow a servant to deprive me of this, for it is a great pleasure to me to be able to show, even by this, that I desire your comfort. Now, Peter dear, am I not better than any servant could be?' And she looked up with that soft expres-

sion of love which invariably soothed him, so that
Prinkle got down beside her on the floor, and
pressed his lips affectionately on hers.

That night the poor fellow retired to bed to
dream of kind Mr Hendry, and Nell as a lady.
Poor fellow, we say; for this dream was destined
to prove as false as any that had preceded it. Nell
knew this, and it was with a heavy heart she saw
him leave for business on the morning.

Peter went about his work in a state of great
excitement; and he turned nervously at every
footfall, so impatient was he for the appearance of
Mr Hendry.

At last the tall, austere man entered. There
was very little of a kind expression on that cold
face of his, and Peter felt the demon of jealousy
rise within him when, over the balustrade, down-
stairs, he saw him pass from one warehouseman to
another and proffer his hand. He thought it was
not such a kindly face after all, and his spirit
wavered when he saw that the other employés
were put on the same footing with himself. Up-
stairs he came, and Prinkle began to work with
vigour, and his heart throbbed wildly when he
heard his master's footstep on the floor. Mr
Hendry passed a pleasant word with every one,
not even overlooking the message boys,—he even
spoke with the lad at Prinkle's side, but to the
astonishment of all, and to the consternation of
Peter, he passed him coldly by, and retraced his
haughty steps down-stairs.

Prinkle was astounded, the muscles of his face became rigid, and his jaw fell. The others noticed this sudden change, and they gathered round him, some for curiosity, and some to offer sympathy.

'It is a damned shame!'; said one of them, broadly. 'If I had done for him what you have done, I would wrench the proud nose from his face!'

'Yes,' said Prinkle, quietly, as if he tried to master himself, '*it is* a shame.'

Then he drew himself up, and calmly walked down-stairs. He saw Mr Hendry pass into the private room, and he followed him.

His master turned, nor did he betray any surprise, but asked,

'Well?'

'I've come for an answer to my letter, sir,' he said firmly.

'I have none for you. There is your letter,' and he tossed the epistle at his feet.

'No answer, sir?' he gasped.

'No, I tell you I have none. If you have any cause for complaint, my son David is master here, go to him.'

'Well, God help us!' cried Prinkle, still striving to stifle his wrath.

'Mr Prinkle, you must guard yourself. I shall allow no such inordinate language. If you feel yourself aggrieved, I suppose you can easily find employment elsewhere.'

This was said with a sneer which sent Peter's wrath beyond all bounds.

'I remember the time,' he cried, 'when you had a different story to tell me! It was when I became an informer for the sake of truth; when I gave you a secret which made you a rich man; when I was the means of ruining Mr Alton, who was a better man, every way, than you are! Don't interrupt me, sir, for I will speak! You treated me then in a different way. When you had need of me, there was nothing too good for me, and there was no promise too great for you to make; but times are changed, and you would throw me off like old boots! You are paying me a smaller salary than the one agreed upon in the engagement I broke for you. Is that honest! It is a shame, sir, and you promised me a better life than this!'

'Silence!' cried Mr Hendry. 'I want no more of your mad talk!'

'Mad talk!' he screamed. 'I wish I could give you more of it!'

'But you shall not!' he stamped.

'I shall!' he cried furiously. 'John Alton was an honest man compared with you! He tried to defraud you of money, but you are defrauding me of the peace of my life; and by your constant worrying you are seeking to crush out the sense of justice which God has planted in the human heart! You know you are! You are treating me as a brute! Ah, sir, if I had the power to give expression to the thoughts which burn within me, I could tell a tale that would make the very stones of London rise and cry shame to your face! Yes, yes, I am mad, but God knows, and you know too, what has brought me to this! Oh, Nell, Nell, my poor Nell!' and Peter wept bitterly, as he fell helpless on the desk.

Mr Hendry could bear it no longer, for his conscience smote him, and he left the room, and passed out into the street.

Prinkle returned to his place, and the warehouseman who had so frankly given his opinion of Mr Hendry's studied slight, came to his side, and endeavoured to soothe him.

'Never you mind, Mr Prinkle,' he said. 'If Hendry has a conscience at all, I'd rather be you than he. My advice to you is to get out of this place as quick as you can,—try some other houses —and even if you take a smaller salary, you may have a better life of it.'

'Ah, it's all very good to speak; but if you were in my shoes, you would know more about it. I would be quite useless to another master, for when I get the least excited, my nerves gets up, and I feel as if I were only in the way. However, if David Hendry gets the good things in this life, I'll have day about with him in the next!'

But all the warehousemen were not so kindly disposed towards Prinkle, for at this very moment a plot was being concocted to utilize his present excitement for the purpose of fun.

'I say, Hopkins,' said one lad to another,

'Prinkle is in excellent condition; don't you think we might have a lark with him? He and I lock up the place to-night, and I have a glorious trick to show you.'

Hopkins was quite agreeable, and he asked what it was.

'Come to the hoist-room, and I'll let you see.'

So the two lads went off together. This room measured some twenty feet square, and it was almost filled with empty packing-cases, piled up on each other to the roof. In the ceiling there was a hatchway for goods, communicating with the two flats above, through which there hung a number of loose ropes for working the hoist.

Jones, the originator of the plot, immediately threw off his coat, and busily set about an explanation of his idea.

'We'll have a rehearsal,' he said.

He thereupon took up a rope which lay on the floor, and commenced making a noose.

'I'm going to hang myself,' he explained; and Hopkins at once entered into the spirit of the thing, rubbing his hands with great delight.

'By George! This is gammon on a gigantic scale!' he cried. And so it was.

A loop was made with the rope, and Jones passed it round his body under his arms, stuffing his armpits with paper so that it should not hurt him. Hopkins then assisted to put on his coat, which he buttoned tightly up to his throat, so that, the lower parts of the rope being hid, it appeared as if it were fastened round his neck. The other end was then put through a pulley in the ceiling, and Hopkins drew him up several feet from the floor, and fastened the rope to an iron hook in the wall.

'By George!' he cried, stepping back a pace. 'It'll do. Jerk your head to the one side. That's it!' and he clapped his hands with satisfaction.

When Jones was taken down, a few things were set in order so as to be ready for the execution, which they intended should take place exactly at a quarter past six; at which time Mr Prinkle would walk his usual rounds to see that the warehouse was right for the night. Jones and Hopkins whispered their intention to several of the other hands, and they all waited patiently for the appointed time.

Prinkle continued at his post all day, but it must be confessed that, owing to the excitement under which he laboured, very little work was done. Singularly enough, neither of the Messrs Hendry had appeared on that flat since the morning, and Prinkle concluded that they wished to keep out of his way. But those who were in the plot were constantly passing through his department, regarding him curiously, and chuckling to each other over the prime condition of their victim.

Six o'clock came at last, and the more advanced among the employés began to leave, so that by ten minutes past, the place was quite deserted,

but for a number of raw youths who waited to
see the play.

'Now,' said Hopkins, when he had fixed up
Jones in the way we have already described,
'mum's the word! You may keep your foot on
this box for rest, but as soon as you hear him
coming, just swing yourself free. If they cut you
down, see that you fall with a dead weight, for
I'll take care that you are not hurt. Now, remember to jerk your neck, and give your body a
twist if you can. There—that'll do.'

Five minutes later, Mr Prinkle changed his
coat, and went to the counting-house for the
keys.

'Well,' he said, seeing the lads all clubbed
together, 'what do you all want here? It's time
to clear out. Where's Jones?' For it was the
rule in locking up that, when the senior hand
went his rounds, the junior should wait in the
front warehouse to watch lest any one should enter.
'Where's Jones?'

'Didn't he go into the counting-house just
now?' asked Hopkins. 'I thought I saw him go
there.'

'No,' said Prinkle. 'He's not there. Surely
he can't have forgotten that this is his night of
locking up!'

'Oh, no,' replied Hopkins, 'for he told me
to wait for him. He promised to walk home with
me.'

'Then it's very careless of him,' said Prinkle,

'but we can't wait here all night. Will you watch the door?'

Hopkins at once agreed, and their hearts began to beat rapidly when they saw Peter start upon his rounds, and make directly for the hoist-room. Immediately they were startled by a frantic yell, and they all rushed to where Prinkle was.

'Murder! murder!' he cried, swinging his arms like a madman. 'Quick—quick—for God's sake, quick!'

'What is it? what is it?' they exclaimed from every side; but Peter could only gasp, and point in the direction of the fatal room.

'He's hung!' he whispered.

Hopkins snatched up a knife and rushed into the place, followed by Prinkle and all the boys. Every one stood back in dismay when, through the dim light, they saw the seemingly lifeless form of Jones dangling among the loose ropes of the hatch! Certainly the spectacle did infinite credit to the artistic power of the actors, for nothing could possibly have appeared more real! With a howl of anguish, which was almost genuine, the boys flew towards their companion, and Hopkins caught him in his arms, when a lad mounted a box and cut the rope above his head. Jones allowed himself to drop with such a dead weight that his friend fell beneath him.

'Stand back—stand back—and give him breath!' cried Prinkle, making his way in among the boys, and taking up his hand.

'Speak, Jones! speak one word!' he conjured, while he chafed his hand. But in the dim light there was no response, and the lad lay as if dead. One little fellow made his way out, saying he was off for a doctor; and the others carried him into the warehouse, and all the place was filled with their hysterical cries.

When they had got him out, Prinkle extemporized a couch by tumbling a pile of piece-goods on the floor, on which they laid him, and they crowded round again, calling him loudly by his name.

Meanwhile, Peter had extricated a piece of paper from the clenched fist, which proved to be a short note to the lad's mother, seeking forgiveness for the rash act! The writing swam before his excited vision, but still he could understand its purport. He pressed his hand upon his brow in the greatest agony, while the tears chased each other on his cheeks.

'Ah!' he cried, 'God help his mother! It was himself that did it! Oh—oh! what will she say! Poor—poor woman, Heaven help her!'

And then he knelt beside the lad again, and implored him, in wild tones, to speak.

Jones was unable to feign death any longer, and he heaved a deep sigh.

'Thank God!' cried Prinkle. 'He lives—he lives! Rip open his collar! Fetch water—quick!—he lives!'

One of the boys, on hearing this, and having no objection to see Jones get a share of what was going, immediately ran off, and returned with a good-sized pitcher of water which Prinkle took, and quite innocently dashed on the lad's face!

This was not in the programme: it was too much for flesh and blood to stand, and the mock suicide sprang with a howl from his couch, and cursed and swore at the man whom he had duped! This gave such a ludicrous turn to the affair, and seeing Jones stamping about and drenched to the skin, they roared and laughed till their sides ached with pain.

But not so Prinkle. If a bolt had fallen from heaven it could not have stunned him more. He retreated to a table, where he rested, and his face was fearful; for every muscle of it was quivering and pale, and a white froth oozed from the corners of his lips. For about the space of a minute he surveyed the scene in silence, and then, without uttering a single word, he staggered up-stairs, firmly grasping the rail.

The lads were too excited now to observe his movements, and they gathered together in a group, and while they discussed what had taken place, they indulged their laughter to their hearts' content.

'It served you right,' cried one to Jones. 'And I'd been sorry to miss the last part of it. It was a long way the best. Gracious, what a figure you cut!'

But Jones did not like to be jeered. 'Away,' he said, 'or I'll put my finger in your eye!'

But the boys were in a mood for fun, and they kept it up with great zest, till the deepening shadows warned them it was time to go.

'Dear me,' exclaimed one of them, 'what o'clock do you think it is? It's twenty minutes past seven! How dark the nights are getting, to be sure.'

'Come on,' said Jones, shaking his wet coat from his neck, 'let us get out of this. We'll need the lantern.' And he went and fetched it from the counting-house.

'Halloa!' he cried, when he came back, 'where's Prinkle?'

'I saw him go up-stairs,' said one. 'He'll be seeing that the place is right.'

'He's precious long about it,' replied Jones. 'See if you can get a hold of him.'

But two of the lads, who had searched up-stairs and in the top flat, returned in dismay, for no Prinkle was to be found.

'This is a pretty go,' said Jones, 'for he takes home the keys. Surely he can't be on this flat?'

'He's not here,' answered one, 'unless in the hoist-room.'

'I wouldn't go there,' replied Jones, with a grim laugh, 'for I might get a glimpse of my own ghost!'

But he did go to the hoist-room, and in an instant he staggered back, trembling in every limb, pale and speechless!

'What is it?' they cried. But he could only

hand them the lantern and point where he had
been.

In another instant they rushed into the
place, and there they saw the form of Prinkle,
still and twisted, hanging from the hatch.

The bull's-eye was flashed upon his face, but
it only revealed a discoloured countenance, and a
dark, protruding tongue. When they cut him
down, Jones was in a frenzy of despair, and it was
now his turn to call Peter by his name! But the
poor man's spirit was far away beyond reach of
his call, and the weary soul had flown to peace and
rest, at last!

Nell waited long and anxiously for Peter, but
though she waited and wearied, her husband never
came.

The lads in the warehouse made a solemn
compact among themselves that no one should
divulge the story of their freak, and they returned
to their own homes with a life's burden upon their
hearts.

The suicide weighed heavily on the conscience
of the elder Mr Hendry, for he believed that he
alone was the cause of Prinkle's death.

Poor Peter was buried at the expense of Mr
Trevor, and, after a time, Nell was taken to live
with Rachel. As the years rolled on, these two
women were drawn to each other by the warmest
ties, and they found a world of peace in the retirement of their cottage in Northumberland.

The Hendrys mourned for the poor man whose

honesty had enriched them, and whose spirit they had crushed with the dead pressure of their power, with that sorrow whose sum and substance consists in an inch or two of unsightly crape. By and by the cloud which was cast upon their warehouse, by this untoward event, was lifted away; and the last we heard of these exemplary men, they were flourishing like green bay trees.

THE END.

JOHN CHILDS AND SON, PRINTERS.

www.ingramcontent.com/pod-product-compliance
Lightning Source LLC
Chambersburg PA
CBHW021037030726
47496CB00006B/1579